AT LEAST I WAS THERE FOR YOU

She had been there. In his house, keeping him company. Making him forget he was sick. But she'd been absolutely no use as a nursemaid. "Alex, you'd kill people with your kindness."

"I would—" She paused. "Okay, maybe I would. But still, I have to finish this house."

"Why? What has gotten into you? You're even more stubborn than usual lately."

"I am not."

"Are too."

She took a step forward, chin upturned in a tease, closing the gap between them. "Am not."

He came closer, his grin widening. "Are too."

His voice had lowered, his gaze dropping to her lips. At that moment, something inside Alex suddenly went hot and liquid. This had been a game, a joke, but the joke died on her lips, as she became very aware of Mack. Of the muscles beneath his T-shirt. Of the way his skin glistened with a fine sheen of sweat. Of how blue his eyes were. Of how his lips curved into just the right kind of grin, the kind that made her want to—

Kiss him.

Where the hell had *that* come from?

BOOK YOUR PLACE ON OUR WEBSITE AND MAKE THE READING CONNECTION!

We've created a customized website just for our very special readers, where you can get the inside scoop on everything that's going on with Zebra, Pinnacle and Kensington books.

When you come online, you'll have the exciting opportunity to:

- View covers of upcoming books
- Read sample chapters
- Learn about our future publishing schedule (listed by publication month *and author*)
- Find out when your favorite authors will be visiting a city near you
- Search for and order backlist books from our online catalog
- Check out author bios and background information
- Send e-mail to your favorite authors
- Meet the Kensington staff online
- Join us in weekly chats with authors, readers and other guests
- Get writing guidelines
- AND MUCH MORE!

Simply The Best

SHIRLEY JUMP

ZEBRA BOOKS
Kensington Publishing Corp.
http://www.kensingtonbooks.com

ZEBRA BOOKS are published by

Kensington Publishing Corp.
850 Third Avenue
New York, NY 10022

All Kensington titles, imprints, and distributed lines are available at special quantity discounts for bulk purchases for sales promotion, premiums, fund-raising, educational, or institutional use.

Special book excerpts or customized printings can also be created to fit specific needs. For details, write or phone the office of the Kensington Special Sales Manager: Attn. Special Sales Department. Kensington Publishing Corp., 850 Third Avenue, New York, NY 10022. Phone: 1-800-221-2647.

Zebra and the Z logo Reg. U.S. Pat. & TM Off.

ISBN-13: 978-1-4201-0036-5
ISBN-10: 1-4201-0036-X

First Printing: December 2008
10 9 8 7 6 5 4 3 2 1

Printed in the United States of America

Chapter One

Mack Douglas wondered some days if Alexandra Kenner even knew he was a man.

She had never looked at Mack the way other women did. Virtually every woman Mack had ever known noticed he was made up of testosterone. Some flirted, some just smiled. Others made their interest quite clear by a shifting of cleavage, a bold invitation to dinner or an even bolder invitation to bed, but Alex—

Alex saw him as a friend. The ugly, curse-of-death *F* word.

Right now, she was swimming laps in his inground pool, her sleek body streaking back and forth in the bright sunshine, while she worked off a broken heart. Earlier that afternoon she'd told him all about how Edward—or the Evil One, as Mack had come to think of him—had turned out to be married. The bastard had been two-timing his wife and Alex.

Some men, Mack decided, just didn't need to live. And Mack didn't really need to hear the details, either, not from Alex.

Especially not while she was wearing a bikini.

She flipped over, the water sluicing down her skin.

He bit back a groan. Shifted from foot to foot. Kept his mouth shut about the effect she was having on him. Again.

He'd never told Alex how he felt. To her, he was just Mack. He always had been. They'd been friends forever, since he saved her from a bee in first grade, and, in turn, she'd given him something to look forward to every morning.

Alex had changed his life when she'd moved next door and become his friend, and he, she'd told him many times, had changed hers. For twenty-two years he'd also seen her as just that—

A friend.

Someone to tell his problems to. Another on his e-mail list to forward that one about the priest and the monkey who went into a bar. The first one he'd call when he scored Red Sox box seats, the last one he'd call at the end of a date when the woman had turned out to think she was the descendant of Marv the Martian.

Then, somewhere along the way, Mack had started to notice Alex. Notice the way she breathed. The scent of her perfume. The shape of her hips, her breasts.

And he'd stopped thinking of her in friendly terms.

It had been, however, a one-sided thought road. For a guy, there were days when that particular avenue was pure agony. Like today.

Alex stopped swimming. "Have you heard a single word I've said in the last ten minutes?"

"Of course," he lied, watching her float on her back in the pool, her breasts poking up in the water, two very enticing flotation devices. Ever since she'd slipped into a swimsuit, his concentration had gone south—and stayed south.

"Uh-huh. So what did I just say?"

"That all men are the scum of the earth. And Edward is king of the scum pond."

Alex laughed. "Close enough." She rolled over onto her stomach, swam across the pool, her strokes even and smooth. Then she hoisted herself out of his pool and Mack had to remember to breathe.

The water cascaded over her breasts, running like a waterfall down every inch of her luscious curves, shimmering along her tiny waist, the arc of her hips, as she climbed up the ladder, then onto the concrete. She swung her long brown hair to one side, squeezed the water out of it, completely unaware of what such a movement made the rest of her body do in that teeny, tiny, hot-pink bikini.

Mack swallowed. Grabbed the beer beside him and knocked back half.

"Thanks, Mack," Alex said, finally grabbing a towel and wrapping it around herself, taking away the best parts from his sight. "I needed that."

I did, too.

With a sigh, he put down the beer. "My pool is open, anytime."

"Despite the fact that you listen about as well as a fence post," she said, grinning, "I appreciate the invitation to come over today. I needed to get as far away from Edward as possible. And I always love your house. To find the best house on the corner, look for the one owned by the carpenter."

"One of these days, you'll let me build you one."

"When I have a need for more than one bedroom." She sat down on the lounge chair and he found himself starting to pray.

Take off the towel and lie back, go for a tan.

"I didn't know what I was going to do after that whole thing with Edward," Alex said. "What kind of guy proposes to a woman while he's still married to someone else?"

"Well, he did say he was separated." Mack figured he'd stand up for his kind, at least a little. Though a big part of him wanted to find Edward, rip the guy's guts out and feed them to the nearest carnivorous animal.

"Separated is *not* divorced, Mack. You know that. Did you date other women when you were married?"

He winced. Why'd Alex have to bring up that topic? If there was one door to his past that Mack preferred to keep bolted shut, it was the one holding the memories of his short-lived marriage. "You know I didn't cheat. I might have sucked at being a husband, but I never ran around on Samantha. And," Mack said, drawing in a breath, "as Forrest Gump would say, that's all I want to say about that."

"Are you ever going to talk about it with me?"

"Nope."

"I thought we were best friends."

"We are. Which is why I'll keep my nightmares in my own bedroom." He grinned. "No sense keeping you up at night pacing the halls in your fuzzy slippers, now, is there?"

"Mack, that's what friends are for. To be there and hear the good, the bad and the ugly."

"Wanna have a sleepover and find out for sure?" Mack asked. Only half-kidding.

Alex rolled her eyes. "You are incorrigible."

"Which is why I'm divorced. What's Edward's excuse?"

"Don't ask me. Frankly, I think he was hedging his bets." Alex's face reddened with renewed anger. "He had the gall to tell me his wife thought they were 'working things out.' He still goes to counseling with her every Tuesday, for God's sake. Yet, all this time he's been living with me and just happened to *forget* to mention that he was married. You don't just forget a wife."

"You do if it's convenient for getting you the next one. Sort of like keeping a spare tire in the back of your pickup for emergencies."

"I am not a spare tire." Alex blew a lock of hair out of her face with a gust and shot him a glare. "Why are men such jerks?"

That word got Mack's attention. Reminded him that he had descended into the depths of jerkdom by standing there, praying for Alex to take off the towel so that he could sneak a peek at her body again. Some friend that made him. He sank onto the lounge chair beside her and handed her a beer. "Because we have very tiny brains and we tend to keep them behind our zippers."

Alex laughed. "Seriously."

Mack shrugged. "I don't know. It's hard to think with this tiny brain."

He wasn't exaggerating, either, given that most of his thoughts right now were running down another track entirely, and being dictated by the brain behind his zipper. Clearly, given his past relationship record and present thought patterns, he shouldn't be the spokesperson for the male population. He didn't exactly make them look good.

Nor was he any better at commitment than Edward was. At least Edward had stayed married. Ever since Mack's single failed attempt—which lasted only slightly longer than the average Hollywood marriage—Mack had steered clear of matrimony—as clear as one man could steer of the institution. He'd sooner put his head through a crosscut shredder than repeat *that* mistake.

Alex sighed. "All I've ever wanted to do is meet one nice guy. Why is that so hard?"

"Why do you want to?" Mack asked, leaning forward, propping his elbows on his knees. "I mean, aren't you working hard on becoming reporter of the year over there at the *City Times*? Why bother adding in the complication of a relationship?"

He, for one, couldn't imagine that kind of future, not in a million years. He'd learned his lesson—the bachelor life was the best one for him. No one to answer to, no one to wonder why he came home late from work. No one to question a damn thing he did, which was why he now stuck to the kind of relationship where he got in quick, got out quicker.

Even if lately all that had begun to feel as empty as a light beer. Was he missing out on some secret the rest of the world knew and he didn't? Or was he just having some kind of weird male hormonal thing?

Probably a vitamin B deficiency. Yeah, that was it.

Alex put aside the beer. "How long have you known me, Mack?"

"Forever."

"And in all that time, did I ever have a normal family? Parents? A golden retriever? Hell, I couldn't have *paid* Oliver Twist to change places with me as a little kid, at least until I went to live with my grandmother. Most kids dream of a pony for Christmas. Me, I just wanted . . ."

Alex drew in a breath, looked away for a moment, making Mack's chest tighten in sympathy, because he knew the moment that had changed Alex's life, the day when everything went downhill.

Then she straightened and became her sassy self again. "Well, who wants to be Oliver Twist, anyway? Annie was the one who ended up with Daddy Warbucks." She grinned.

"And the dog, don't forget the dog." At the mention

of the three-letter word, Mack's mutt, Chester, got to his feet and padded over to them, tongue lolling, tail wagging. His whole body shaking with include-me-in-this-too. The tan dog was a mess of breeds—long ears, a short tail, and a squat, barrel body.

Alex bent down and patted Chester. He looked up at her with complete adoration, his tail whirling like a helicopter rotor. "Look at him. Anyone else would have called this dog a lost cause, but not you."

"Are you saying my dog is ugly?"

"He's not a Yorkie pup, let me put it that way." Alex rubbed Chester's ears and he let out a doggie groan.

For the first time since Mack had rescued Chester from behind a Dumpster on a construction site a year ago, Mack was jealous of his own dog.

"But he's cute."

"Like his owner?"

Alex laughed. "Since when do you fish for compliments?"

Since he'd started wondering what Alex thought of him. Since Alex started paying more attention to his dog than to him. "Hey, I'm a guy. My ego is always in a fragile state."

Alex's laughter deepened. "*Nothing* about you is fragile, Mack." She scratched Chester under the chin and the dog flopped onto the ground, offering up his belly for the same manual adoration.

Mack swallowed hard. He would have started eating Alpo just to trade places with his dog. "Well, just having a dog doesn't mean your life is on the right track."

A dog hadn't filled in all the gaps. Hadn't helped quiet the continual craving in Mack's gut for something—what, he didn't know—but something he was missing. Like a platter that wasn't on his personal buffet. He'd tried everything in his life to find that dish, but it hadn't worked.

Maybe he just needed a vacation. A break from the

mundaneness of work. Yeah. A couple weeks on a beach, and he'd get this . . . this sense of dissatisfaction out of his system. And maybe also shed this constant want for what he couldn't have.

Chester spied a squirrel in the yard and scrambled after it.

Alex sat back and let out a sigh. "I have almost everything I ever wanted, careerwise, and what I don't have, I can get myself. I can make that part of my life work like a watch, but when it comes to relationships, I've got two black thumbs. I'd just like *something*, or rather, *someone*, that's normal in my life."

"You've got me."

She laughed. "You, my hulking friend, are far from normal." Alex leaned back, turned her face up to meet the summer sun. "I'm serious. All these years, I've been dating, and it's the same old story. Single woman in the city finding jerk number seven hundred and sixty two. I want a change. I want a man like me."

Mack arched a brow. "Like you?"

"Someone who wants to cut through the crap of a relationship, be honest and maybe . . . I don't know, settle down, at least for a little while. Except . . ." Alex paused.

"The whole idea of settling down scares the crap out of you?"

"Yeah." She laughed. "I guess we're two of a kind that way, aren't we?"

"Absolutely. I wouldn't come within a hundred yards of an altar again if you paid me." He'd learned his lesson there. Should have been smart enough not to even attempt it in the first place. He wasn't cut out for the stifling blanket of marriage, and had made Samantha's life miserable.

He knew, because she'd told him. A thousand

times. Then she'd slammed the door so hard it had cracked the jamb. The next time he'd seen her had been across the table in her attorney's office.

"But I'm ready to take a chance now," Alex said. "Be a grown-up."

He laughed. "A grown-up? Now that sounds boring."

"What's boring is the dating rat race. I am so *sick* of it. I'm D-O-N-E. I want a solid, stable relationship."

He mocked a yawn, teasing her. "How fun is that?"

"Is it so unusual to want a man who comes home when he says he will? Give me one dependable guy who doesn't think honesty is a sexually transmitted disease, and I'll be happy for the rest of my life."

Mack thought about that for a second. In his current role as representative of the male population, he made all men look like hedonistic liars. Okay, so some of them were. Hell, he'd been known to have a few of those tendencies once in a while.

Maybe more than once in a while.

"So, what are you going to do if you find this needle in the X-Y haystack?" Mack asked.

Alex raised and dropped one bare shoulder. Mack's hand curled tighter around his beer. The cold glass bottle was no substitute for the warm skin a few feet away.

"Maybe," she said. "I might even fall in love."

He grinned. "I'd say you have the falling in love part down pat."

She leaned over and smacked him. "Thanks a lot."

When she moved like that, Mack had to grab his beer so he wouldn't stare down her bikini top again. Why couldn't Alex wear a one-piece, like other women? Why did that damn towel have to keep slipping?

She drew in a breath, raising her breasts. Up. Down. Up. Down. "What would you say if I told you I even considered getting married?"

He put a hand over his mouth, feigning shock. "I'd probably faint."

"Well, I did. I know, I know, next to you, I'm one of the most commitment-phobic people out there. But for a second there, when Edward proposed, it didn't sound as scary as I thought it would. Until I found out he was married." She wagged a finger in Mack's direction. "Then I wanted to kill him."

"Good thing you didn't. It's kind of hard to meet Mr. Right when you're sitting on death row."

She stuck out her tongue at him. Ten years ago, he'd have found that funny. Now it made him want her. Wanted to capture that tongue in his mouth, curl his own around hers. His groin tightened and his pulse began to thunder in his temples. Damn, he needed a date—with someone other than Alex.

"Edward may have been a jerk, but he made me think. Maybe it *is* time I grew up, settled down. Became a big girl. But no kids. That's not me. Definitely not me." A shadow fell over her face and she looked away.

Mack's heart broke for her all over again. He reached out a hand in Alex's direction, but she was too far away for him to touch.

Always too far. Always drawing into herself, away from him, from everyone.

Oh, Alex, he thought, will you ever forgive yourself?

Then she straightened, and the shadow washed away, replaced by her normal sunny countenance. "But marriage sounds . . . nice," she went on. "Like that one dessert I never tasted in the restaurant, but everyone tells me is really great."

A sweet, slow smile took over her face, a smile that socked him in the gut.

Holy Mother of God. He needed to find a way—if only for his own peace of mind—to get Alex out of sight. Then maybe he could forget her. Move on. Think about other women for a change. Women who didn't want the kind of permanence Alex had just described. The kind that caused his throat to swell, his chest to constrict. No way was he going to voluntarily sign up for the kind of pain patrol his father and best friend were already walking. The kind of pain he'd already experienced. Only an idiot put his head in the guillotine twice.

But he also wasn't going to keep on flogging himself with Alex's presence, either. "What if, uh, what if I helped you?"

"What do you mean?"

"Helped you find a man. One who isn't a jerk? Who actually has more than one brain cell and walks without dragging his knuckles on the ground?"

She laughed. "You mean you'd help me find my happy ending? Get this Cinderella a prince?"

He nodded. Told himself it would be a happy ending all around. Alex would finally be loved the way she deserved to be loved, and he'd stop wanting something he couldn't have.

Because as much as he cared about Alex—and if there was ever a person in his life he had cared about more than himself, it was Alex—there was one thing he refused to do.

Screw up their friendship.

All his life, Mack had protected Alex. Taken care of her. Drawn her under his bigger wing and sheltered her from the storms of middle school, bad prom dates and, most of all, the scars left by her childhood. He couldn't go into a relationship with her now, knowing full well he'd never be able to give her what she wanted, needed and deserved.

Mack might be a cad, but he wasn't one who would ever put his own baser needs ahead of Alex's basic needs.

"You'd really do that?" she asked. "The man who once made a speech—a very convincing speech, I might add—to a roomful of beer-swilling buddies comparing marriage to Alcatraz, only without the perks of prison?"

"That was years ago."

"Try six months, Mack."

"I never said *I* was considering getting married again." He shuddered. "I'm simply being a good friend."

Alex snorted. "And what's in it for you?"

"You'd quit bugging me, for one."

"I don't bug you." She considered the statement. "Okay, maybe I do. I am here an awful lot."

He tipped his beer her way. "Proves my point." And every time she was at his house, in his pool, in his living room, the torture of her presence only became more agonizing. For five seconds today, he'd thought maybe—just maybe—he and Alex could give it a shot. Then she'd blown that plan out of the water with her announcement that she was looking to settle down. Get married.

If he'd been a betting man, he'd have laid twenty-to-one odds Alex would have been the last to fall to the marriage bug. But fall she had and he had no intention of succumbing, too.

Not even for Alex. He'd seen firsthand how promising forever and ever could explode and disintegrate into something far afield from what people imagined on their wedding day. He'd stick to himself, and his dog, thankyouverymuch, and avoid the unhappy ending. Why sign up for the inevitable?

He only prayed Alex would end up different. Because she was worth much better. She was worth a man who would love her without reservation. Without strings.

And then, he could finally quiet this fascination with her. Go back to being just friends. Because as much as he wanted Alex—

He wanted her friendship far more.

"Why should I trust your taste in men?" Alex asked. "What's made your track record so good?"

"Hey."

He grinned. "Listen. I'm a guy. I think like a guy. Which means I can weed out the psychopaths, the sex fiends and the addicts looking for a mommy."

"If you do that, you won't have any friends left." She gave him a teasing smile.

Mack's chest tightened. He took another swig of beer. "I'll find someone normal." Someone boring. Someone who wouldn't turn her on, make her into the sex kitten he suspected she could be—

Okay, not going down the right mental path. Mack reined in his thoughts and tried again. "A man you can bring home to Grandma and still enjoy waking up with every morning."

Though the thought of Alex waking up with anyone else but him nearly made Mack crack his beer bottle in half. All the more reason to get her fixed up, and fixed up fast.

She thought a minute, chewing on her bottom lip. Mack watched, fascinated, as her bright white teeth tugged on the crimson skin. Damn, it was hot out here.

"All right. I'll try it your way." Alex turned her dazzling smile on him, the one that made it almost impossible for Mack to think straight. "If all works out, then I'll get married and finally get out of your hair. And, even better, I'll finally stay out of your pool. After all, what are friends for, if not for setting you up?" She slipped off the towel and laid back on the lounge chair, totally oblivious to the effect she and that slim excuse for a swimsuit had on him.

Mack groaned inwardly and guzzled the rest of his beer.

He shot to his feet. Alex was right. The best thing he could do was introduce her to a man who would marry her.

Alex was never going to see him as anything other than a friend, the guy she leaned on when things got tough, the one she confided in, the shoulder she cried on. For so long, he hadn't minded filling that role, but now—

Now, damn it, he did.

And at the same time, he needed her to do the same for him. *What we have here, Douglas, is a hell of a conundrum.*

"It's a deal," he said. "I'll find a Mr. Perfect for you."

Then he stripped off his shirt and dove headfirst into the deep end, trying to get away from her and the fantasies that bikini conjured up.

Trouble was, he suspected he was already in way over his head with Alex.

Chapter Two

After the engagement that never actually engaged, Edward did what he always did—left Alex to clean up the mess. He jetted off to the Bahamas, or maybe it was Bermuda—Alex had stopped listening after the words "I'm married"—leaving only a note in the apartment they had shared.

Sorry to have to remind you at a time like this, darling, but this is *my apartment. And since we're no longer together, it's time you moved out. I'll be back in a few days. That should be enough time for you to get resettled.*

Best wishes,
Edward

She took the note, written on Edward's distinctive monogrammed thick linen card stock in his precise script, wadded it up into a tight ball, then chucked it at Edward's favorite vase: a Chinese cloisonné. The hard paper missile landed squarely in the center. The vase teetered on its narrow pedestal and Alex charged forward to catch it, but her steps on the bouncy wood floor only shook things up and tipped the scales, bringing the bright red-patterned container crashing to the floor. And five thousand flowers shattered into five gazillion.

Well. That's what Edward got for writing on such heavy damn paper.

"Resettled, my ass," she said to the shrapnel. But without anyone around to hear, the words had as much punch as a two-year-old.

She gave herself ten minutes to rant. Ten minutes to be really pissed off and curse Edward's name six ways to Sunday. Then she told herself to get over it and make a plan.

She started packing, pulling her books off the shelf and putting them into a box in the closet. The same box she'd used to move in a year and a half ago. Pretty sad that she hadn't even thought to throw it out. Maybe, in the back of her mind, she'd been holding on to the box, knowing this wouldn't work out.

What she needed was a life change. A *major* life change. Something that would get her out of a job she hated, out of relationships she hated, out of apartments that weren't even hers, and into something—

Permanent.

A life with legs. The one thing she'd never had.

Alex's hand lighted on the book that had defined her adolescence. Willow Clark's *The Season of Light*. A coming-of-age story about a troubled young girl named Jensine McCallister who lived in a small town and dreamed of more. Alex flipped over the book, threadbare from its many readings, and read the back cover bio about the author, even though she already knew it by heart:

Reclusive author . . . Boston area . . . never granted interviews. Only wrote one book in her career.

The words "Boston area" leapt out at Alex like they had been written in neon. Then the others followed suit. Reclusive, never granted an interview. What a coup a story like that would be.

Alex smacked the book against her palm. Of course. Why had she never thought of that before? All this time, she'd been searching for a story idea that would wow her editor. She'd thrown him profile after profile, hoping he'd give her the go-ahead on any of them, so she could finally score a position in Features and climb her way out of the fashion pages.

If she could track down—and interview—the inaccessible Willow Clark, essentially, do what no one else had ever done before, then Joe would *have* to give her a job in Features. And she could kiss stilettos good-bye forever.

Alex tucked the book into her purse, then went back to packing. Tomorrow, as soon as she got to work, she'd start searching all the interlinked newspapers' and media databases, and find Willow Clark. Getting the interview from there should be a piece of cake. After all, Alex had an advantage she was sure none of the other reporters had had.

She'd read the book. *Really* read it. And maybe if Willow Clark saw that kind of passion, she'd be more apt to talk.

"You disappointed me, Alex."

Alex turned and found Renee Wendell, standing in the doorway and holding two coffees, one an iced frappuccino with extra whipped cream. "Hey, what a great surprise. You and the coffee." Alex stopped packing and dusted off her hands. "What are you doing here?"

"Reading your mind." The leggy brunette strode forward and placed the foamy concoction into Alex's hand. "It's the job of the former maid-of-honor-to-be to bring caffeine fortification and emotional support after the jerk of the century skips town." She looked around Edward's apartment. "I really thought I'd find more death and destruction, though."

Alex shrugged. "What's the point?"

"Revenge? Pain? Making him pay for being such a complete asshole?" Renee sat on the black leather sofa. After three kids, Renee's figure had taken on more curves, but she was still beautiful, with a wide, genuine smile and big brown eyes. "Do I need to go on?"

Alex laughed, then plopped into the opposite armchair, laying her coffee on the end table. Skipping the coaster. Let it leave a water ring, damn it. That alone would freak out neatnik Edward.

The exhaustion of the entire betrayal overtook her, and she draped her arms over the chair's sides, suddenly wishing she could turn back the clock and unring this bombshell bell. "Believe me, I thought of blowing up his apartment. Putting all his suits into the incinerator. Smashing his tie tack collection."

"He has a *tie tack* collection?"

"His first name is Edward, Renee. Does he sound like the kind of guy who would collect race cars?"

"Get me a hammer. I'll smash 'em myself." Renee laughed. "That's just nuts."

"What the hell did I see in him?" Alex shook her head.

"Same thing you see in every guy you date, Alex." Renee ran a hand over the edge of the couch, then met Alex's gaze with the kind of honesty only a best friend could have. "Security."

Was that what she had been doing? Seeking some kind of Band-Aid for her childhood in Edward? Alex shuddered. Next time she'd just buy an alarm system and a Doberman. "Look how well that worked out.

Now I'm boyfriendless. And homeless. Edward left me a very polite note kicking me out of his apartment."

Renee muttered a very unflattering curse under her breath. "We're definitely taking that tie tack collection with us. My three-year-old is all into Bob the Builder. He'll have a lot of fun demonstrating 'Yes, we can,' with Tony's hammer on those suckers."

Alex laughed. "I feel better already."

"See?" Renee gave her a helpful smile. "Focus on the positive."

"Remind me. What's the positive in this?"

Renee thought a minute. "You didn't end up a bigamist."

Alex rolled her eyes. "Oh, gee. Missed my chance to be on CNN."

Renee tipped her coffee cup in Alex's direction. "There's always next year."

Alex rose. "First, I have to find a place to live."

"You could live with me."

"And sleep where? In the closet? With three kids, you and Tony are cramped in that apartment as it is."

Renee ran a finger around the rim of her cup, the good humor washed from her face. "Yeah, well, we might be one less soon."

The bottom dropped out of Alex's stomach. Not again. Renee and Tony had been doing so well lately. Hadn't they? "What do you mean?"

"Nothing. Forget I said anything." Renee waved off the words and brightened, though her cheer rang a false note. "Tony and I had a fight this morning and you know I get all dramatic over that crap."

Alex studied her friend's face, but the mask of "everything's fine" had slipped back into place. Renee wore that face well. "Are you okay?"

"Me? Sure. Just peachy." Renee got to her feet and

turned, searching the apartment. "Where's today's *Globe*? We need to look in the classifieds. There's bound to be an available apartment."

Alex took a step closer, for the first time noticing the redness in Renee's eyes. The strain in the lines on her face. The flush in her cheeks. But she let it go. For now. "I'll get the paper. And the shredder."

"For what?"

Alex grinned and the sting of betrayal began to lift with the energy of new action. "Edward's not going to need his ties if we're taking the tie tack collection, now, is he?"

Renee Wendell had learned to lie from the day she said "I do."

She lied to her husband. She lied to her friends. She lied to her kids.

And most of all, she lied to herself.

That she was happy. That her marriage was okay. That she could juggle all these balls in the air and catch them, throw them back up and catch them again.

That she wasn't seriously thinking about having an affair with another man.

"Renee, are you listening to me?"

Renee looked up from her menu, from the words that had been a blur almost from the second she sat down in the diner, and stared at her husband. He'd asked her a question and she scrambled to find the thread of the conversation that she had dropped. Birthday presents. Their middle child. Had she bought them yet. "Yes, Tony, I'll buy the presents after work today. Before I pick up the kids and cook dinner and help with homework."

He frowned. "You don't have to get bitchy about it. I can go to the store, too."

She let out a sigh. Lately, she'd felt pulled in twenty directions. Helping Alex this morning, dealing with Tony at lunch. The constant needs of the kids, her job. And where was she in all of this? Lost in the shuffle, like that second black sock in the washing machine. "You wouldn't know what to buy."

"Kylie is my daughter, too, you know." He folded his arms on the table, his dark brown eyes meeting hers, a lock of chocolate hair falling across his forehead. He needed a haircut. She'd mention the fact, but that would only set off a new argument. And she needed *that* about as much as she needed to get pregnant again. Frustration filled Tony's features, the look so familiar, Renee could have drawn it in her sleep.

Once upon a time, when they looked at each other they smiled. Laughed. There'd been no tension, no fighting. Those days seemed a million miles away, as far away as her husband had moved emotionally. From her. From the kids. From their lives.

"What is Kylie's favorite TV show?" Renee asked her husband. "Her favorite color? What doll did she ask us to buy for her birthday? She may be your daughter, Tony, but you aren't plugged in to what she wants. At all."

He sat back, anger sparking in his eyes, red flushing his cheeks as if she'd slapped him. "Maybe if you let me—"

"Maybe if you were home more often."

"I'm not having this argument again, Renee." He let out a gust. "Can we get along today? Please? For her birthday at least?"

"Of course," Renee said. She'd play the happy wife role again. Bake the cake. Set the table, light the candles, sing the song and smile all the while. And the act would continue, while she wondered where the hell her marriage had gone and how something that had once felt so right could have gotten so badly derailed.

It hadn't taken long for Alex to realize her housing options were limited. She and Renee had combed the classifieds, trying to find a place that fit Alex's lean fashion-reporter's pay and her Edward-dictated timeline. And came roach-free. Hitting all three marks was impossible.

Unless she wanted to opt for a cardboard box under the Tobin Bridge. Plenty of room at the inn there.

She could move in with Mack, of course, but living with him—

Well, it wasn't entirely out of the question, but the thought of watching him parade in and out with the hussy of the week didn't sound appealing. He was her friend, and he had a great pool, and a great body and a lot of other great qualities, but his taste in evening companions . . .

Not so great. And that, Alex knew, would get on her nerves in five seconds.

Not to mention Mack was, well, Mack. Her best friend. Living with him twenty-four/seven could do the one thing she had studiously avoided all these years: hurt their friendship. She'd sooner choose the cardboard box than mess up the symbiosis between them.

As for relatives, the pickings were even leaner. She'd never known her father, and her mother had died when she was five.

Alex had been born when her mother was seventeen, and even though Josie Kenner had tried, she'd never been much of a mother. She'd gotten pregnant too young, and been nothing more than a kid raising a kid. Forgetting that she couldn't keep on partying and staying up late, with a toddler in tow.

It wasn't until Alex went to live with her grandmother that she had any kind of normalcy. A schedule. Someone there to cook her meals, give her cookies, read her books.

Show her what a home could really be.

Alex had a few aunts, uncles and cousins scattered around the country, and one odd cousin, Phoebe, living in Newton, in a basement apartment. Phoebe, however, kept a triple-thick layer of heavy-duty foil on her windows, because she'd watched *War of the Worlds* one too many times.

Either way, Alex had no intention of staying in Edward's apartment, even if it meant moving to a Motel 6. At least someone there would leave a light on for her.

Twenty minutes later, Alex had most of her possessions packed. Seeing how little of her life had been joined to Edward's made it clear he'd never really made room for her. Not in this apartment, not in his heart. The furniture was his. The pots and pans. The electronics.

But the ties were gone. The tie tacks now in the back of Bob the Builder's cement truck. Alex chuckled. "*Yes we can* make Edward a little miserable, too." She locked the door and left with the last box.

All Alex took with her were some books, CDs, clothes, her laptop. Pretty symbolic of her life, actually. Thus far, she hadn't settled down long enough to accumulate anything.

She'd told Mack yesterday that she wanted to have a normal life, to get off this revolving wheel of bad decisions. Maybe even get married, make a life with someone else.

To do that she'd need to at least buy a sofa. And for a sofa, she'd need a home.

A little after four, Alex gave up the search for an apartment and drove to Merry Manor for her weekly visit with Grandma Kenner. Her grandmother had lived here for nearly five years, a choice she'd made after selling her house in Dorchester shortly after the last of her old neighborhood friends moved away. Grandma had said she wanted a place that offered something to do, and someone to do those things with. The place was bright and airy, and offered the full continuum of care, which gave Alex peace of mind that her grandmother would be okay, should anything happen.

Grandma was pretty much all the family Alex had, and making sure Grandma, who was now in her eighties, was safe and healthy, topped Alex's priority list.

On the grounds of Merry Manor, Grandma's familiar red kerchief and bright pink sweater stood out like a poppy in a field of lilies. Alex caught up to her—Grandma Kenner walked several miles every day and moved surprisingly fast for a woman her age. "Hi, Grandma."

"Alex!" She drew her granddaughter into a White Linen–scented tight hug. "How's my favorite granddaughter?"

Alex laughed. "I'm your only granddaughter."

"Well, if I had others, you'd still be my favorite."

They fell into step together, strolling along the azalea and other flowering shrubbery that decorated the path. A number of other elderly people walked along it, too, or wheeled along in wheelchairs. Some had help, others moved along unassisted. Nursing staff dotted the landscape, keeping a careful watch on the residents.

"How are you?" Grandma asked. "Planning a wedding

yet? You know I have that new dress from Macy's and all I need is a party to wear it to."

"Edward and I broke up," Alex said. Every time she said the words, they got easier, and surprisingly less painful. Maybe she hadn't cared as much about him as she'd thought. She told her grandmother about Edward's wife on the side and her newly homeless status.

"Should I have him killed for you?" Grandma asked. "There's a guy in here, ex-CIA, he knows people."

Alex laughed. "No, Grandma, but thanks for offering."

"The guy should at least be maimed. Tortured a little. Any man who hurts my Alex deserves a painful ending."

"Don't you think you're a little biased when it comes to me?"

"Just a little." Grandma wrapped an arm around Alex and gave her a soft kiss on her hair. Alex leaned into the touch, holding tight for one long second. Comfort, warmth. Familiarity. She found them all in that embrace, and always had.

"If I could find a place to live I'd be fine," Alex said when she pulled back and resumed their walk.

"I'd let you live here with me, but it's a seventy-five-and-over community. You're too pretty to pass for a senior citizen."

"Ah, a bright side. I could use one of those. So far, all the available places I've found come with Chuck E. Cheese's cousins for roommates." Alex sighed. "Or, they're so overpriced, it's ridiculous. I either need to get into a new field or get a raise because fashion reporters don't make crap for money. Working toward your dream job is highly overrated."

Fashion reporting was not her dream—feature writing was. Alex had yet to earn a spot on those coveted front pages, but she had taken every assignment she could that would get her closer to that goal. Someday, someday soon, she'd be there.

All she needed was that one piece, the golden ticket that would get her editor to sit up and take notice, to realize Alex had the chops to do more than write Top Ten Tips for Kissable Lips.

And Willow Clark was that ticket. She knew it.

Except she had to find Willow Clark. And get the biggest hermit since Harper Lee to agree to an interview.

"You know . . . there is one place where you could live," her grandmother said slowly.

"You know something available?"

Grandma nodded. "A house. It, uh, needs some work."

"A house?" Alex thought about that for a minute. Homes were the kind of permanence she'd never invested in. The kind of putting down roots she had studiously avoided all these years. But where had that gotten her so far?

Alone, and regretting one incredibly stupid relationship after another.

Maybe taking a different path would yield a different result. It certainly couldn't get any worse than the near slide down Bigamy Boulevard.

"Carolyn!" called Betty Andrews, one of Grandma Kenner's next-door neighbors. She came toddling over to them, pushing a walker that squeaked a little as it rolled along the cement path. Her oversized floral dress swung like a bell around her. "I've been looking for you."

"Here she comes again," Grandma muttered under her breath. "The Grim Reaper's Happy Helper."

Alex bit back a laugh.

"Have you had your cholesterol checked today?" Betty asked. "Mine is nearly two hundred. Why, I could have a heart attack this minute. Die right in front of you. And have I told you about my gall bladder? I have a mass, Carolyn. A *mass*. Doctor thinks it might be cancer."

"Did he *say* the word *cancer*?"

"Well, not in so many words, but something's in there, and that something, it could be cancer." Betty leaned in, her light blue eyes wide. "I'm looking at a one-way ticket to the amusement park in the sky. Any day now, *kaput!* I hope you have your affairs in order, Carolyn, because it could happen to you, too. In fact, we're all meeting tonight in the recreation room to have a writing-your-will party."

"A party. To write wills." Grandma shook her head. "Doesn't sound festive."

"It'll be fun. We'll have chips and dip. Margie's bringing hummus and Dave is making his walnut brownies. You really should come. You can never start preparing for the afterlife too early." Betty wagged a finger and gave Grandma a look of dire warning before spinning her walker around and wheeling away.

Grandma let out a sigh. "These people drive me crazy."

"What people?"

"The doom-and-gloomers. Can't escape 'em around here. It's like the cloud over the Addams Family house is always after me, except here it's got a power wheel-chair. Which is exactly why," Grandma began, turning toward Alex, "I want you to move into that house. Fix it up, get it ready, and then . . . I can, uh, follow."

"I thought you liked it here."

Grandma put a hand on her hip. "Alexandra, do you think this place is me? I've tried to fit in, tried my best, but it's depressing. All these people talk about is aches and pains in their hips and joints, and next thing you know, I feel like I'm falling apart, too. Not to mention, the staff runs this operation like a military academy."

Alex chuckled. "You're exaggerating."

"Well, maybe, but I really don't like living by other people's rules." Grandma stopped by a maple tree and turned to face her granddaughter. "I'm an old woman, and I may need some help in my later years, but I don't want to spend those years being told when to eat my meatloaf and what time to play canasta. I may joke about life around here, but there are many days the schedule feels a hell of a lot like prison. Only we're sitting on death row."

Alex's heart clenched. Grandma Kenner was eighty-one. She'd lived such a long life. Who knew how much longer she had? And if she wanted to live somewhere other than Merry Manor, then she had every right to do that.

"So will you do this for me?" Grandma asked.

Alex combed her memory banks for a second house but came up empty. "I thought you sold your house years ago, Grandma."

"I did. But I've sort of kept this one in reserve. A . . . backup plan. An escape route, really, to get me out of this joint." She smiled. "It works for both of us. You want to move on, dear. You need something to help you do that, literally." Her grandmother reached out and took her granddaughter's hand in hers. Grandma's palm was soft with age, skin paper-thin, an interstate highway of veins visible. "This little house is perfect for both of us."

"But, Grandma, I don't know the first thing about fixing up houses."

"You can read, can't you? Hold a hammer? Besides, like I said, the place needs hardly any work. You'll have it done in a weekend." Grandma waved a hand in dismissal. "Two, tops."

Alex shook her head. "I don't know."

They reached Grandma's condo. The building was linked, as most of the private residences were, to all the other condos and the main building in the front, and faced the grounds in the back. It had the illusion of a home, with the safety of nurses in the rear. "I think you're exactly the right person to handle this. Plus, it's about time you put down some roots. Roots help you get a crooked tree straightened out, and your life, darling, has become a crooked tree." Grandma laid a hand of concern on Alex's arm and gave her a soft smile. "I'm saying this as your grandmother, as someone who loves you. It's time you grew up."

Alex laughed. "Last I checked, I was twenty-seven. That's grown up."

"In numbers, yes. But dear, you have all the commitment of a fruit fly, and I mean that in the nicest way."

"I almost got engaged to Edward."

"Almost only counts in horseshoes," Grandma pointed out. "You do know how fruit flies end up if they don't settle down and breed, don't you?"

"Now who's the doom-and-gloomer?"

"You can't keep flitting from banana to banana, Alex. Find another fly. A bumblebee. I don't care, as long as you settle down, make a life, and give me some great grandkids before we're both wearing bibs and I can only recognize them by rubbing their fuzzy heads."

Alex chuckled. "You're exaggerating."

"Maybe. But I do it out of love. Only out of love."

They entered the sunflower-yellow kitchen. Bright white curtains framed the windows, and a small glass table sat beneath the window, decorated with two floral-patterned placemats. Grandma crossed to the stove, retrieved the teapot, filled it at the sink, then put it on a burner and turned on the flame. "Speaking of living alone," Grandma said, "how's Mack?"

"Same as always. A total pain in the butt."

Grandma laughed. She put a plate of frosted cookies on the table, then slid into the opposite seat. "Maybe so, but he still knows the way to an old girl's heart. He brought these treats by yesterday. Not only did he bring me some, he brought enough for the whole east wing. He's got half the Merry Manor women in love with him."

"They fell in love over cookies?"

Grandma winked. "At my age, you'll take what you can get. Either way, Mack has good stock. I always did like that boy."

"He's a man now, Grandma. A year older than I am."

Grandma waved a hand. "Decades younger than me. A mere boy in Father Time's eyes." Then she leaned in close and studied Alex's face. "What about Mack?"

Alex picked up a cookie and took a bite. "What do you mean, what about Mack?"

"Maybe *he's* your fruit fly."

Alex exploded in laughter. "Mack? God, no. He's a *friend*. As a boyfriend, he'd be a disaster. Not that he isn't attractive, but because he's . . ."

"He's what?" Grandma prodded.

"Incorrigible," Alex said, using the word she'd called Mack earlier.

Grandma smiled. "Sometimes those ones are the most fun."

Alex rolled her eyes. "Let me put it in your kind of terms, Grandma. I'm looking for a sturdy oak tree, not a wild tumbleweed. Besides, my biggest priority right now is a roof over my head, not a man."

"True. You probably should find the yard before you

try to plant a tree in the lawn." The teakettle whistled and Grandma rose to turn it off, then she filled two mugs with hot water and cinnamon-apple teabags. She returned to the table and slid a mug toward Alex. "That house is the perfect solution all around. A place to live, a new start, and plenty of hard work to get that dreadful Edward out of your system."

Alex cast a glance out the window. Clouds marched across the sun, obscuring it for one long second, then moving to allow light over the earth again, like a symbol of Alex's days ahead—sunshine on the horizon. Wasn't that exactly what she'd decided she wanted? Something more permanent? A place to put a sofa? She took in a deep breath, and with it a new sense of resolve. "Okay. I'll do it."

"Wonderful! This could be just the thing to shake up your life," Grandma said. "Change things. Put you on a new path. I think you'll see, Alex, dear, that life throws you a few curves, and if you take them, you might be surprised at what you find waiting for you around the corner."

An hour later, Alex sat in her Honda and stared at the set of keys Grandma had given her. One of these unlocked the front door to a new beginning. Her first step toward something forever.

A home.

Alex's heart beat faster and her throat constricted. She'd avoided permanence for so long, sidestepping the strictures of a mortgage because tying herself to anyone or anything meant—

They might let her down.

Like her parents had. Like Edward had.

But this time, the power lay in her own hands, literally. She could choose to change her destiny, to paint and carpet her way to the perfect picture she'd always wanted.

Alex inhaled, drawing in the scent of the ocean through her open window with the breath. The clean air burst in her lungs along with a song of hope. Of newness.

She ran her thumb over the main house key. Could this slim piece of metal be a way of turning a mess into something resembling a life? Could she really straighten out a lifetime of bad decisions by putting down roots?

She leaned back, closed her eyes and let her mind wander down familiar paths. When Alex had been little, she'd spent so many nights picturing a Utopia, the ideal world she desperately wanted—and she imagined what it would be like to exist out there, somewhere. Now, that world—or at least the beginnings of it—was within her grasp.

As her mind drew the images, she could almost see them, hear them, touch them. A flower-lined walkway, filled with pink impatiens and white geraniums, waving their happy faces. A golden retriever waiting by the door—tongue lolling, massive paws planting an oversized puppy hug on her chest. Rooms filled with overstuffed furniture calling out to visitors to sit a while, surrounding them with comfort that fit like a hug. Cabinets overflowing with every kind of food from chicken noodle soup to chicken and broccoli rice. And most of all, warm light bathing every surface, casting its golden glow over the wood, the carpets, kissing the house like Midas himself.

Making it home.

Alex's hand closed over the keys. She could do this. Tackle a little spackle.

After all, how hard could it be?

Chapter Three

"Do you want the bad news . . . or the bad news?" Mack asked, shielding his eyes against the sun.

Alex stood beside Mack on the lawn in front of her new potential residence, the late-June heat beating down on them. She'd been here for ten minutes, and couldn't shake the feeling that this house looked familiar. Something about the slope of the roof—what was left of it, anyway—the curve of the driveway, if she could call the smattering of gravel and tar a driveway . . . the short, clumpy expanse of dried yellow lawn . . . It all struck a chord of memory, one that flitted away before Alex could capture it.

"Neither," Alex said. "Lie to me."

Mack grinned. "This is a great house. You'll be very happy here." Then he turned on his heel and headed for his truck.

Trepidation quadrupled Alex's heart rate and she ran after him. "Mack, don't go. Don't leave me here."

He sighed. "Okay, truth. Bulldoze it, Alex. Torch it. Sell it. Whatever you do, don't try to take this on yourself."

"It's not that bad." She squinted at the building. "Is it?"

Mack opened the door to the pickup and swung his

body inside. "You know the Titanic? I'd sooner try to fix that up for a pleasure boat than take on this house."

Alex groaned. "Mack, you don't understand. My grandmother is expecting me to renovate this house. She wants to live here."

"Why? She already has a place to live."

"Yes, but she wants to move here. And I need a place to live right now."

Mack hopped back down and returned to Alex, his gaze connecting with hers. So aware of her every breath. The scent of her perfume, the way a single tendril of her hair curled around her jaw. "Live with me." The idea was out before he could stop it. Insane, completely insane.

And yet, he found himself praying for her to say yes.

"That would be imposing. I can live here."

He arched a brow at the dilapidated three-bedroom Cape Cod–style house Alex had called him to look at late that afternoon. He'd hated to tell her how horrible the place was, after hearing the excitement in her voice, but he couldn't, in all good conscience, let her think this sorry excuse for a house was habitable.

Had her grandmother bought this place sight unseen on eBay? Mack couldn't believe anyone would pay good money for a place this bad. "Alex, I wouldn't let my dog live here, and I'm not saying that to be mean. The roof is leaking, the front door is about as secure as Scotch tape, and there's no air-conditioning. It's at least ninety-eight degrees today. You'll melt."

She smiled. "I'll survive. You know, when I was a kid, we didn't even have air-conditioning at my grandparents' house. You didn't have any, either. Both of us grew up just fine."

"You can't take this on, Alex," he insisted. His carpenter's eye assessed the house again. They'd already done a walk-through, which had revealed such a long list of problems, Mack had stopped keeping a mental tally when he reached one hundred. "It needs everything. New plumbing. New electrical. New roof. New windows. And when you do that, you have to put in new walls, new flooring. Basically, get out the full catalog from Lowe's and circle one of everything."

Her face fell. "Really?"

He shifted his weight, wishing he could soften the blow. Maybe if Alex saw the reality of the situation, she'd give up this crazy idea of fixing the unfixable. He knew her—she could be as stubborn as an angry hornet. "What kind of budget do you have?"

"Budget?"

"Let me guess. Small. Very small."

"My grandmother said it just needed a little TLC. She didn't talk budget." She gave him a hopeful smile. "You know me. I'm good at TLC."

Mack roared with laughter. "You, sweetheart, are totally bad at TLC, and you know it as well as I do."

She thrust her fists onto her hips, anger flashing in her green eyes. "Who took care of you last year when you had the flu?"

"You call dumping a can of Campbell's into a pan, then letting it burn because you got so distracted beating my ass at poker, taking care of me when I had the flu?"

"At least I was there for you."

She had been there. In his house, keeping him company. Making him forget he was sick. But she'd been absolutely no use as a nursemaid. "Alex, you'd kill people with your kindness."

"I would—" She paused. "Okay, maybe I would. But still, I have to finish this house."

"Why? What has gotten into you? You're even more stubborn than usual lately."

"I am not."

"Are, too."

She took a step forward, chin upturned in a tease, closing the gap between them. "Am not."

He came closer, his grin widening. "Are, too."

His voice had lowered, his gaze dropping to her lips. At that moment, something inside Alex suddenly went hot and liquid. This had been a game, a joke, but the joke died on her lips, as she became very aware of Mack. Of the muscles beneath his T-shirt. Of the way his skin glistened with a fine sheen of sweat. Of how blue his eyes were. Of how his lips curved into just the right kind of grin, the kind that made her want to—

Kiss him.

Do way more than kiss him. Take him to bed. Hell, take him on the floor of this house right now.

Where the hell had *that* come from?

She'd known Mack forever. He'd always been her friend, never a man to date. She'd kissed him once, back in high school, in a terrible fumbling, awful, let's-get-this-over-and-see-what-it's-like way, and it turned out to be terrible.

She'd never before seen him as a man who made every part of her tingle with anticipation when his smile tipped up just a little bit more on one side than the other. Never before had she had to remind her heart to beat when he shifted his weight, and seemed to inch closer.

"I . . . I . . ." But nothing else came out. She stuttered the vowels and that was it.

His grin quirked higher. "Giving up so soon, Alex?

I've never seen you quit an argument in the middle. What happened? Cat got your tongue?"

He tipped her chin with his finger and for a second she forgot to breathe. She was tempted—so very, very tempted—to dip down and take that finger into her mouth and taste Mack's skin. She watched his lips, watched his every movement, every breath.

What the hell was she thinking? This was *Mack*, she reminded herself again.

Mack, her *friend*. Not Mack the Sex God. Mack, the guy she had known all her life and never found the least bit interesting. She had to be hormonal. That explained it all. It was time for her period, past time, actually, and she was a raging ball of PMS.

"What, uh, what were we arguing about?" she asked.

Damn, his cologne smelled good. A subtle mix of juniper, sandalwood and other scents she couldn't name. Why had she never noticed it before? She inhaled again, drawing the scent in deeper, holding it in her lungs.

"You. Living with me. Because you can't live here."

He tiptoed his touch across her jaw. Alex's lips parted. Her throat went dry.

"And I believe you were saying that you were afraid that if you moved in, you'd be unable to resist my manly charms."

She burst out laughing—an explosion of nerves at how close Mack had just come to reading her mind. "What manly charms? Last I checked you were about as charming as an armchair."

"Hey." He stepped back, his hand dropping away.

Thank goodness. She shuffled back a little, too.

"I take offense to that."

His face fell, and for a moment, she thought she might have hurt him, then the look disappeared.

"So, are you going to try to tough it out here, or take me up on my offer?"

How easy it would be to rely on him. Again. To reach out, let Mack's broad shoulders take the load. For one minute, Alex wanted to do just that. To dump the entire problem of her messy life into his lap.

Just like always.

But what good would that do? Her life had become a mess because she had yet to straighten it out herself. To take control. She had a chance here to do something constructive, to quite literally build a different life. What had Grandma Kenner said?

Putting down roots could straighten out the tree.

Well, if past history was any indication, Alex could use a little straightening. And what better way to do that than with a hammer, some nails and a lot of hard work?

Hard work she did on her own, without relying on Mack, who had always been her tree. It was best to be here on her own, especially since this particular male oak was looking more and more attractive by the second.

She looked up at Mack and smiled. "Nope, I don't need any help. I'm going to do this one on my own."

"You're insane, Alex."

"I can do this." She spun around and looked at the house, feeling recharged. Renewed. Again, that feeling of déjà vu tingled up her spine, but the memory danced just out of reach.

She shrugged it off, and went back to assessing the workload ahead of her. It didn't look *too* bad. And they did have books at the library for this kind of thing. She had some savings, a Home Depot credit card. Grandma said she'd contribute to the costs, too. That should be enough. Right?

Either way, it was part of the new start. One she was

determined to make, come hell—or high construction costs. "I'm doing it. I'm pulling a Jensine."

"A . . . what?" Mack asked.

"A Jensine. From the character in *The Season of Light,* Willow Clark's book. In fact," Alex leaned closer even though there was no one around to overhear her, "that book has inspired me not just to make a change in my life, but a change in jobs. I'm going to do what no reporter has done before and land an interview with Willow Clark." Alex let out a sigh. "That is, once I find her. *And* get her to talk."

"*The Season of Light?* Sounds like a girly book."

She smacked his shoulder. "*The Season of Light* is my favorite book in the universe. It's *the* coming-of-age novel for every teenage girl in the world."

Mack snorted, teasing her. "Well, in that case, I'll put it right at the top of my to-be-read pile."

She laughed. "You should. You might learn a thing or two about girls."

"I already know a thing or two." He closed the gap between them. "Or ten. About girls. And women."

The breeze ruffled Mack's hair. Alex ached to do the same. Insane. Mack had always made it clear he had no intention of ever getting serious, of settling down, ever again. Doing anything that even smacked of getting involved with him would be emotional suicide. She'd already danced on that precipice enough with men like Edward.

"Do you want me to help you?" Mack asked.

"Uh, with what?"

"Getting an interview with Willow Clark. I know a lot of people in Boston. You know how it is, that 'six degrees of separation' thing. Someone's bound to know someone else. In fact, I think I built a house for a librarian. I bet she has a connection or two that could get you a lead."

With little effort, Alex could have access to the author she'd admired all her life—and a one-way ticket to the front page. Mack would snap his fingers and solve Alex's problem, just as he had when he'd talked to the principal in junior year and covered for her when she'd skipped school to go to a concert. Just as he had signed on the dotted line as a cosigner for her first car. Just as he had a dozen other times.

And where would that leave this tree? With weak roots that still hadn't learned to stand on their own.

"No," Alex said. "I don't need you to call in a favor. I won't be much of a reporter if I couldn't handle my first feature assignment alone. I'll do this one myself."

"Why? I don't mind helping you. Really."

"No," she replied, firmer now. "I can do this on my own. I have to, because up until now my life has pretty much been an out-of-control mess. I'm taking charge, with that story, and with this." She strode toward the house and stepped up onto the porch, intending on making a statement, à la the climactic movie scene just before the hero leaves to slay the dragon. She grabbed hold of one of the balustrades, swung against it, and felt like a kid again. Felt so much like a kid that she had the weirdest sense of having swung on that wood post before. "And now, I can finally do something concre—"

The balustrade gave way, sending Alex tumbling to the ground. So much for slaying the dragon. Mack rushed forward to right her. "See? Do you need a clearer sign than that? This place is a piece of crap, Alex. Please let me level it and start from scratch."

"Nope." She got to her feet and brushed the flakes of paint and clumps of dirt off her shorts. "I'm taking control of my crumbling life by starting with this crumbling house."

"What the hell are you talking about?"

"It's a metaphor, Mack." She shrugged. "I can't explain it. I look around this place, and I feel like I have to do this. Not just for my grandmother but for me, too."

Mack shook his head, muttered something under his breath that sounded like "insane asylum," then headed off to his truck. Alex thought he'd just climb inside and leave, but he returned with a large metal box. "Here. If you insist on doing this, then at least take some tools." He flipped open the lid, revealing a stash of carpentry tools. Alex had no idea what most of them were, though she did recognize the screwdriver and hammer.

Oh, shit, she was in over her head. Way over her head. But at this point in her brave new speech, it would take a presidential order to get her to admit that to Mack.

"Promise me you'll at least wear some safety glasses. I'd rather you didn't end up a one-eyed invalid at the end of this. You'd still be beautiful with an eye patch, maybe even a little sexier." He grinned, then handed her some plastic goggles before he headed off to his truck again, still shaking his head.

"Thanks for the vote of confidence," Alex said, waving the glasses at him. "It's good to know I can count on a friend's support."

"If I were your friend," Mack said as he climbed into the red Ford, "I wouldn't let you do this. I wouldn't let you do half of what you've done lately."

Then he left, leaving Alex to wonder what the hell he'd meant by that.

Chapter Four

Mack stood outside the small ranch-style house on Pinewood Street and said a little prayer that this time would be the time. The one that turned everything around, and set this corner of the world to rights.

Yeah. And miracles popped out from under rocks all the time, too.

Nevertheless, Mack wasn't going to give up easily, because he wasn't the kind of man who did. So he strode up the solid concrete stairs, noting they were in need of a coat of paint, rang the bell and steeled himself for the worst.

"I'm not here." The words were a grumble, but Mack could still hear them, even from the other side of the glass circle in the middle of the front door.

"Then why are you talking to me?" Mack shouted back from his place on the porch. A summer breeze whispered past him, giving a slight sway to the wind chimes hanging on the end of the porch, leaving with a tinkle of music.

"Because I'm hoping you'll get the hint and leave me alone," the voice replied, closer now to the glass.

"I need help, Dad. Can't figure this one out on my

own." Mack held up a sketchbook in his hand, a set of designs he'd brought along. A ruse, really.

"I didn't raise an idiot."

Roy had a point. Mack did know just about everything there was to know about carpentry, thanks to his father. Over the years, Roy had shared all his knowledge with his son, which had provided Mack with virtually all the mental tools he needed to run one of the most successful custom home construction and renovation businesses in the greater Boston area. He'd grown up at his father's knee, going to work with his dad on Saturdays—falling in love with the smell of freshly cut wood and with the idea that he could construct something with his own two hands. For a long time, construction had been the way he'd conversed with his dad.

Until last year. When Roy had pretty much stopped talking to anyone.

Mack didn't really need help, and his father probably knew that. He was here only to get Roy out of the house. Get him away from the TV, the dark room he'd kept to ever since Mack's mother, Emma, Roy's wife of thirty years, had taken off in a convertible with their lawyer. She'd left their marriage a dozen times, but this time it had been for good.

Roy had come home from the grocery store, read the note she'd left on the kitchen table, shut the front door and kept it shut ever since.

Finally, the door opened, swung open, really, with no clear invitation for Mack to enter. But enter he did, stepping into the cavernous darkness of the house where he'd grown up. The first house Roy had ever built.

It was small by today's standards, a three-bedroom ranch, with nothing too fancy, "just what a man needs," as Roy always said. It had seemed to be the perfect fit for the practical Roy and for Emma, the only woman who had ever managed to coax a smile out of the gruff, no-nonsense carpenter. Until she'd left. Now it seemed too big. Too empty. And too damn dark.

"Well, don't just stand there letting the heat in," Roy said. "Shut the damn door."

Mack did. The darkness only multiplied. He turned on the lamp on the end table, meriting a warning from his father about the cost of electricity, which he ignored. "You can't go on playing the happy hermit forever, you know."

"Do I *look* happy to you?"

"Exactly my point."

His father scowled, then headed into the kitchen. Mack kept the book of sketches with him and followed behind. He helped himself to a soda out of the fridge, then sank into one of the chrome and vinyl chairs that ringed the Formica table. Nothing had changed in this kitchen for half a century, and Mack suspected, without an intervention from Martha Stewart herself, nothing ever would. "What's on your agenda today, Dad?"

"Why do I have to have an agenda? I'm retired."

Mack gave up on that line of questioning. It hadn't gotten him anywhere in a year. It wasn't going to get him anywhere today. "I've got this house out on Cherry Street I'm building. The client wants these cabinets built in the basement media room. Trouble is, the space is a little too small. On top of that, I have to work around the heating ducts and a waste pipe coming down from the first-floor bath. I remembered you had a similar situation with that Somerville house back in, what, '92—'91?" Mack paused, hoping his father would correct him, knowing full well which house it had been and what year it had been.

Roy shrugged. Didn't answer.

Mack sighed. Fiddled with the sketchbook. He paused a long time, then decided he had to say it sometime, even though he knew it would set off an argument he wasn't sure he had the stomach to fight. "Mom's the one that left, Dad, not you."

Dark clouds gathered in Roy's eyes and he pushed away from the table. "Don't talk about your mother."

"She wouldn't sit around like this, if it was her," Mack pressed, following his father. "And you know it."

"You don't know what you're talking about. Leave me alone."

"Why? So you can wither away like some houseplant that doesn't get any sun?" Mack crossed in front of his father, waited until Roy lifted his gray head and met Mack's gaze. Roy's lighter blue eyes had filled with anger and hurt. "I'm tired of seeing you like this, Dad. Come out with me. Come work a few jobs. It'll do you some good."

Roy wheeled on him. "What would do me good is if your mother would come back."

Mack ran a hand through his hair. "Dad . . ."

"Until she does that, I'm not leaving this place." Roy stalked out of the kitchen and headed down the basement stairs, his footsteps thudding heavy and hard as he descended into an even darker silence.

Alex's entire body shuddered and shimmied, and had been for the better part of Saturday. She suspected she would never walk straight again.

And she'd yet to make more than a small dent in tearing down the walls.

Damn. She'd thought this would be a hell of a lot easier. The TV shows made all that home repair stuff look simple, wrapping up a whole room renovation in a half hour, transforming entire houses in an hour. The hosts put a tool in Average Annie's hands, and wham-slam, she was knocking down a wall and erecting a new one before the first commercial break.

Yeah, well, apparently they kept a hidden home improvement team off camera, because Alex wasn't getting much of anything done in an entire day, never mind an hour.

Discouragement weighed heavy on her. She blew her bangs out of her eyes, dropped down onto an overturned five-gallon bucket and lowered the reciprocating saw to the floor. Okay, so she wasn't Harriet Homebuilder. She wasn't even Harriet's stepsister. Or distant cousin thrice-removed.

Mack had been right. This place was a disaster. What had Grandma been thinking?

Alex reached into the cooler beside her and pulled out a diet soda, opened the can, then took a long swig. The fizzy carbonated beverage slid down her throat, settling in her empty stomach with a slightly acidic burn.

Alex glanced around the house—and that eerie feeling returned again.

She *had* been here before. She knew it.

But when? The only house she remembered living in was her grandmother's.

This house had been abandoned for a long time. Most of the wallpaper had peeled off the walls in long strips, like a mummy losing its wrappings. The drop ceiling had lost enough tiles to expose an even worse situation above with dark concentric rings spelling water damage, either from the roof or the second floor. Or both.

She should check out the rooms upstairs and see if

something was leaking. A place like this, empty for so long, had surely been vandalized. Not that she'd know what to do about a leak, but hey, at least she could see where the problems were. Better informed than ignorant.

Alex climbed the stairs, her sneakers sinking into the divots in the worn shag carpeting. She paused at the top, then entered the first bedroom on the right. The pale brown paint on the walls gave them an odd cast of color. Alex brushed a palm across the surface, and with it, she whisked off a thick layer of dust.

The walls weren't brown.

They were pink.

Pink. For girls.

Alex stared at the wall. Rubbed another circle of dirt away. Tiny hairs rose on the back of her neck and her throat began to close. She snatched her hand back from the wall and stumbled back, reaching for her cell phone.

She punched in Grandma Kenner's number, her fingers trembling as she hit the digits on the Motorola. "Grandma, tell me about this house."

Tell me it's not what I think.

"I, uh, don't know that much."

Tell me it's the house of a friend.

Alex caught the lie in her grandmother's voice. Grandma Kenner had never hid anything from her before, not that Alex knew.

Tell me it's someone else's house. Please.

She backed away from the pink walls, turned and hurried down the stairs, back to the main floor. She stopped and leaned against the staircase, her heart hammering in her chest, still wanting to think this was some other place, anywhere but . . .

"Grandma, *whose house is this?*"

A beat passed. Another. "Do you remember it at all?"

Did she remember? Alex pivoted and ran a hand over the living room walls. Instead of drywall, they had been covered with rough pine, stained a dark, almost ebony color. The surface seemed to claw at her skin, scratch her palms.

The memory slammed into her, hitting in a barrage of images.

She'd been running, playing a solitary game of pretend. Her hair caught on the corner of the wall. A sliver of wood grabbed hold like the trees in the *Wizard of Oz* and held on to her ponytail as she ran by, yanking her to a stop with a painful pinch.

Alex's hand went to the back of her head and she swore she could still feel the spot where she'd lost those strands.

Then she moved away from the wall and the pictures began filtering in, as real as if she'd stepped two decades into the past. A broken doll on the carpet by a red pool created by a spilled cup of Kool-Aid. Alex watching a flickering television from her perch on the couch, careful to avoid the spring that poked into her leg if she didn't sit just right. Standing by the windows, waiting, always waiting, for her mother to come home. A stranger playing babysitter, one of an endless parade of temporary friends.

She covered her mouth, cutting off a gasp.

No. Not this house. Of all the houses in Massachusetts, the millions of possibilities—

She didn't want to believe it could be this one. Not *this* one.

"This is . . ." Alex swallowed. Her heart began to race, and in her mind the memories sputtered like the old TV used to—eating cereal straight from the box for lunch, for dinner, for every meal, because there'd been no milk, no bread, no bananas. Nothing else in the cabinets. "This is her house."

"Your house," Grandma corrected. "Where you lived as a little girl."

"This isn't mine. It's hers." She shook her head, wandering to a built-in hutch in the corner and seeing now a vague memory of dishes there. Not many, just a few, a ragtag collection of plates and cups. Castoffs. Other people's leftovers.

The cupboard below. She'd hid there once.

"Your grandfather and I bought it for your mother when you were born. She left it to you when she died. You were too young, so I held on to it, paying off the mortgage, the taxes. So that when you were old enough—"

"When I was old enough, I'd what? Want to live here again?" Pain alternated with anger, catapulting one over the other, like an emotional game of leapfrog. Alex struggled for breath, for composure. For her brain to accept the impossible. "Hell, no, Grandma. *Burn* the place. Tear it down."

"You're still very angry."

"Don't you think I have every right to be?"

"Yes, you do, sweetheart, but . . . sometimes forgiveness is the best path to finding your way out of the forest."

This was what Alex got for having a grandmother who loved to garden. Every lesson was wrapped in a nature analogy. Even lessons Alex didn't want to hear. "She's dead, Grandma. There's no need to forgive anyone." Or talk about her. Or be in her house. Or be here at all.

"I didn't mean forgiving just your mother, Alex. My daughter wasn't a perfect parent, Lord knows. She had her faults, but you've been awfully hard on yourself, too."

A tightness started in Alex's chest. She let out a breath, easing the sensation, but not the arrow of truth Grandma's words had delivered. But Grandma hadn't lived here. She hadn't known how much Alex wished she could go back and undo a hundred different moments. Moments that still stung, needles in her skin, her heart.

She ran a hand down the glass front of the cabinet, the edges having the ring of familiarity but the distance of years. "This is really the house where I grew up?" Alex knew the truth but still couldn't accept it. Couldn't believe the place she'd lived in as a child still existed.

"It's where you started out. That's not the same thing." Grandma paused a long moment, and Alex could almost feel her trying to send a mental hug. "I knew if I told you this house belonged to your mother, you'd take a blowtorch to it before you'd set foot in it."

Alex huffed. "I still might."

"Don't." Grandma let out a long, slow breath. "The one thing the doom-and-gloomers around here have shown me is that you have to bring chips to the party."

"What's that supposed to mean?"

"That even when you have bad news, or something awful to deal with, you still have to make the best of it. Find the good in the bad. There is some good there." Grandma's voice softened and Alex could almost hear her smile. "Look how you turned out."

"That's all your doing."

"I'd love to take the credit, dear, but I can't. Your mother was far from perfect, but she loved you."

Alex snorted. Loved her? What had her mother known about love? What had she taught Alex about love—except that it could hurt? "If she loved me, she wouldn't have lived the way she did. She would have put her kids first."

"My daughter should have done a lot of things that she didn't do, but she *did* love you, you need to know that. And maybe in that house, you'll find out how much she did. All the clues are there, if you look hard enough. Don't you want to know about her? About you?" Grandma paused. "You hardly remember anything. You were so little, sweetheart."

Alex didn't respond. She bit her lip and turned away, but the conversation lingered in the air.

"You can do this, Alex. It'll be good for you, too." Grandma's voice held the same note of firmness that had delivered lectures on everything from taking vitamins to eating oatmeal on winter mornings. "You can't keep letting your past rule your future."

"It's not."

Grandma harrumphed.

"Okay, maybe it is. A little." Alex looked around the rooms again, seeing them now not as a challenge but as a disaster she couldn't possibly tackle. No, she couldn't. Not this house. "But starting here? With this?"

"What better place to start than back at the beginning? You can't figure out where you're going if you don't look at where you came from." Grandma paused. "And no one said you had to stay there, Alex. It's yours. Do with it what you will. Keep it, sell it. I don't care. But your mother left it to you for a reason and because she did, I think you should at least hold on to the house for a little while. Maybe see what secrets it holds."

A house that was, as Mack had said, a dump. A complete monstrosity. It needed an unbelievable amount of work before she could put it on the market.

Assuming Alex even wanted to do the work now that she knew the history.

"Do you know how much work is involved here, Grandma?"

"Yes, I do, honey." In Grandma Kenner's voice, Alex could tell she meant a lot more than renovating the money pit of a house. "But take it from this old lady who has made her fair share of mistakes. This is the kind of hard, hands-on work that changes the soul."

Alex stared at the cell phone for a long time after they hung up, as if the slim Motorola might chirp back with a better solution, before finally slipping it back into her pocket.

Keep the house. How could she do that? When the past contained within these walls was too difficult to face, too much to handle? She closed her eyes, the images coming back in flashes, like a jerky eight-millimeter movie, flashes seen through a child's eyes. She remembered so little about her mother.

She'd had long brown hair, green eyes. She often wore short denim skirts. And T-shirts. She'd loved T-shirts with sayings, though Alex had been too little to read the words.

There'd been music, lots of loud music, and people, lots and lots of people. Her mother had lived life like it was one long party, seeming to forget she had a child who needed her. Alex, beneath the table, playing with her dolls, while the people laughed and danced, and ate, and kissed, and her mother pulled her out from time to time, like her daughter was an accessory she'd just remembered. Hardly ever home, never living a normal, sit-down-to-dinner or read-books life. Even when her sister had been born. And then that awful day.

Alex caught her breath, and it hurt, sending fire down her lungs.

The open door. Beyond it—Brittany—so still, so very still.

Alex closed her eyes, but the memories kept coming, a wave of them, the ones she tried never to think about, pushing past the mental locks. She saw her mother now, grief-stricken, running, running out the door, getting into her car, and taking off too fast, too upset.

She'd run a red light, kept going past the guardrail, and left Alex alone.

Alex sucked in the stale air around her, swallowed hard. God. She hadn't thought of that day in years. Alex closed her eyes, pinched the bridge of her nose and tried to block it, but the image of her baby sister appeared again. Alex wrapped her arms around her body, shivering against a sudden chill, even though it was at least ten degrees hotter in the little house than outside. She shoved the memories back into the mental box and locked it tight.

God, no, she couldn't handle this. It was too much.

Her grandmother might think renovating the house would make Alex work through whatever issues she might have with her childhood, but this hammer-and-nail therapy wasn't going to work.

Nevertheless, Alex needed a place to live. And this place stood empty. Unused. Granted, it was also a piece of crap right now, but it was an *available* piece of crap Alex happened to own.

The smart thing to do would be to work on it. Make it habitable.

Then sell it.

Take the money and move the hell on. She'd come this far—she could make it that much further.

Could she? Really? Here?

It was too much, too much to take. Too much to do. Too much for her. Hot tears edged at the corners of Alex's eyes, but she pressed the heels of her hands hard into her eye sockets and refused to give in to defeat. To the past. She'd get beyond this. Just like she did before.

Work. Work on the house. And stop thinking, for God's sake.

She crossed the room and reached again for the electric saw. Before she turned it on, her front door opened. Or, rather, it fell into the room, the hinges at that moment apparently deciding they'd had enough of holding on to the jam.

With the sun bursting behind him like an announcement of salvation, Mack walked in. He stepped calmly over the broken door, as if he saw that kind of thing every day. "So, when's the housewarming party?" He held out a potted plant and grinned.

The floodgates gave way and Alex burst into tears.

He dropped the plant onto the fireplace hearth and crossed to her. "Hey, I didn't mean to make you cry. I know I'm no Robin Williams, so forgive my lame attempt at a joke. And the plant, just throw it out. Seriously. Throw it out the nearest window. It'll make you feel better. I swear."

"I-I-c-can't . . ."

"Sure you can." He plucked the pot off the fireplace and put it in her hands. "Just chuck it. Let it take root wherever it lands. Call it avant-garde landscaping."

"It's not that, it's . . ." She swiped at her face, then looked up at him, the damn tears still coming, mad as hell at herself for crying, for letting the house, the memories it triggered that had been sitting at the corners of her mind, get to her. "This is the house where I grew up."

Mack paused, confusion knitting his brows, then the
light dawned in his eyes, and his entire face softened.
He stepped forward. "Oh, God, Alex. How . . . ?"

"My mother left it to me." She let out a chuff, but
the breath caught in her throat, lodged like a log. "My
grandmother thinks renovating it will be some kind
of therapy."

Now Mack closed the gap, his hands reaching for
her, his touch on her bare arms as comforting as a
flannel blanket, his blue eyes filled with an understanding that came from knowing her since she'd
learned her ABCs. The tightness in Alex's chest eased
a bit. "And what do you think?"

"I think . . ." She drew in a breath, held it, then let
her gaze travel over the space. "I think maybe she's
right. But I don't know if I'm strong enough for this."

"You?" A wide smile took over his features. "You are
the strongest person I know—outside of maybe Arnold
Schwarzenegger. Before he was the Governator. He's
let his pecs go all to hell since getting into office."

His words had their intended effect—she laughed,
and a bit of the heaviness lifted from her shoulders.
What would she do without Mack? Every time she
needed him, he was there, the only person who could
see through the clouds in her life and find the sunshine.

"Where do I start, Mack?" She sighed, and tears
threatened her eyes all over again, thinking of all that
lay ahead, tasks too huge for one woman. Coupled with
everything else—trying to launch a new job at the
newspaper, rearranging her life. When she took on a
To Do list, she did it big. "Where the hell do I start?"

"Right here, Alex. With this." He cupped the pot of
geraniums. The bright red flowers wiggled a little, like
they were waving at her. "Just do it, Alex. Open the
window and let 'em rip."

She wanted to laugh but couldn't because now she really had started to cry. Not just because of the house, or the truth that had smacked her hard in the gut, but because of Mack, being there, with a stupid pot of geraniums, and his dependable-as-sunshine goofy grin. "I c-c-can't. The damn windows are p-p-painted shut."

Mack crossed to one of the windows, ran a finger along the edge, then turned back to her. "Yep, they are. Well, that just means you have to throw harder." He reached out to Alex, tugged her over to one of the windows and gave her a pat on the shoulder. "Now throw that sucker. Like Sammy Sosa."

She gaped at him. "*Through* the window? But it's closed."

"So? What better way to get rid of some of that frustration and get a start on the demo? Personally, I prefer a sledgehammer, but we can start with this." He gestured between the plant in her hands and the window. "Go ahead. Do it."

"But—"

"I may not know a lot about what happened here," he said, his voice soft against her neck, tender with the friendship of years, "but I do know there's a lot you'd like to erase. A whole lot of holes you'd like to punch in that past." He squeezed her shoulder and met her gaze, knowing her so well, so very well. "Not to mention the holes you'd like to punch in Edward's selfish face."

She swiped at her face and nodded.

"Then start right now, Alex."

Mack had gone insane. He expected her to throw a plant through the window?

On purpose?

She turned back to him, to tell him no, when her gaze caught on the empty rooms. Rooms that held the echoes of crying nights, missed chances, empty promises.

This house. This damn house.

She barely remembered these rooms, but they still tickled at the edges of so many other bad memories. A childhood no one should have had to live. A mother who had tried but failed, and a child who'd been too young to fix anything, even her own sandwich.

Then she thought of the past few days, of Edward, of how he'd lied and connived his way into her bed and her heart.

Bastard.

"Go ahead, Alex," Mack urged. "You'll feel better."

"I hate this house," Alex whispered, then she hefted the weight of the pot in both hands and swung forward, putting her entire body into the movement, letting go as she did. The heavy pot of geraniums went flying, hitting the glass at the same time Mack yanked her back, out of the shrapnel spray.

In an instant, it was over. A spray of glass and bright red petals littered the floor, a light summer breeze filtered in through the jagged open circle, and Alex had the beginning of landscaping. Sort of.

Lightness filled her chest, as refreshing as ice cream on a hot day, as swimming in the middle of August. But more than that, she felt oddly like she had accomplished something. Made a change. Erased a little of what had been here before.

She turned to Mack and started laughing. "That was insane."

Mack just grinned. He moved toward the window, inspecting the damage. "Yep, I was right. Single pane. Not even insulated. You'd need to replace it, anyway, to have any kind of protection against the winter. Too bad I don't have more plants."

Reality inserted itself into the temporary reprieve she'd felt. Smashing windows wasn't the most practical method of home improvement.

"That would only make for more work. I've got enough of that on my hands right now." She sank back onto the bucket, dug in the cooler for a second soda and handed it to him. "What are you doing here? I thought you pronounced this place DOA."

"I did. But once it became clear you were going to be stubborn about this, I took pity on you." He grinned. "And I returned."

"I'm glad you did."

"So you really want to do this, huh?"

She crossed her arms over her chest and nodded. "The best way to erase a bad past—or, more specifically, my bad past decisions, is to start with taking out the carpet and knocking down the walls, if that makes sense."

Mack considered her for a long time. "It makes perfect sense, Alex."

For the first time since she'd walked through that front door, she felt like she had an ally. She wasn't alone. Just like back when she'd first met Mack and her world had instantly expanded when he'd offered her half of his PB and J and a listening ear. And here he was, doing the same thing with a geranium. She smiled, then wrapped her arms around him in a tight hug. "Thanks, Mack."

He stiffened. How odd. Never before when she'd hugged Mack had he turned into a statue, like she had the plague.

"You're, uh, welcome."

Alex looked up at Mack. His features had become unreadable, his expression stony. "Did I do something wrong?"

"No."

"Okay," she said, then started to move out of the embrace, when he pulled her back, into his arms. His strength went around her, with warmth this time, her body curving perfectly into his, fitting as if she'd been made for him.

There was no coldness in this hug. Nothing strange. Except . . .

Heat grew in her gut. Her pulse began to race, and his arms didn't feel comforting, but . . .

Sexy. Desirable. She found herself wondering what it would be like if he touched her in other ways.

Mack cleared his throat and stepped back, the strange tension between them broken, evaporated as if it had never existed. "Anytime you, uh, need some more geraniums, I'm your man."

She worked a smile to her face, still trying to sort the jumble running through her. "I'll keep that in mind. But first, I have a lot of interior work to do."

Mack looked around the space, assessing it again, then turned back to her, reading her face as easily as the newspaper. "You know the best part about renovation?" He moved behind her, put his hands on her shoulders and spun her slowly around the room. With one hand, he pointed toward one section of the room after another. "You can forget what happened here, erase it entirely. Create your own vision. Close your eyes, Alex. See that vision. Imagine this house, not as it was, but as it can be. A new wall there. Some built-in shelves here."

"This is crazy."

"Try harder. Tell me, what's on those shelves?"

She opened her eyes and shook her head at him. "There aren't any shelves, Mack."

He slid his palm over her lids, shutting her vision

into darkness again. "Picture it, Alex. Try. What's on the shelves?"

She sighed. Paused. For a long moment, nothing came to mind, nothing to erase the images of the tattered, ruined house that stood here now. Of a broken, interrupted childhood.

And then, the shadows gave way to light and a vision began to take shape. "Books," she said. "And flowers. Fresh flowers."

"Good. And on the windows?"

"White curtains." She saw them, truly saw them, as if they were hanging there. The image took shape, then took flight from her lips. "Simple, plain, hanging to the floor. Nothing too fancy. Nothing to distract you from the view. Of . . . daffodils. Tulips. Rosebushes. All the landscaping outside, waiting to burst into spring color."

"It sounds wonderful."

"It sounds like"—she opened her eyes and turned back to him—"like I'm rewriting history, in a way."

"Exactly." He brought her full circle to meet his gaze. "And creating a whole new future, too."

"But what if . . ." She bit her lip. "What if I can't? What if it's too much for me to handle?"

"That's where I come in," he said and he smiled again. "I'm your renovation buddy."

She laughed. "That's what you're calling yourself?"

Mack shifted, and the movement brought him closer to her, within inches. Sharp, heated awareness sparked along Alex's nerve endings. He reached out and danced a fingertip along her jawline, the movement meant to be a tease, but awakening instead a fire inside her so strong, she nearly quivered with the sudden rush.

"Something like that," he said, his voice low, dark.

Alex stood there, transfixed, her lips parted, waiting—for what, she didn't know—but suddenly, the conversation about the house had ended and a conversation of a very different sort skated just beneath their words. "You're planning on staying," she asked, the words escaping on a breath as her gaze met Mack's, his blue eyes as dark as an ocean at night, "for the long haul?"

"As long as it takes," he said. His finger slid slowly along the curve of her jaw, then drifted away. Yet his touch seemed to still burn on her skin, the places he'd merely whispered against left seared. "If there's one thing I'm known for, it's getting the job done. And doing it right."

Alex gulped. "We are talking about construction here, aren't we?"

His smile curved upward, sparkled in his eyes. "Of course. Unless there's something else you need me to do?"

The question hung in the air. With a few words, Alex could turn the tide of their relationship, upend the friendship and turn it into something—

Something very, very hot.

She knew Mack and knew, without a doubt, that he would be good in bed. She'd heard, after all, a hundred times over from the girlfriend of the week how amazing Mack was. How considerate. How talented in the bedroom.

But in the end, she'd undoubtedly be shuffled off to join the women who shared memories of Mack, and nothing more. In the process, she'd lose the very things she treasured most about him.

And probably, lose him. Not to mention her dignity, and her heart. Not a risk Alex wanted to take.

"No," Alex said, stepping back to brush invisible dirt off her shorts and forcing herself back into work mode. "I don't need anything else. Though I might want to hire a more talented landscaper."

"What, you don't like how I changed things?" he asked, referring to the geranium scattered across the front lawn.

"No, Mack. All you did was make more of a mess," she said. Meaning everything else.

Chapter Five

Mack had one philosophy that had worked for him every day of his life.

Hard work would take care of any problem.

Apparently, that philosophy didn't apply when it came to Alexandra Kenner.

Seeing Alex in those little denim shorts and hot-pink tank top, her body coated with a fine sheen of sweat, as she worked with everything from his sledgehammer to the reciprocating saw, had his mind running down some seriously physically frustrating paths. Not to mention that window of vulnerability she had opened today, which had nearly broken his heart and made him want to scoop her up, take her home and never let her go. That alone told him he needed to do something other than stand around and watch her.

So he worked more. Hit things harder. Drove home too many nails to count.

But none of it distanced him from thoughts of Alex. He could have built three Eiffel Towers and still had enough pent-up frustration left over for the Taj Mahal.

Alex paused in sweeping up the debris from the last wall they had knocked down. Earlier that day, Mack had ordered a Dumpster, and together the two of them had made at least five dozen trips out there. His arms ached; he could only imagine how Alex's felt, but she'd kept up with him, refusing to slow down or take a break longer than a few minutes.

Mack had talked her into opening up the space between the living and dining rooms, giving the small house a wider, more modern layout. Already, the house had additional light, felt breezier, homier. She pressed the back of her hand against her forehead. "How do you do this work all day, Mack?"

"Easy. I'm the big, hulking man, remember?"

She laughed. "Seriously. I'm beat."

"Want to call it a day?"

Alex looked around. "It doesn't look like we got much done."

"Are you kidding me? We knocked down two walls, stripped off the old plaster and lathe in the living room and dining room, hauled all that debris out to the Dumpster *and* took down the old light fixtures in both rooms. I'd say that's a lot. You're a workhorse."

"Don't let anyone ever say you don't know how to flatter a girl."

Mack did know how to flatter a girl. But when it came to Alex . . .

Well, she was different.

And when she inhaled, as she did just now, the slight movement doing the same thing to her as it did to everyone else—making her chest rise—her skin released the jasmine notes of her perfume, the raspberry scent of her shampoo. But to Mack, that ordinary act set off a cavalcade of fireworks in his gut.

His hand curled tighter around the two-by-four in his grip. Every lesson he'd learned in Man 101 flew out of his head. He thought of nothing but pressing

her to the wall and trailing his mouth down the warm
expanse of skin beneath her jaw, to the valley between
her breasts, then lifting her shirt and teasing his
tongue over every sweet inch of flesh until she cried
out and he found a release from the agony of want—

And not having.

Because Alex was his friend, and had made it clear
that was all she wanted from him. Friendship. If he
started acting all "manly" with her, he knew he'd
screw that up. But sometimes—

Sometimes he wanted to do exactly that.

"Do I have plaster dust on my nose or something?"
Alex asked.

Mack realized he was staring at Alex. Way to go. He
cleared his throat and tossed the timber onto the pile
in the corner. Then he grabbed the broom from her.
No way he could keep watching her hips sway around
the room like that. "No, sorry. Guess I'm tired, too."

"You? The big, hulking man, tired?" She gave him a
teasing grin.

"Yeah. Exactly." He started sweeping, stirring up a
furious cloud of dust, avoiding Alex and the turmoil
stirred up inside his body. That desire dust storm was
a lot more volatile than any sawdust on the floor. He
kept his back to her, concentrating every ounce of his
attention on the sawdust and wood chips before him,
but still seeing only Alex's hips, ass, breasts—

God, he wanted her. He wanted everything about her.
Her lips, her body, her mind. He'd never craved anything as much as he craved her. The broom's bristles
bent at a 45-degree angle with the force of his efforts,
the dirt pile growing larger by the second. But still it
wasn't enough.

If he didn't keep himself busy—and busy to the nth
degree—he'd end up throwing Alex to the floor like

a caveman and finally putting into action all those fantasies that had played in his mind for years.

A sure way to take their relationship to the next level. And also a big way to act like a jerk. Alex had just broken up with a total jerk. She needed his help. A shoulder to lean on. Not a Neanderthal.

He glanced over and saw Alex watching him. A slight, distracted smile danced across her features. His chest tightened and he paused for a moment, mesmerized. Alex's tongue slipped out, flickered across her crimson lips, and Mack quit breathing.

"Maybe you should, uh, stop, Mack."

"Stop what? Sweeping? But I'm nearly done."

"Go home." She stepped forward, her hand wrapping around his on the handle. Warm palm meeting his, the touch so soft, yet so strong. "It's late. You've, umm . . . probably put in a full day on your own construction site, too. Yet here you are, still helping me."

"I said I would." He stared at Alex. What was up? All of a sudden she was kicking him out? When he was thirty seconds from being done with the cleanup?

"Yeah, but . . ."

Her hand still lay atop his, her grip secure, warm. He couldn't help but imagine her hand on top of another piece of his anatomy. Definitely not the way to keep his thoughts out of caveman territory. "But what, Alex?"

Alex shifted one shoulder, whether to answer his question or to alleviate an itch, Mack didn't know, and her tank top slipped, the strap sliding down her arm, exposing a slim white satin strap and a whole lot of bare skin. Mack reached out, slid a finger beneath the cotton and let his touch ride along her skin until the strap was back in place. "You, uh . . ."

"Oh. Thanks."

She didn't move. Neither did he.

"I should finish," Mack said.

"Finish . . . what?"

"Finish what I started," he said, knowing damn well that he had stopped talking about the floor a long time ago. His touch lingered along her skin, rising with her every breath, heat on heat. Desire coiled tight inside him. He took a step forward, releasing his grip on the broom, leaving her to hold the wooden handle. His other hand slid down her bare arm, covering her warm, sweet skin with his palm, then drifting over to her waist to bring Alex to him, pressing her lithe body to his hard, hot one.

Alex's mouth opened, her wide green eyes capturing his. "What are we doing?"

"Starting something," Mack said.

"Starting what?"

In answer, Mack bent forward, closing the gap between them slowly, not sure he should do this, not sure at all that tipping the equation was wise. Before his lips could meet hers, a car alarm went off somewhere outside, blaring its insistent horn song to the neighborhood. Alex jerked back, breaking the contact, the tension, as quickly as a pin pricking a balloon.

And deflating the hope that had risen in Mack.

She spun away from him and went to work again with the broom, finishing where he had left off, bending over and scooping the debris into a plastic pan as she talked. "Ever since we've been kids, that's all you've ever done is help me out, Mack. Maybe it's better if you don't do that this time." Her voice trembled as she spoke. From nerves? From anger?

She'd picked up the conversation as if nothing had transpired. Clearly, Alex hadn't felt what he had. And she wanted nothing more than business as usual.

"Alex, I don't mind, really."

"It's not that I don't appreciate the help," she went on, barreling forward without hearing him, "but I don't want you to kill yourself to bail me out. Again. I can't keep expecting you to save me every time I get myself into a jam. And this one is a major jam, complete with a whole lot of emotional grapes."

There was nothing left on the floor to clean, but Alex kept on sweeping and scooping. What the hell was up with her today?

Him.

That was what was up. She was pissed at him. He shouldn't have tried to kiss her. He knew better, damn it.

Mack took both the broom and dustpan from her and put them against the workbench. "Hey, you're done, Martha Stewart."

"I'm just making sure every last bit is gone. I can handle cleaning up, Mack. You can go home."

"Are you kicking me out?"

"No. But there's really no reason to stay." She sipped at her soda, avoiding his gaze.

"I don't mind helping you. That's what friends are for, right?"

"Friends, yes, not gluttons for punishment. Seriously. I took this mess on." She made a sweeping gesture of the house. "It's my job to tackle, not yours."

Maybe so, but Mack saw the house as a way to both tempt and torture himself. He could spend more time with Alex—a win and a lose situation all at once. A win because it helped appease this constant throbbing need to see her, be with her, inside him—

And a lose because it just made that throbbing need worse.

Okay, so maybe he *was* a glutton for punishment.

Still, he didn't understand why all of a sudden she wanted him out of here when not three hours ago they'd agreed that he was going to help her. Especially when she must have realized by now this job was too much for one woman. "You want to renovate this place, right?"

She nodded. "Yeah."

"And you are not Joe Builder."

She sighed. "True. If there's one thing I learned today, it's that no matter how many episodes of *Trading Spaces* I watch I'm never going to turn into a contractor."

"Good. I'm glad you agree with me. For once." He grinned. "So you're stuck with me. Day after day. For long hours, working side by side."

She swallowed hard. Looked away and started fiddling with a pile of nails on the temporary workbench he'd made out of some plywood. "I can't let you do that."

Mack stepped forward and tipped her chin up to meet his. Alex's green eyes were wide, almost luminescent in the overly bright light cast by the halogen lamp set up in the corner. Her lips were cherry red, moist from the soda, and so damn kissable, they could have been a commercial. "It's not a favor, Alex. This is good for me, too. I've been the boss man of my company, sitting on my butt and directing people way too long. It's nice to be working with my hands for a change. Reminds me why I went into construction in the first place."

She considered that for a moment. "Okay. But if you insist on helping me, then I'll pay you. Keep it a business-only transaction."

He grinned. "Last I checked, you didn't have any money."

"I have some. I have a job."

He released her chin but didn't move away, just kept inhaling her perfume, wanting her with a nearly painful desire. He knew he shouldn't do this. Knew he'd already treaded way too close today, but couldn't stop himself.

Torture and pleasure at the same time. Damn, even dogs learned faster than he did. "You're a reporter, not a Rockefeller. And if you're here with me all the time, you won't be doing much reporting."

"True."

"Go to work, let me do the heavy lifting, and you can help after you're done at the paper. I can get you materials at cost, which should make a difference in your budget."

"Mack, friends or not, I can't let you do all this for nothing. What do you want?"

You. A bed. One very long weekend. And a can of whipped cream.

Mack cleared his throat. "Nothing."

She put her fists on her hips. When she looked at him like that, he had trouble breathing, because her breasts perked up and her eyes flashed, and everything about her came alive. And made everything within him do the same.

"Come on, Mack, there has to be *something* I can do for you."

"My father—" he blurted out before he could think.

Damn. He hadn't meant to say that. He'd just been scrambling to come up with something before he mentioned a motel room instead.

"Your father what?"

"Nothing." He went back to work with the broom.

She got in front of him. "Will you talk to me?"

Mack wasn't a spill-his-guts kind of guy. He liked to keep his guts right where they were, tucked inside. But with Alex looking at him, her green eyes wide, the urge to open up to her doubled. Just like when he'd been a kid and he'd snuck over to her grandmother's house in the middle of the night, crawling into the window of Alex's room, because he'd gotten scared when he'd overheard his parents arguing long into the night. Alex had gotten out her Monopoly game and made him play until he forgot every bad thing that he had heard in his living room.

He let out a breath. "My dad needs a project. Needs *something* to get him out of the house. He's locked himself inside there since my mother left him. This house is the sort of small challenge he needs."

"*This* is a small challenge?"

Mack laughed. "Okay, it's bigger than that. But it's not as big or as much pressure as building a house. And it'll give me an excuse to drag him someplace every day."

"Gee, when you put it that way. Drag him over here, kicking and screaming . . . How can I resist?" She put out her palm. "Should we shake on it?"

Shake hands?

Mack had a better idea. He'd much rather seal the deal with a kiss. He took a step forward, desire rocketing through him fast, furious, pounding in his head, when Alex misinterpreted his movement and took his palm, pumping his hand vigorously.

"Good, we have a deal." Her smile widened. "Now, if you can find me a hot guy who doesn't think lying is a part-time job, my life will be complete."

Once again, Alex had reminded Mack that she thought of him as a friend. Not a potential boyfriend.

Reminded him of the promise he'd made that day by the pool. Clearly, a moment of delusional thinking. But also the best course. He had all the staying power of runny glue, and she wanted a man with bondability.

All his life, he'd done what he could to ensure Alex's safety. Happiness. Why would he deny her this?

Even if, when he looked down into Alex's eyes, his hand still gripping hers, every nerve in his body sang at her touch, acutely aware of her presence. Even if he wanted her in a way he'd never wanted any woman before.

"Hey, what about me?" he asked, giving her a grin. Saying it like a joke. Not meaning it that way at all.

"You?" she laughed. "Mack, no offense, but . . ."

"What?"

"You're a great friend. The guy every woman calls when the power's out and she needs someone to keep her company. Or she needs a date to some family function just to shut Aunt Eloise up about her shriveling ovaries. But you and I both know you are not settling-down material, and that's what I'm looking for. A guy who wants to put up a fence and build a future. Make plans."

He took a step closer, filling the gap between them. "You? The woman who has run from anything resembling a plan all her life?"

"Hey, we all have to grow up sometime."

"Maybe so. I tried it myself, Alex. Believe me, there's a lot of false advertising out there about being part of the white picket fence life."

She sighed. "Mack, all I want is to be happy. Maybe I won't find everything I want with a white picket fence, but I think it's about time I tried, don't you?"

His gaze roamed over her face. Then down her lithe figure and back up again to those deep green eyes, so vibrant they were like a meadow in spring.

Alex was right.

She'd never be happy with him. Not in a relationship, at least. And if Mack wanted to do what was best for Alex, he'd keep his promise to introduce her to a man who wouldn't break her heart.

In other words, a man as far removed from himself as possible.

"I'll find you a Mr. Perfect," Mack said, moving away until he no longer caught the scent of raspberries. "After all, isn't that what friends are for?"

Chapter Six

"Tell me again why I'm wearing this ridiculous thing," Alex said on Sunday night. She stared down at her skirt, and saw far too little material and way too much leg.

"Because this guy might just be the one and don't you want to meet Mr. Right for the first time in something that screams hot?" Renee turned Alex toward the mirror and gave a little flourish wave. "See? Doesn't that make the perfect first impression?"

"It screams harlot. He'll think I'm a prostitute."

Renee grinned. It was the first time she'd smiled in three days and at this point, Alex would have worn Go-Go boots and a Miracle Bra to keep a smile on Renee's face.

"Look at the upside," Renee said. "If he mistakes you for a hooker, it might just turn out to be a very lucrative part-time job. A win-win now that you've taken on that money pit."

Alex rolled her eyes, then took one more assessing glance in the mirror. For a first date, this ensemble—a black leather skirt, high heels and a red scoop-neck top—topped the too-sexy meter. Mack would undoubtedly agree.

Or would his eyes light up with appreciation if he

saw her? Would that familiar grin curve across his face, and instead of teasing her like one of the guys, tell her she was beautiful, desirable?

Whoa. Where had that come from? Since when did she worry about what *Mack* thought of what she wore? Since he'd gotten close enough to kiss her the other day. Since he'd muddied the waters of their friendship by making her wonder if she'd read desire in his eyes—or just imagined it. Like she was imagining him desiring her now.

Clearly a sign she needed a different outfit.

"I'm changing," Alex said.

"You'll regret it," Renee said. "Your ovaries are aging by the second, you know."

"Thanks for the reminder," Alex said, ducking into the closet, peeling off the outfit and opting for the second choice she'd brought along—black jeans and a turquoise V-neck top. She stepped out and flung out her arms in a ta-da gesture. "This is more me."

Renee mocked a yawn as she moved around the bedroom picking up stuffed animals and little toys that had been left behind like a Hansel and Gretel crumb trail. The kids weren't home but evidence of them was in every nook and cranny of the tiny apartment. "That's like putting a Buick in the driveway when you could have been revving a Firebird down the street. Which do you think will get a second glance?"

"Maybe *you* should wear the skirt. Nothing gets a husband raring like a miniskirt, right?" Alex gave Renee a hopeful smile. "Go on down to Tony's brother's house and talk to your husband. You two need to work things out, hon."

Renee turned away and busied herself with folding three other rejected shirts. The hunch had returned to her shoulders. "Tony living there is only temporary. He'll be back."

Worry tightened in Alex's chest. Should she probe? Let it go?

Thus far, her friend hadn't talked about what was going on in her marriage. Why she had given up on it—for the third time in eleven years—and why she had been alone in this apartment for three days. She simply clammed up whenever Alex brought up the subject.

Maybe Alex should talk to Mack. He and Tony were good friends. Mack had to know something. Perhaps he could intervene, figure out what was going on between the two of them. Or at the very least, convince Tony to come home.

Alex reached out and laid a hand over Renee's, stopping her from refolding a sweater for the fourth time. "Renee, I'm just worried about you. I care about both you and Tony, and the kids. I want to see everything work out."

Renee put down the sweater. "Aren't you going to be late?"

"I have time."

"Well, I'd love to talk, but I don't have time right now. I have . . . plans."

"You never mentioned any plans." What was Renee hiding? And why did she refuse to talk about the issues?

"Tony picked up the kids after dinner and took them to Putt-Putt, which leaves me totally alone for a couple hours. I'm going to pretend there isn't a huge stack of laundry waiting for me in the other room and just enjoy myself." Again, another smile, but nothing that told Alex any information.

When it came to her personal life, Renee had been

pushing Alex away more and more lately, and Alex couldn't figure out why. A wall had gone up, a wall between Renee and Tony, a wall between her and Alex, and Renee wouldn't let anyone in. On the outside, Renee acted normal, but her emotions were guarded, closed, as if she were hiding something. Even at work, she'd stopped going out to lunch with Alex, when it used to be a daily occurrence. Now, she begged off, saying she was too busy or had other plans, or had a meeting. Yet, more than once, Alex had seen Renee leaving the office with Bill Rhinehart. For companionship?

Or something more?

Whenever Alex asked, Renee ducked and dodged. In all the years Alex had known Renee, they'd never had secrets. But the nagging feeling that Renee was hiding something now refused to die.

"Why is he picking you up here?" Renee asked, returning Alex's thoughts to the present.

To her date. With Mack's choice for Mr. Right. Alex could only imagine what that could be.

"As far as Mack thinks, I'm living here. And I can't have my date dropping me off at that house. That place is just plain embarrassing."

"Not to mention unsafe." Renee wagged a finger at her. "It's a construction zone, Alex. You shouldn't be living there. If Mack found out—"

"He's not going to. Besides, I have no place else to live, Renee."

"You could live here."

"And sleep where? No offense, but your apartment is the size of a postage stamp and you already have three kids."

"Mack has a huge house."

"Mack is like Casanova on speed. There is no way I'm living with him."

"Maybe . . ." Renee began, smoothing a hand over the pile of clothes and avoiding Alex's gaze, "it's more about not wanting to see Mack bringing home other women."

"What's that supposed to mean?"

"You can't tell me you don't have a thing for that man. He is seriously hot."

Hot didn't begin to describe Mack or how her body had reacted to his the other day. Hot didn't begin to touch how close she'd come to kissing him. How she'd toyed with the idea, turning it around in her mind a hundred thousand times since. But lust didn't always lead to good sense, and Mack and her together definitely didn't make good sense.

"Renee, he grew up next door to me. Lived at my house as much as his own. He's practically my brother."

"Yeah, well, he *isn't* related to you." Renee rose and replaced the shirts in the closet before returning to her lecture. "And you should be thanking God for that fact, because that would be a cruel twist of nature if he was. You should rethink Mack."

"Why do you always think there's something between Mack and me? He's just a friend, Renee. He'd never date me, and vice versa."

"He's a man, Alex. You're a woman. That's basic sex math."

"Sex math? Is that some class I missed in high school?"

Renee laughed. "Obviously."

"Mack isn't interested in me. Ever since we were little, the man has acted like I'm as interesting as a potted plant and as annoying as a wasp. Either way, if he was interested in me, why would he be fixing me up with guys like Steve? I'm telling you, Renee, he does not have a thing for me." Alex picked up a forgotten

T-shirt and concentrated on folding it, avoiding Renee's gaze.

"Do you find him attractive?"

"Well, of course. He's a good-looking guy." Alex's attention remained on the shirt she was folding, but her face had reddened.

"Is there a buzz of electricity when you're around Mack?" Renee moved closer, dipping her head to study Alex's face.

"Certainly not."

"You're lying."

Alex finally looked up and met Renee's eyes. "Okay, maybe a little. But nothing is ever going to happen between us. Mack is way too unpredictable and unstable and uncommitted for me."

"There is that." Renee sighed and sat on the edge of the queen-sized mattress. "And, believe me, you want a man who believes wholeheartedly in marriage. You can't carry that ball alone."

"Renee." Alex sank onto the bed beside her friend. "What's going on with you and Tony?"

"I don't want to talk about it." The doorbell rang. Renee sprung to her feet, clearly glad for the interruption. "There's your date. Go have a good time."

"Only if you promise that when I get back, we'll talk."

"Answer the door," Renee said, waving in that direction. "Don't keep him waiting too long."

"Maybe I should cancel the date and stay here. With you."

"Me?" Renee brightened and together they left the bedroom. "I'm fine. Really. I'm going to make a ton of popcorn with too much butter and cry my way through *Sleepless in Seattle*. And when you get back, I want details about your date. Let me live vicariously through you. Okay?"

Alex bit her lip, considering. The doorbell rang again, and she decided Renee did look better. Less upset than earlier. "Okay. Wait up for me."

"I will. Now go open door number one so I can see what surprise Bob Barker sent over."

Alex crossed to the door and pulled it open. She hadn't been quite sure what to expect when Mack had offered to fix her up. She knew Mack and Mack's taste in women—thin, blonde, vacuous—but as to his taste in dates for her, she'd been dubious.

Oh, how she had misjudged Mack. A young George Clooney stood in the hallway, a spray of white roses in one hand and a wide smile on his face. "Alexandra?"

"You must be Steve."

He put out his free hand. "Steve Rowen. It's a pleasure to meet you."

She shook his hand, finding a warm, firm grip. No zing of attraction went through her, but she chalked that up to the fact they'd just met. Not to mention she'd had a long day of hard work. That was it. She was tired, so not being bowled over immediately by Steve was to be expected. She invited him in, taking the flowers from him as she did. "Thank you. They're beautiful."

"Mack said you like roses. White especially."

Alex fingered one of the silky petals and inhaled the delicate fragrance. "I do. I wonder how he knew that."

Steve shrugged. "I guess he pays attention."

He had? Mack, of all guys. She'd known Mack forever, but never expected him to remember a detail as minute as her favorite flower.

From her position on the sofa, Renee gave Alex a smile of Grade-A approval. "This is my friend, Renee," Alex said. "Why don't you two chat for a minute while

I put these in some water? I'm sure she's dying to get to know you."

Steve good-naturedly sat down across from Renee and submitted to a rapid-fire inquisition, while Alex trimmed the roses and set them in a vase, pouring in the little packet of preservative. What he did for a living—accounting, just like Renee. Where he lived—Newton. How old he was—thirty. If he had ever been married before—once, for two years. No kids, one dog that the wife got in the divorce. He drove a Toyota. Loved the Red Sox and hated country music. Allergic to shellfish, wouldn't eat broccoli if you paid him.

"Can I have him back now?" Alex asked. "Or do you want to hook him up to a lie detector?"

"We'll save that for the second date." Renee grinned, then waved them on their way.

A half hour later, Alex and Steve were seated in a quiet restaurant. Elegant surroundings, with a hum of instrumental music playing in the background. Waiters who whispered in and out like smoke to whisk away crumbs and empty dishes.

Steve was attentive. Nice. Charming, even. He was good at conversation, interested in Alex's job, her opinions on everything from politics to books. He had every quality she should have looked for in a man.

Including the fact that he didn't have a wife on the side.

But she didn't feel any electricity. That little internal roar of desire, that trigger that told her this was the one.

Nothing. No click. No hum. No sexual buzz.

He was nice. Just *nice.*

She found her mind wandering, to thoughts of Mack. Now there was a man that a woman—not her, of course, but other women—would feel a jolt of electricity with on a first date. He had something about him. That grin, maybe, or that sparkle in his eyes, that drew a woman in, captivated her, and made her feel like no one else existed.

Like earlier today with the sweeping. For a moment there, she'd been caught in a web with Mack, forgetting he was her friend. She'd seen him as—

A man.

A man who rarely stayed alone for long. A man whose bed was rarely without female company. A man who was probably on a date right now, too.

The thought of Mack out with another woman, giving somebody else that grin, laughing at her jokes, just as Steve was doing here, sent a prickle of something—Alex knew it couldn't be jealousy—roaring through her.

How crazy was that?

She simply wasn't paying enough attention to Steve. She had a polite, charming guy doing his level best to get to know her. She'd be insane to think of anything else right now.

She shook off thoughts of Mack and refocused on Steve, fighting the urge to yawn. It had to be all the extra work on the house that had her so tired. Not her date.

For the rest of the meal, Alex smiled and engaged in the conversation, talking to him like a work colleague, forcing herself to stay interested and awake by pretending he was someone she was interviewing— and feeling oddly like this *was* an interview, not a date. In the end she insisted on picking up half the tab for dinner, then begged off early, telling Steve she had to work in the morning.

"Are you sure?" he asked. "I know this great jazz bar off of Washington that has the best martinis."

"Any other night, really, I'd love to, but martinis and trying to get that interview with the new dress shop on Newbury Street and then writing the story by deadline tomorrow . . ." She put out her hands, then shrugged. "Not the best mix. I had a great time tonight, though."

She'd already said that three times. Any more, and he'd begin to think she was lying. She smiled at him. Attractive man, really. Dark hair, green-blue eyes. A chiseled chin, fit body, not too tall. He'd worn a tie—ten points in his favor—and hadn't had a single bad habit or annoying trait. All around, he'd been—

Nice.

Ugh. She was beginning to hate that word. And hate Mack for sending her a man who had so many good points, she couldn't even think of a reason to tell him to go home.

They were standing on the stoop of Renee's apartment building, the soft light from above bathing Steve's features in a golden glow. Alex had briefly considered having him drop her off at the house from hell—as she'd started affectionately calling her "project"—just to see if that would scare him off, then realized Steve was such a gentleman, he'd probably offer to hang her wallpaper.

Steve stepped forward, one arm slipping around her waist. Alex waited, thinking that now, *now* she would feel that charge, that burst of anticipation—but no, nothing, not so much as a flicker of want. Surely, though, plenty of relationships had been built on great conversations with attraction coming later.

But the disappointment in her gut weighed heavy and again her thoughts strayed to Mack. Was he, too, standing on some woman's porch? Holding her in his arms? And was she thrilling at his touch? Anticipating his kiss? And more . . .

Was he anticipating kissing her? That surge of not-jealousy rushed through Alex a second time. What was wrong with her?

"I had a really great time, too," Steve said.

His voice had dropped into the lower-decibel ranges. Men were so obvious. They laid out all the road signs. The I'M GOING TO KISS YOU NOW signals that were as obvious as the old Burma-Shave roadside signs. Step closer. Arm around waist. Deep voice.

The trouble? Alex had no desire to kiss Steve Rowen. Instead, she found herself thinking one very insane thought for a flash of a second—

She wanted to be kissing Mack. To be in *his* arms. To feel his chest against hers. His lips pressing down, taking her—

Now that was crazy. Completely insane. Mack was a friend. Nothing more. An annoying friend, at that.

She did *not* want to kiss Mack Douglas.

Steve moved in for the kill—that's what Alex got for mentally debating for so long—and Alex was caught. Either wriggle out and be completely obvious about her lack of desire or just stay there and hope he was quick. She opted for the latter, turning her face so that he ended up with a half-mouth, half-cheek kiss.

Steve drew back. A mixture of confusion and disappointment showed in his eyes. "Well, good night then."

"Good night." Alex gave him a smile, then turned away. "Thank you, Steve. I really did have a great evening."

Oh, God. She'd said it *again*. Now she was encouraging him. That's what she got for trying to be polite.

"Would you like to go to a concert on Saturday?

There's one of those music-in-the-park events in Mansfield. If you like jazz and picnics."

Alex hesitated. Maybe tonight had just been an anomaly. She'd been tired—bone tired—from all the work on the house. And Steve wasn't terrible. Hadn't she had plenty of friends who had started out with no sparks, then found those sparks the more they dated?

Of course, she couldn't think of a single example right now, but that didn't mean they didn't exist.

"Sure. That sounds great."

Immediately, Steve's features went from dim to 100-watt. He beamed at her, released her from his waist-grip with a second quick kiss on her cheek, then said good-bye and hurried down the stairs and off to his sensible, so very accountantlike Toyota.

Alex let herself into Renee's apartment, sidestepping toys and Barbie dolls. A single light burned on the end table in the living room. Despite her promise, Renee had gone to bed. A note on the kitchen table said they'd catch up later over a latte.

Once again, Renee had managed to avoid discussing what had gone wrong with her troubled marriage. Maybe Alex should stop worrying. Let Renee and Tony figure it out on their own.

But as Alex left to get into her car and head back to her own house—and to a blow-up bed in a drafty room—she cast one more worried glance in the rearview mirror at Renee's building. And suspected more secrets were hidden behind that shut door than just a marriage on rocky ground.

Chapter Seven

Renee went to work on Monday morning in the *City Times* office, carpooling with Alex, and trying her damnedest to feign interest in Alex's rehashing of her date. But it was like slogging through one more episode of *Dora the Explorer* and holding back a scream that the friggin' backpack was right under the stupid monkey's nose. Not that she didn't care about Alex, but she had bigger problems on her mind.

Problems she couldn't share.

Because if she did, Alex would hate her. Hell, she hated herself. And she needed to find a way out, one that wouldn't destroy everyone's lives. And yet, wouldn't leave her still stuck in this thick mud of unhappiness.

"He sounds great, Alex," Renee said, forcing her own issues out of her mind.

"Yeah, he was. Too great. Too nice." Alex shifted the vase of white roses in her lap. Renee had brought them along today to give to Alex. No sense keeping them at Renee's, where romance seemed to have died a long time ago.

"How can a guy be too nice?" Renee asked.

"I don't know. There just weren't any . . . sparks."

"Trust me. Sparks aren't all they're cracked up to be." Renee clutched the steering wheel and stared at the red dominoes of brake lights ahead of her. Two more exits of this stop-and-go hell and they'd be at the office. Two more exits before she had to make a decision. A choice. "They make you rush into things you probably shouldn't do."

"Like get married too fast?" The question was a gentle one, but they both knew Alex meant Renee's rush to the altar at seventeen.

"Yeah. Like that." And like thinking about jumping into bed with the first man who seemed to understand a stressed mother and a forgotten wife. The first man who'd made Renee feel sexy and beautiful, not tired and old.

"Are you okay?" Alex asked. "You look pale."

Damn. She clearly hadn't taken enough time with her makeup this morning. "Um, after Tony brought the kids back, the three-year-old was up a lot last night. He has a summer cold. Couple that with being out late, and it all knocked the kids off their schedule. I didn't get a lot of sleep." That part was true. The why wasn't.

A Volvo cut in front of Renee's minivan. She laid on the horn and let out a curse.

"You want me to drive?" Alex asked.

"I'm fine."

"Renee, I know you and you are totally not fine. I really wish you'd talk to me. I can't be the only one living a soap opera here." Alex let out a little laugh.

"It's nothing, really. Normal mommy stress." Renee forced a smile to her face and showed it to Alex. The see-I'm-totally-okay proof. "A preschooler, a nine-year-old, a preteen with raging hormones and a husband who can't get motivated enough to change an empty roll of toilet paper entitles me to some road rage."

Alex laid a hand over her friend's and gave it a squeeze. The sign of empathy sent a slice of guilt running through Renee. Would Alex be so willing to support Renee if she knew the truth? Knew that Renee had been having lunch three times a week with Bill Rhinehart in accounting? That for the past three months, Renee had been flirting with the idea of an affair?

"I'm here," Alex went on, "anytime you need me, either way. And I say we plan a girls' night out soon. Get a sitter, or dump the kids at Mack's house, and go out on the town. Go out for pedicures and margaritas."

Renee laughed. "Dump the kids with Mack? If there's one man who couldn't handle *a* kid, much less three, it would be Mack. Didn't you see him at our barbecue on Memorial Day weekend? You'd have thought my kids were the next *Invasion of the Body Snatchers* the way Mack was backing away."

Alex chuckled. "He did look terrified. But he just needs experience. What better way to get experience than by babysitting?"

"My kids would be better off being raised by wolves than left with Mack." Renee put on her directional and moved into the lane for the exit. Today was one of the few days she was grateful for the Boston traffic jam. She welcomed anything that delayed her arrival at work. Anything that put off making the decision ahead of her.

Cheat on her husband or remain true. Bill had made it easy. He'd arranged the hotel room. All the details. All she had to do was say yes.

How bad would it be, though, to have one afternoon with another man? A man who appreciated her, a man who would look at her with love in his eyes, who would pay attention when she talked?

A man who didn't resent her for chaining him to a marriage he hadn't wanted. A life he didn't even enjoy.

The same man who had walked away from his marriage last week. Renee kneaded at her temples and tried to shove thoughts of Tony to the back of her mind. She'd end up starting her day with a headache she didn't need.

"Speaking of wolves," Alex said, "I have a meeting with Joe later this week, on Tuesday morning. I think I've finally got a story idea that will make him sit up and notice me as a feature reporter. I went in early in the morning and did a little research Saturday on the Web—thank God for Google—and it's looking good."

"Really?" Renee asked, forcing herself back to the conversation. "That's great. You've wanted that position forever."

"It'll be a hell of a lot better than covering fashion and food. *Real* journalism is what I went to college for. What I've dreamed of." Alex laid out her fingers, picturing an imaginary newspaper page. "Above the fold, front page, first section, with my byline."

"Local writer solves Jimmy Hoffa mystery, huh?"

"Something like that." Alex grinned. "But I don't want to say anything about it yet, in case I jinx things."

"Doesn't features pay a lot more, too?"

"About double. And the bump in pay couldn't come at a better time."

"That reminds me, Noah, how is it going with that ark?"

When Alex had told Renee the other day about the house she had inherited, Renee had thought her friend was insane for taking on such a monumental project. When she'd shown Renee pictures of the house she'd taken with her digital camera, Renee had considered admitting Alex to an asylum. The place wasn't just awful—it was beyond repair. Sort of like Renee's marriage, only there weren't any nails and hammers to shore up what had gone wrong between Renee and Tony.

Hadn't she already tried a hundred times over to fix her marriage, only to see it crumble again and again? At a certain point, she just needed to face facts and realize it was over, and no matter how hard she searched, she'd never find that thread that had brought them together in the first place.

Renee tried to listen as Alex told her about the repairs she'd been making to the house with Mack's help, but her mind kept returning to her marriage, then to Bill, then back to her marriage, like a stuck record.

They'd reached the parking garage for the *City Times*. The shadow of the building seemed to engulf the car as Renee pulled into the concrete structure. Dread filled Renee's stomach, churning with the toast she'd eaten earlier. She prayed a space would be hard to find, that she could delay arriving at work for another ten minutes, but no, there was an open one near the elevators. Renee parked, then she and Alex got out of the car and headed over to the elevators.

She forced herself to concentrate on her friend as they rode to the tenth floor. "So your grandmother thinks this will be some kind of therapy?"

Alex nodded. "Even if she's right, I'm renovating, without the side order of psychoanalysis, then I'll sell the place. Grandma will be disappointed, but there is no way I can hold on to that house."

"Too many memories?"

"Not so many, but . . . . enough." Alex let out a breath and leaned against the faux wood wall of the elevator.

Renee knew the basics about Alex's childhood, but little more. About the father she had never known, the too-young single mother who had never quite given up her partying ways until it was too late—and she'd died, leaving Alex to live with her grandmother. When it came to the first few years of her life, Alex rarely talked about what she'd gone through. Either way, Renee could tell just by the way Alex avoided the subject and kept her heart carefully guarded that growing up that way had left emotional scars.

Knowing her friend had gone through that because of a distant mother only doubled Renee's frustration with Tony, who had never seemed to plug in to their marriage. To being a dad. She didn't want any of the three kids to turn around as adults and wonder why Dad hadn't been there. But every time she tried to talk to Tony, the argument fell on deaf ears—or he walked away.

"Anyway," Alex went on, her voice visibly brighter, "all those flipping-houses shows said the biggest profits come when you do it yourself, and Lord knows I could use a profit. I won't even tell you my bank account balance. It's embarrassing for someone my age. I should have listened to my guidance counselor and become a doctor."

"Except you're squeamish around the sight of blood."

"There is that." Alex chuckled. "Good thing there are books on home repair."

Renee rolled her eyes. "Lord save us from the people who think they can build the Eiffel Tower with a little help from Borders."

"You are so off my Christmas list."

The elevator doors *whooshed* open and Alex and Renee got off, stepping into the chaotic reporters' section of the *City Times*. The noise from two dozen sets of typing hands and simultaneous conversations, along with three televisions tuned to the major networks, hummed through the room. It was like being surrounded by a hundred beehives.

"So this Steve guy," Renee asked when they reached Alex's desk, "do you think he might be the one?"

"I don't know. I didn't feel anything when I met him. Not so much as a blip of attraction." Alex dropped her purse on her desk, on the few inches of free space among the fashion magazines and manufacturers' samples, all vying to get their mascaras or stilettos onto the pages of the *City Times*. She cleared a few more inches of space and set the vase of roses down, too.

"The lust thing is highly overrated."

"Maybe. But the whole night I kept thinking about—" Alex shook her head and started flipping through her stack of pink message slips.

"Thinking about who?"

"This is going to sound crazy, but . . . I kept thinking about Mack, wondering what he was doing. Who he was out with."

"Maybe you do have a thing for him," Renee said.

"I don't." Alex dropped the pink slips to her desk. "Okay, maybe I do. But he's *Mack,* Renee. One of my best friends. I'd be crazy to go out with him and ruin a great friendship. Plus, the man is so commitment-phobic, he could be the poster boy for bachelors worldwide."

"He was married once."

"For about a minute. And he got divorced. Plus, you forget he's fixing me up with other guys, for Pete's sake."

"Maybe you're right," Renee conceded, deciding that even if Alex was hiding her true feelings about Mack, she wouldn't probe into it now. Her own life was messy enough. "My guy-reading skills are pretty rusty."

Alex shot a quick glance at Renee. "How are things going with Tony? Did you two talk last night when he brought the kids home?"

"Things will be fine," Renee said quickly. Too quickly,

she realized, because Alex's brows shot upward. "I have to go. I'm, uh, late for a meeting."

She was late for a meeting. Of sorts. But she didn't tell Alex it was with another man. A man who had made Renee feel like she was a woman again. Reminded her that she was indeed desirable. Funny. Intelligent. Something other than the tired mommy and overwrought wife who washed Tony's briefs. The same woman whose husband hadn't touched her in six months.

Leaving Renee to wonder: if he wasn't touching *her*—

Who was he touching instead?

Chapter Eight

Mack had been at it for three hours and had yet to find any satisfaction. Sweat drenched his shirt, exhaustion plagued his muscles, but still he kept up the same pace, trying to work Alex out of his system.

Didn't work.

With every piece of wood he tore down, every nail he ripped out, he still kept hearing Steve's excited voice on his cell phone . . . *"Mack, she was fantastic. Thank you for setting me up with her. Alex is just amazing. Wonderful. I can't wait to see her again. You didn't tell me she was beautiful. I mean, you said she was pretty, but she's a friggin' knockout."*

Mack's blood pressure rose again, just replaying those words in his head. At the time Steve had said them, Mack had clenched his cell phone so hard, he'd cracked the little plastic case. *"Yeah, she's okay."*

"Okay? Mack, you really are losing it. Alex Kenner is a catch and a half. I can't wait to get to know her better." Steve's chuckle was deep. The kind in man-speak that meant more than playing-Monopoly-on-a-Friday-night and what's-her-favorite-color better. *"A lot better."*

"You lay a—" Mack bit his tongue.

"What'd you say, Mack?"

"Nothing. Have a good time." Wasn't this what he'd wanted? What he'd planned? What Alex had asked him for?

Yeah, if that was so, then why did it suck so much?

Mack had clicked off the phone, then threw it onto his bed. He took a long, cold shower. He'd headed to the job site of the newest house his company was building on Larchwood Street. Ended up taking out his frustrations on most of the construction crew. And still didn't feel any better. What he needed was good old-fashioned work with his hands, not playing supervisor. Not doing paperwork. He put Larry, his second in command, in charge of the Larchwood Street house, then headed to Alex's monstrosity to work Steve's call out of his system.

Mack ripped another two-by-four out of the wall, the wood splintering at the base where he'd forgotten a nail, and threw it into the growing pile of debris. He bent over, slammed out the nail with a hammer, then tossed that one, too, into the pile. He sunk the claw end into the next section of wall and pulled, tearing out another hunk, throwing that to the side, moving fast onto the next one.

Alex. Amazing. Wonderful. Knockout.

He'd show Steve a knockout. With his right fist.

So far, most of Monday was gone, and Steve's words still marched through his head like perky high school cadets. What he really needed was to get good and drunk.

And find another woman. Any other woman.

"Hi, Mack."

Any other woman but her.

Mack spun around. Alex stood in the center of the room, wearing shorts that should have been considered illegal and a tank top that probably was. She held out a cold soda in his direction. In her other arm, she cradled a vase with flowers. White roses. Damn.

He'd been the one to suggest them. He'd practically driven Steve to the damn florist. What the hell had he been thinking?

"What are those?" he asked, even though he knew the answer.

"Flowers. I thought they'd brighten this place up a bit." Alex smiled. She inhaled the scent of the blooms, and a smile curved across her face. "They're from Steve. Aren't they gorgeous?"

"Yeah. Gorgeous." Right now, he wanted to rip those flowers out of Alex's hands, throw them out the window and stomp them into the ground. The tidal wave of jealousy rising in his chest nearly choked him. For Pete's sake, they were just flowers. Not a ring.

The problem: they were flowers in *Alex's* hands, from another man. Up until yesterday, Alex had been Mack's fantasy. Not that he owned her, but, damn it, he hadn't thought he'd been sharing those images, not until that phone call from Steve.

Clearly, he was going to have to kill Steve.

"You seem awfully grumpy. What's up with you?" Alex asked.

How could he tell her that she'd walked in on him at a very, very bad time? When he'd been thinking about her. Wondering what she was up to. Picturing her in his arms, his groin hardening at the thought of her. If it was true that men thought about sex every four seconds, those researchers hadn't met Alex Kenner, because Mack thought about sex with her every four hundredths of a second.

He swallowed hard. His body steeled, his heart rate bumped up a few notches. His fist curled tighter around the hammer.

"Mack? Seriously. What's the matter? Is it something with the house? Did *I* do something?"

"No. It's . . . nothing." He drew in a breath. Watched her do the same. Her breasts rose, fell. Did it again. Damn. "It's everything."

She licked her lips, and that was it. He was a goner. Hell, he'd been a goner the minute she walked through the door and said his name. He dropped the hammer to the floor, crossed to Alex, jerked the vase out of her hands, then the soda, and laid both on the workbench beside her.

A little *O* of surprise widened her mouth, then escaped her in a *whoosh* of breath when he swooped her into his arms. He crushed her body to his, and before he could think about what he was doing, or the wisdom of his actions, Mack did what he should have done a long time ago.

And kissed Alex.

Chapter Nine

Alex couldn't have been more surprised if the entire Boston College marching band had burst into the room and started belting out 50 Cent's top-ten hits.

When Mack took her in his arms, brought her to his chest and kissed her, Alex froze. Stunned, she didn't react at all at first. But that lasted all of a split second before every switch in her body flipped to ON.

Then, she forgot Mack was a friend. Forgot she wasn't supposed to be attracted to Mack, forgot she had, up until this point, never really considered Mack kissing material.

Okay, she had. More than once, but only in moments of clear lunacy. Because Mack was her friend.

But a friend didn't set your body on fire when he kissed you. A friend didn't make the world turn on end, then send it reeling in and out of focus.

His lips captured hers, hard, fast. He was fire against her skin, so hot she was sure she was going to spontaneously combust—and enjoy doing it, too. Her body arched against his, her nipples peaked, straining against her bra, the lace an agony of fabric, while everything inside went hot and liquid.

Mack's tongue dipped into her mouth, swept across to join hers, and she groaned against him, the desire swift and strong. Her hands roamed up his back—muscles so hard, they were like the lumber holding the framing together—and clutched at the cotton of his shirt, wanting his skin. Wanting him in a way that astonished her.

Then the heat gave way to a surprising tenderness. Mack reached up, cupped her jaw, his thumb rubbing back and forth, easy, gentle, sweet, and another kind of fire, one of yearning, erupted in Alex's chest.

This kind spelled vulnerable. Open your heart. Let him in. Oh, God, oh, God, oh, yes, oh—

Oh, no. No. *No.*

Mack was not the kind of man she wanted. Not at all.

Alex jerked back, out of Mack's arms, stumbling across the floor. "What . . . what was that?"

Mack stared at her for one long second, then shook his head, bent over and picked up his hammer. "A mistake."

"That's it? That's all you have to say? You kiss me, out of the blue, then"—she paused to take in a breath, her lungs heaving still—"and you say it was a mistake? What, of mistaken identity? Did you stumble into the Playboy grotto by accident?"

The grin she knew as well as her own curved across his face. "I'd never confuse the Playboy grotto with this place."

She scowled. "Then why did you kiss me?"

Mack turned away, swiped some nails off the workbench and started slamming them into a two-by-four, driving the metal home with swift, even strokes. "I don't know."

A three-year-old could tell he was avoiding the question. Alex considered pressing the issue, then thought again.

Did she really want to know the answer? Because whatever Mack said would tip the equation between them even more. If she let it be, she could just write that kiss off. Pretend the heat, the work, had gotten to him. Or some rogue mosquito had given him malaria.

Yeah, that was it.

And she'd kissed him back because—

Because he'd caught her off guard. Nothing more.

Get back to work. Get back to *anything* other than that.

"So what are we working on today?" Alex asked, strapping on one of the leather tool belts Mack had brought with him. She'd gotten pretty adept at wearing the heavy apparatus yesterday, and had grown comfortable with the sensation of the leather pouch and tools banging against her hips.

But today, the whole thing reminded her of Mack. Mack's body against hers. The hammer hanging off the belt slid against her thigh and reminded her very much of Mack's erection, unmistakable a moment ago.

He'd found her sexy? Wanted her that much? And, Alex knew, just by the steady thudding of her heart, the buzz running through her, that she had wanted him, too.

She definitely needed to get out of the heat.

"New walls and constructing some built-ins," Mack said. "We demoed, now we're going to construct."

Alex looked at him, studying his blue gaze, searching for something, anything, that would tell her what had just happened. "What exactly are we constructing here, Mack?"

He paused a beat, then broke the eye contact. "A house, Alex. Nothing more."

Disappointment curdled in her gut, but Alex pushed it away. Mack was right. Hadn't they tried this, once before, years ago and hadn't it been awful? From here on out, Alex was going to learn from her mistakes. No way was she going to go down the wrong path with any man ever again.

And definitely not with Mack.

Even if this grown-up version kissed much better than the fumbling teen he had once been, in that one kiss they'd shared years ago. Even if the grown-up Alex had this constant drumbeat of desire running through her every time she looked at Mack. Something she hadn't had back in the old days.

Either way, the older Alex knew better.

Mack had always been the guy next door. The guy, truly, underfoot. She'd practically grown up with him, seen him as a brother.

Her best friend.

How stupid would it be to mess all that up with sex? She could lose Mack, and if there was one constant Alex couldn't bear to lose—

It was Mack.

Besides, Mack didn't believe in long-term relationships. He'd made it clear, over and over again, that his brief foray into marriage had been a major mistake he'd never repeat. From now on, he'd said more than once, anything lasting longer than a weekend was a long-term commitment.

Alex wanted, no, needed, much more than a weekend. She needed a man who would give her his heart— and park his shoes in the closet forever. Mack wasn't that man.

"Are you going to help me?" Mack asked.

Alex realized she'd just been standing there, holding the tools and serving as nothing more than a mannequin. "Of course."

For a few minutes, they worked together and didn't communicate except in construction terms. "Hand me that drill," and "Where do you want me to hold this?" Words that conveyed constructing physical walls and kept those emotional walls firmly in place.

She had to force herself to concentrate on remodeling and not on him. It had to be the heat, because she'd never been this distracted by Mack before. And she'd spent a hell of a lot of time with him over the years.

"So, what's your plan?"

"Plan?" she echoed.

"For the living room."

"Oh."

What had she expected him to say? Her? He'd meant the room, of course. Not them. That, Alex reminded herself, was a good thing. She was not at all interested in Mack for a relationship, regardless of what had just happened.

Regardless of that kiss. That incredible, amazing, earth-shattering kiss. Yeah, that.

Or the firestorm he'd stirred up inside her. Or the way he'd reminded her that he wasn't just a friend, he was a man. A very attractive man. One who knew how to turn everything inside her to Jell-O with one touch.

What else did he know how to do? And how much would she enjoy the other tricks he had up his sleeves?

Mack started talking about running pipes for plumbing and heating, retreating into jargon that went in one of Alex's ears and out the other. She just agreed, not knowing what she'd agreed to, but glad to have something to do besides kiss Mack again.

"Well, let's get to it," Mack said, picking up his hammer again.

"Yeah, sure," she agreed again, though her mind still wasn't quite on the house. Not a good sign. She scrambled for another topic. One that didn't involve watching Mack's muscles ripple as he hefted two-by-fours into place, slipped a couple of nails between his

fingers and drove them home with his hammer—
making her think only of how he could drive something
else home with the same rhythmic pounding.

Desire twisted in Alex's gut. She inhaled a sharp
breath and paused, her hand curling around a pile
of nails.

Talk to him. About something. Anything.

"So, uh, have you talked to Tony lately?" Alex asked.

"Every day." He stood a second timber beside the
first one, then nailed them together. "He is my concrete supplier, after all."

"What do you think is going on between him and
Renee?"

Mack stopped hammering, turned to face Alex, his
cobalt eyes wide with surprise. "I thought you knew."

She shook her head. "Renee won't talk about it.
And, believe me, I've tried. She avoids the subject,
avoids me. I planned to talk to her last night after I got
back from my date, but she'd already gone to bed."

Her concern for Renee had grown every day since
that afternoon back in Edward's apartment. Something
was going on in the Wendell marriage, something
more than the stress that had always plagued it, and
Alex, who loved them both, hated to see the relationship self-destructing. But short of staging a Dr. Phil intervention, she couldn't do a whole lot about it, either.

"What they probably need is time alone," Mack said.
"I'm sure they'll work out their problems if they just
spend time together. Talk and . . . you know." He left
her to fill in the blanks, being a little less direct than
his usual self.

"I agree. That's why I've been staying here, even
though Renee keeps trying to talk me into moving in
with her. I figured they didn't have a chance of . . . working it out, like you said, with a third wheel around." Alex's

face heated. Weird, because she had never gotten embarrassed talking about sex with Mack before, and he had never avoided the subject of sex with her before, always treating her just like one of the guys. Of course, he probably hadn't kissed one of the guys like that before . . . "So I moved in here." She gestured toward the front hall, where she'd stowed her air mattress. "It's a win-win all around, as far as I can tell. Because of the construction, the house is open and vulnerable at night, and I don't like to leave it empty. It could get vandalized."

"Are you crazy? You're not seriously staying here, are you?"

Oh, shit. She hadn't just told him that, had she? That's what she got for trying to fill in the conversational holes. "I'm fine. Sure, it's a little spooky at night, but—"

"There's no air-conditioning. No security. You are *not* staying here," Mack repeated.

"I'm not five years old. I don't need you to tell me what to do."

"Apparently you do." Mack crossed to the rolled up air mattress, picked it up and tested its weight. "This is no type of bed for you. It's about as thick as a piece of paper. You need a *real* bed, Alex."

His eyes met hers, filled with a heat she'd glimpsed just before he'd kissed her, then it was gone, erased as fast as it had appeared, and she told herself she'd imagined it. "I don't need anything fancy, Mack. And I don't want to leave the house unsecured."

He scowled. "If I promise to put in some security, will you quit staying here?"

She thrust her fists on her hips. "And where am I going to stay? Grandma Kenner doesn't have the room in her tiny little condo and it's against the rules for her to have long-term visitors, anyway, not that I could pass for a senior citizen either way. Staying with Renee only gives her an excuse to keep Tony out. And Edward is back home in our apartment, which belongs to him, anyway. I wouldn't go back to him if you paid me. I could rent a place, but I'm pouring most of my income into here."

"Then stay with me. I have a huge house, and all that space is just going to waste. I've already asked you once. This offer is expiring quick." He grinned, but the seriousness stayed in his gaze.

She shook her head. "Mack, we've been through this. I—"

He took a step closer, the air mattress dropping from his hands, landing on the floor and rolling away. "Not to mention, I have that pool. Think about it, Alex. Wouldn't that be a hell of a nice way to end your day after working here? Taking a dip in that cool water?"

The pool. Mack in the pool. Half-naked, stroking through the water . . . "But—"

"And a real bed. With a good mattress. Which would be a hell of a sight better than that piece of crap." He pointed at the roll of plastic that had stopped by the wall.

Mack in the morning. In a towel. Wet from the shower, hair curling against his chest. Skin glistening, just aching for her to taste—

What was wrong with her? Where were all these thoughts coming from?

She couldn't forget living with Mack meant seeing Mack in his element. With other women. Women who might join him in that bed. In that shower. In that pool. Alex shook her head. "I shouldn't—"

"You shouldn't argue with me." He moved closer. "This is the kind of thing friends are for, right?"

"Is that what we are, Mack? Friends?"

"Of course."

"Then what was that a few minutes ago? Because

friends . . ." Alex drew in a breath, one that trembled through her veins, and she had no clue why. "Friends don't kiss each other like that, last I checked."

"Well, maybe some friends do." He paused. "Okay, most friends don't."

"None that I know of."

"It was an anomaly. It won't happen again."

"Good." But why did the word escape her lips and lose its impact? Why did disappointment sink like a stone into her stomach? Why did she want him to promise more of the same? She didn't want him to kiss her. She didn't want to get involved with Mack. She didn't want to mess up a good thing. "It was a bad idea. It . . . complicates things."

"That it does. And you know me," Mack said. Still close, inches from her. A breath away from her touch. "I'm not good at complications."

"No, you're not." Exactly why she'd never considered a relationship with him.

"So, will you stay with me?" he asked.

Stay with Mack. Swim with him in the pool. Stay down the hall from his bedroom. See him outside the shower, the kitchen, with the towel, and then that same towel dropping—

"Will you talk to Tony?" Alex asked, quickly, getting her mind onto something other than Mack without a towel. "Get him to move back home with Renee?"

"Are you blackmailing me?"

"Simply making a deal."

He chuckled, then put out a hand. Alex slipped her palm into his much bigger, rougher one. His hand engulfed hers in a second. Warm, secure. "Sure."

"And promise me you won't give Tony your usual 'marriage is the work of the Devil' speech?"

"You know I only reserve that one for you."

She rolled her eyes. "You are incorrigible."

"I try my best," Mack said. Then he leaned down, so close to her, he could have kissed her again with only a whisper of effort. Every ounce of Alex stilled, waiting, hoping, even as she told herself any kind of kiss with Mack was a bad idea. A very bad idea. "And maybe one of these days, you'll let me corrupt you, too."

And, oh, for one second, Alex wanted him to do that. Very, very much.

Hoo-boy. Had she just made the worst decision of her life?

Chapter Ten

Renee hid in the ladies' room.

Okay, so it was the coward's way out. Dodging the question from Bill Rhinehart about going to the Westin hotel this afternoon. The one afternoon she had free. Her middle child was going home with a friend after school, the oldest one had play rehearsal, the preschooler was in day care. Her boss was out at a meeting and wasn't coming back, so slipping out of the office wouldn't be a problem.

Renee had no one expecting her to be anywhere until after five o'clock.

Her stomach churned. She clutched her gut, sure she was going to puke, then decided to face facts. She was no more cut out for having an affair than a walrus was for living in the tropics.

She turned on the tap, splashed some cold water on her face and refreshed her lipstick. Then she stared at the face in the mirror. A face she didn't recognize. "What are you doing?" she whispered to her own reflection. "What the hell are you doing?"

She pressed her palms to her cheeks, meeting hot

skin. Maybe she was getting sick. Or maybe she was just embarrassed to even think about cheating.

She'd grown up a good Catholic girl. The kind that went to Mass every weekend, had worn her First Communion dress with pride, sworn up and down she would follow every Commandment. Where had she gone off track?

Was cheating on her husband a sin if her husband had checked out of the marriage before it barely began? If they'd gotten married for all the wrong reasons, and stayed together because they'd thought they were doing the right thing?

And had only made it worse?

Renee swallowed and faced herself again. "Either shit or get off the pot, Renee. You can't sit on the fence forever." Then she grabbed her purse and exited the restroom.

"Renee." Bill's voice, soft, concerned, came up from behind her. He caught up to her in the corner of the hall, out of sight of the rest of the office. A large potted plant—something with huge leaves, Renee couldn't have said what it was if her life depended on it—blocked them from prying eyes.

She bit back a laugh. How ridiculous they looked, behind a potted plant. Subterfuge. Affairs. At her age. She had three kids, for God's sake. She drove a mini-van. She brought snacks to soccer practice. She was a walking, talking, cliché—

And she was staring into a pair of brown eyes that looked at her and found her pretty, and being touched by a hand that wanted her, and wondering when the hell her own husband had stopped doing that.

"I can't," she said, the guilt so sharp, it twisted her gut again, knotting it as tight as a ball of yarn.

"I know," he said. "I know this is hard for you. We

don't have to do anything. I just wanted to say I'm here for you, if you want to talk." His hand rode up her arm, igniting that spark of fire that had left her. How long ago had it died? How long since Tony had touched her and she'd felt that heat? Felt wanted? Desired? His thumb traced a lazy circle around her shoulder. "Or anything else."

Renee swallowed. *Anything else.*

Did she want anything else? Sort of like adding a dessert onto an already full plate. Bill's eyes were kind, compassionate, but the patience in them had a thinner edge than they had three months ago when the two of them had first started going out to lunch. In the beginning, their afternoon meetings had been nothing. They'd talked about work, then drifted into conversations about music. Books. Renee had found herself dying to go to lunch, craving someone to listen to her, to find her interesting again, to look at her and notice she'd worn her hair down, or to say that blue shirt looked good with her eyes. Bill had attracted her mind first, and then her body had followed suit like a puppy trotting along behind a treat.

Then one day outside the diner, she'd stumbled, he'd caught her, and as if it were the most natural thing in the world, he'd kissed her. She'd yielded into that kiss, needing it as much as she did the words, because the loneliness had become as much an appendage as her right arm, and when Bill had touched her, he'd made a dent in a bottomless hole.

She'd felt noticed. Like he knew it was her under those lips. Not some blow-up doll in bed. Somewhere along the way, Tony had stopped paying attention, stopped realizing she was even there. Their lovemaking had become a perfunctory play so often performed, it could have been *Cats.*

But was she ready to take that next irreversible step? She twisted her hands together, and when she did, her fingers struck the tiny diamond Tony had given her eleven years ago when they had no money but a lot of dreams. Once, she'd thought no other men existed except Tony. Couldn't imagine ever loving anyone but him. Falling into anyone's arms but his.

Tears pooled in the corner of Renee's eyes. Her chest tightened and she knew a part of her still ached for that dream. Until that hope died, too, she couldn't do this.

"I'll see you tomorrow, Bill," Renee said, then slipped past the plant and into the open. Before she did anything behind the leaves that she would regret.

Unlike wine, his father's mood did not improve with time or age.

"What is it going to take to get you to stop showing up on my doorstep?" Roy asked.

"You, helping me at that house."

"I'm no longer in the construction industry." Roy flipped out the footrest of his La-Z-Boy and turned on the television. Pat Sajak and Vanna White bloomed to life on the thirty-five-inch color screen. "I'm retired, in case you haven't noticed, which means my days consist of nothing but sitting around on my ass."

"And figuring out five-letter words for *moron*?"

Roy shot him a glare. "You're welcome to pull up a chair and throw out a guess. Like *idiot*."

Mack laughed, and noticed his father holding back a smile of his own. "Come on, you know you're bored out of your skull. It wouldn't hurt you to put in a couple hours here and there doing something constructive."

Roy watched Vanna touch a couple of screens,

turning the white boxes into letter *N*s. "Like what? If you say some bullshit like art therapy, I'm throwing you out of here."

"A house that needs some serious TLC."

"I've done more than my fair share of those."

"This one's different."

Roy snorted. Mack waited. Vanna touched a couple more boxes, and *A*s appeared. The audience applauded like she'd just turned water into wine.

"Different how?" Roy asked.

"It's Alex's house. Where she grew up."

"With Carolyn?"

"No. With her mother."

That got his father's attention. Roy shifted in the La-Z-Boy and faced Mack. "She had a house? I always assumed her and Alex lived . . . I don't know. In a car or something."

"Yeah, me, too. Alex didn't talk about her childhood much. Except to say it sucked."

The wheel spun in the background, click-clacking its way around the circle, the contestants clapping with wild abandon. Everyone rooting for that trip to Vancouver. "And how do you figure into this?"

"I'm helping her. The place is a dump and she's in way over her head."

Roy shook his head and turned back to Vanna and Pat. "You doing it for free?"

"Dad, she's a reporter. She doesn't make much."

"*Brangelina in Love,* you idiot."

"What?"

Roy pointed the remote toward the TV. "What the hell is wrong with these people? They keep wasting their money on vowels. Can't they guess the puzzle already? Clue: *People* magazine. Look. All but one of the consonants have been guessed. A *monkey* could figure it out now. Why throw away your money on an *O*, for God's sake?"

"I don't even want to know why you're so familiar with *People* magazine headlines." Mack leaned forward and flicked the POWER button to OFF. "That alone is proof you're spending way too much time at home."

"Hey! I was watching that. Kenny was trying to win a boat." Roy pointed the remote at the Magnavox, but Mack slid in front of the infrared sensor, blocking the magic eye.

"You do realize how ridiculous you sound, don't you? Reading gossip magazines, getting hooked on *Wheel?* Come to the house. Help me out."

Roy scowled. "I sold most of my tools."

"Bullshit."

His father shrugged. Wiggled the remote from side to side, thumbing the POWER button. "Will you move?"

Mack kept blocking the TV. "I'll share my tools with you."

"I'm retired."

"You're becoming a joke, Dad. You have to get out of—"

"I don't have to do a goddamn thing!" Roy shouted, exploding out of the chair. "Not a goddamn thing, not until—" He cut himself off and let out a curse. "Just get the hell out of my house, will you?"

"Dad," Mack said, his voice soft, his hand on his father's arm. "It's been over a year. She's not—"

"Don't say it. Don't you *dare* say it."

Mack let the sentence go. But he held on to his father, refusing to give up. "Come help me, Dad. Just for a day or two. Nobody knows how to fix a house like you."

"If I knew how to keep a house together," Roy said, his voice scraping past his throat, "my own would still be standing."

Then he shook his head, flung the remote toward the chair, spinning on his heel and leaving the room. The remote bounced off the La-Z-Boy. The big red POWER button hit the corner of the end table, blasting Vanna and Pat onto the screen again. Kenny was crying.

One spin too many and he'd gone bankrupt. No boat for him.

"I know how you feel, Kenny," Mack said. "I'm drowning here, too."

Chapter Eleven

Tony had a three beer and one tequila shot lead by the time Mack got to O'Malley's Bar late Monday night. Boomer sat beside him, a couple of empties to the side. The small, crowded sports bar was noisy, most of the patrons busy rooting for the Red Sox on the overhead widescreen TVs, even as their home team trailed six runs behind Chicago. Nevertheless, red-and-white pennants hung from every available nook and cranny, a visual testament to O'Malley's undying support for his beloved baseball team.

"Mack!" Tony raised his shot glass in Mack's direction. "The king of the bachelor posse! The only one smart enough to throw off the bonds of marriage! My hero!"

"Here, here," Boomer said, raising his own beer. Kenny "Boomer" O'Brien had been friends with the two of them ever since high school, a third leg in the bar buddy triangle. "Gives me some hope I can keep on dodging that bullet, too."

Mack ambled through the crowd and over to the bar. "Coors Light." He nodded a greeting at Boomer.

"Don't wimp out on us. Start like a man." Tony slid his shot glass over to Mack. Had those words come out slurred? No, Tony decided. It was the music. Too damn loud. Made everything he said blend into the background.

"I can't be doing shots, Tone. I have to work in the morning, and so do you. Boomer here is the only slacker." Mack slid the squat, heavy glass away and toward Finn, the bartender.

"Hey, that's a low blow." Boomer shifted his stout frame on the stool. "I'm between careers right now. But I'm *working* on the job thing."

Mack raised a brow. "Working how?"

"Every day I wake up at noon, get the paper off the porch and recycle it." Boomer laughed. "Then I go looking for a woman who wants to take care of my needs. With this as part of my resume," he patted his beer belly, "that's hard work."

"Now there's a real full-time job," Mack said, then shook his head. "You ever think about growing up?"

"Don't do it, Boomer," Tony said. "If you do who's going to pass out on Mack's lawn?"

Boomer tapped his beer bottle against Tony's shot glass. "Exactly. What's our motto, boys?"

"'Growing up is for wimps,'" the three of them said together, though Tony thought Mack didn't sound as hearty as usual. Whatever. The guy had been moody lately. Probably wasn't getting any. He went for his shot glass again.

Mack stopped him with a hand of caution. "Tony, seriously, lay off. You don't normally drink this much. Plus, you have a job where you operate heavy machinery. The surgeon general has a warning about that, you know." Mack let out a chuckle, which Boomer echoed.

"Yeah, that and smoking. The guy is a total party pooper," Boomer scoffed.

"So, I'll blow off work." Tony shrugged off Mack's touch, then grabbed the shot glass, the golden liquid inside spilling a little over the edge in his haste. He went to knock back the tequila when Mack grabbed his arm again and brought the glass back down, sloshing the liquor onto the laminate surface of the bar. "What the hell are you doing?"

"Stopping you from a bad hangover and an even worse decision. Slow down, man."

Tony scowled. "You're not my wife."

"Good thing," Boomer said. "Mack would look like shit in a dress."

Mack laid his arms on the bar and leaned forward. "Speaking of Renee, why aren't you home with her instead of out with us?"

Tony didn't answer that question. Why wasn't he home with his wife? Because his wife didn't want him there. Hadn't wanted him in months. Years. But how could he tell his friends that? Instead, he choked down the last of the tequila and signaled for another beer. "Let's call some of the other guys and make the rounds tonight. Hit some of the regular haunts. Like old times." Again, the words seemed to blend together in his ear, becoming a smushy soup of sounds, but Tony brushed it off. He wasn't drunk. Not nearly drunk enough.

Not if it still hurt, and it sure as hell did. Why had he ever gotten married? The whole thing had been a mistake since the words "I do." He'd rushed into it, rushed into kid number two, kid number three, as if he thought adding more and more to the marriage stew would make him feel like a husband.

It hadn't. Instead it had increased the feeling of suffocation until he'd wanted to scream. To run away. To ditch the marriage, the job, all of it. If he hadn't loved the kids so much, he would have walked away.

And then there was Renee.

Damn. There were still days when he looked at her, or

caught her smiling, and his chest squeezed tight. And he remembered all over again why he'd fallen in love with her.

But those days were fewer and farther between. Instead, guilt filled the crevices left in his marriage. So he'd walked out last week, and started sucking down one beer after another, hoping one of these days the guilt would go away, and he'd find an answer. A way out that wouldn't destroy them and destroy the dream.

But most of all, destroy the hope that he still saw in all their eyes. The hope that Tony—daddy, husband—would somehow save the day.

Mack got back to his house a little past midnight, after driving a passed-out Tony home. He'd helped Tony into the apartment, avoiding Renee's disapproving gaze, who'd clearly assumed the two men had been out partying. Mack didn't tell her he hadn't even finished his own beer, that the only way he'd gotten Tony to stop drinking himself to death was by telling him they were leaving to pick up some of the other guys.

Then, when Tony fell asleep in the truck, Mack just brought him home, instead of back to Tony's brother's house, where his friend had been staying ever since his marriage had gone on the rocks. Again. For years, Mack had been making sure Tony got home. And it was getting tiring.

If this was what being married long-term was like, Mack wanted no part of it.

Mack dropped his keys into the dish by the door, then crossed to the living room. He stopped short when he noticed a light on, bathing the space in warmth. His gaze followed the path of amber, over the caramel leather sofa, then down a pair of long, lean, creamy legs—

Alex.

Mack took in a sharp breath. He moved a few steps forward, now eyeing the path past her legs, over her shorts, her torso, to her face, then to the flickering light from the TV dancing across her features.

She'd fallen asleep on his couch. His heart clenched, and he had to swallow twice before he could breathe again, because a feeling so foreign, so tender, so protective, rose in him. Tight and fierce, making him want to stop the world and hold this moment, hold her.

Forever.

Whoa. Where had that come from? He was used to desiring Alex. To being her friend. But this—this feeling of permanence, of wanting to preserve everything about this moment—was new.

He ran a hand over his face. He was tired, that was all.

She stirred and stretched, her body extending the length of the couch, slow and sexy, like a cat. Then she opened her eyes and a smile curved across her face. "Mack. You're home."

Home.

The word hit him hard, like suddenly being wrapped in a blanket that he hadn't asked for but felt surprisingly warm. He lived in a house, yes, but a home?

Well, he hadn't considered these walls, this dwelling, a home until . . .

Now.

"Yeah," he said. He cleared his throat. "I, uh, tried to talk to Tony."

"And?"

"And he was drunk."

Alex's face fell. "Did he say anything about him and Renee? About them getting back together?"

"He pretty much passed out in my truck. So I brought him home, instead of to his brother's house, though I'm not sure I made the right choice. Renee gave me the evil eye. I think she blames me for contributing to Tony's drunk and disorderly conduct, but he was already three sheets to the wind when I got to O'Malley's." Mack sank into the opposite armchair.

Alex sat up and ran a hand through her hair. Falling asleep had mussed the long brown locks, giving them a tousled, sexy look. The urge to reach out and run his fingers through those tresses nearly overpowered Mack. He splayed his palms along the arms of the chair and stayed where he was.

"I'll talk to Renee. Put in a good word for you."

"Don't bother. In Renee's opinion, I'm part of Tony's bachelor posse. Thus, I'm part of the bad influence." Mack grinned.

She laughed. "You are good at being a bad influence." Then she pressed a hand to her stomach and sat back against the sofa. "Man, I don't feel so well. I laid down because I was a little nauseous earlier. That's the last time I order in Chinese for dinner."

"You could cook." Mack gestured to the right. "I have an entire kitchen at your disposal."

She made a face at him. "And so could you, Betty Crocker. I'm just as exhausted as you at the end of the day. And just as untalented in the domestic department."

He chuckled. "Point taken. I'll stock up on pizza rolls and make sure all the take-out menus are front and center."

Alex rolled her eyes. "Ugh. Don't even mention those. Or that Egg Foo Yung will be Egg Foo Rerun."

"Come on," Mack said, rising and crossing to Alex. He put out his hands to her, and waited until she put her palms into his. He hauled her to her feet. She swayed a little with the force of the movement, nearly hitting him. Again, that protective measure swooped over him. "Time to go to bed."

Alex paused a beat, her green eyes meeting his. Mack's pulse tripled, everything else within him stilled. The urge to kiss her rose within him, as strong as a tidal force, but he kept it at bay. He knew already where kissing Alex got him.

Rejected.

Alex broke the tension with a laugh. "If I didn't know better, I'd think you were taking care of me."

"Don't get any ideas," he said. "You know I'm not that kind of guy."

"Of course."

But then Mack bent down and swooped her up into his arms. She let out a protest that he ignored, while he carried her down the hall, to the third bedroom on the right, the one he'd set up for her, and didn't release her until they reached the bed. She thought he'd just drop her on the bed, then walk away. Or do something silly, like hit her with a pillow, like in the old days when they'd been kids and Mack had stayed at her grandma's because his parents had been fighting. Back then, sleepovers with Mack had been all about popcorn and pillow fights.

Instead, Mack's arms stayed around Alex's body—tight, secure, as firm as steel girders. He stilled, his blue eyes staring into hers. He drew in a breath, and she watched, fascinated, as his chest expanded, then dropped with the exhale. She reached up a palm, sliding against the lettering of his T-shirt, fingers dancing over CARPENTERS NAIL IT EVERY TIME. The hard planes of his chest filled her palm. All that strength, solidity. *Man.*

"Alex."

Her name was a growl, and she knew. She *knew.*

Mack wanted her. And, damn it, right now, she wanted him, too. All that electricity she'd been searching for with Steve—and, hell, even with Edward, despite his stupid tie tack collection—it was here, right now, in this room, crackling between them, nearly hot enough to ignite her skin.

Suddenly desperate to have Mack, to touch not just him, but his skin, Alex roamed her palms up Mack's back, her nausea gone, forgotten. She roamed her palms up, raising his T-shirt with the movement, then retracing her path down again, bare skin meeting bare skin. The sensation lighting a fire in Alex so bright, she swore she'd never felt this kind of desire for a man before.

"Oh, God, Alex," he said again, her name now deep in his throat—the word almost tore out of him. Any traces of sleepiness faded away as desire coiled inside Alex, twisting tight in her pelvis, pooling warmth between her legs. She shifted against him, wanting more, and Mack gave it to her, leaning down and kissing her.

He captured her mouth, sliding his lips along hers with a fierce hunger, cupping her face with one hand. Then he stretched his length above her, giving Alex more access to the wide expanse of his back, his waist, the tease of skin above his jeans. She explored it all with her hands. He reached up above them, tangling his fingers in her hair, holding her tight, closer still to him and, holy God, Alex nearly screamed with how good one kiss could be.

Mack slid his tongue into her mouth, tasting her, teasing her, and they danced together. She arched against him, her mouth wide, her heart hammering in her chest, a thunderous roar. Her breasts brushed against his chest, sending sparks of sensation rushing through the thin fabric of her shirt, racing along her veins.

Alex pulled away, meeting his dark, desire-filled gaze with her own. "I want . . . more."

He grinned. "Anything you want, the answer is yes."

He ripped off his T-shirt, threw it to the side, then drew her on top of him.

Now her hands had free access to explore every inch of his chest, to touch everything she had fantasized about over the last few days. The muscles that had rippled mere inches away from her as he'd worked on her house and turned her on in ways she'd never thought a man with a hammer could. He let out a slight gasp when she slipped her palms over his nipples, then arched up and brought his mouth to hers again, a deeper kiss, his tongue probing the depths of her mouth, giving her a preview of sex. Between her legs, his erection hardened, as stiff as the beams that held up her house.

"I want more, too," Mack murmured against her mouth.

Alex drew back, giving Mack room to slide his hands beneath her T-shirt. His wide, strong hands engulfed her breasts, covering the lace of her bra, but it wasn't enough, not nearly enough. Alex jerked on the hem of her shirt and helped Mack pull it over her head, not caring where it went as long as it was gone. Then with a flick of his thumb and forefinger, the front clasp of her bra sprung apart, and her breasts were free from their lacy bondage, released to his touch.

"Beautiful," he whispered. "Absolutely beautiful."

She felt her face flush. "I'm glad to meet your expectations."

"Oh, you do, Alex. More than you know." Then he raised his head, starting with a trail of kisses that ran down her throat, into the valley above her chest, and then, *yes, oh, yes,* onto her breast, circling the nipple with lazy circles of his tongue before finally sucking the sensitive tip gently into his mouth. She nearly screamed as the sensations exploded within her.

She climaxed, the orgasm hitting her so hard, so

fast, she swore she heard it ring in her head. Musical chimes. One time. Two. Three.

A good five seconds passed before Alex realized the chimes weren't in her head, but rather coming from the door.

Mack pulled away and let out a curse. "Whoever that is, I'm going to kill him."

"Damn. That was the doorbell. I thought . . ." She felt her face heat.

He grinned. "You thought I was that good?"

"Well, you weren't bad." She gave him a teasing smile.

The doorbell rang again, seeming twice as insistent. "Next time," Mack promised, trailing a finger along her lips, "I'll try even harder." Then he swung off the bed, tugging on his T-shirt before crossing to the door. "I'll be back. Very soon. Don't move. At all."

But as soon as the bedroom door shut behind Mack, and cool air swept over Alex with a dose of reality, she did indeed move. She rose, got dressed again and ran a hand through her hair.

What had she been thinking, getting sexually involved with Mack? He was her best friend. The one she relied on for everything from broken hearts to broken windows. Everyone knew what happened when you turned a friendship into a relationship—

The friendship got lost. It drowned in the aftermath. What if things didn't work out? What if she and Mack broke up? And they would. She knew Mack's pattern as well as she knew her own shoe size.

Get in, get out quicker. The only long-term relationship he'd ever had was with his dog. He didn't want what she wanted, had made it clear a hundred times over that he and marriage, or anything smacking of commitment, were a bad idea. Not that Alex had a much better track record. The only truly serious re-

lationship she'd been in had been with a man who
was still married.

If she and Mack got involved, there was no *if* about
it, they *would* break up. It was inevitable. And, what was
worse, they would never be able to go back to where
they had been before. And she would have lost the
only person in the world who truly understood her.

Every relationship Alex had ever been in had im-
ploded. She couldn't let that happen between her
and Mack. No matter how good the sex could be—

The friendship was far more important.

Chapter Twelve

"I've missed you, baby."

The woman cleaving herself to Mack's body like English ivy purred against his chest and roamed her hand up his chest. With nothing more than a word, he could have her in his bed, and have this aching need ignited by Alex answered.

The problem?

Alex had been the one to awaken his desire, and she was the only one he wanted to satisfy it. But doing that came with strings, and Mack wasn't so good at strings.

"Deidre, what are you doing here?" Mack stepped back, disengaging himself from the blonde.

"I ran into Boomer at O'Malley's and he said you were lonely tonight. So I just had to come over." Deidre's hand went lower, over the clasp of his jeans, to cup him. "So I could really *come* over." She laughed, deep and throaty. "And I can see you are *very* glad to see me."

She wasn't the one who'd raised that erection, but he didn't tell Deidre. Five seconds, that's all it would take, to have Deidre naked and beneath him. And he'd be satisfied, without the complicated web that came attached to starting a sexual relationship with Alex.

Not to mention the complications of sleeping with your best friend. A best friend who'd made it clear she was looking for a guy to settle down with, to give her the whole picket fence life. Alex knew that he, of all people, was the last one on earth she should be looking at for that. Hadn't he completely screwed up his own marriage? He could still hear the slam of the front door when Samantha had walked out.

He couldn't bear to hear Alex do the same thing.

"Mack," Deidre said again, now rubbing against him in a way that left no doubt about her thought process. "Come on."

"Deidre, I—"

"Do I have to give you a visual to get you started?" A teasing smile took over Deidre's face and the buxom blonde stepped back, then, with the flick of a button, opened her long black coat to reveal a sheer blue teddy. A couple of shoulder shrugs and the coat was on the floor, and Deidre was back up against Mack, a lot more naked than she had been just a second earlier. "Now, if that's not a hint, I don't know what is."

"Oh, it's a hint all right. I get the picture, Mack."

He wheeled around to find Alex standing in the doorway, the hurt that filled her eyes as deep as his pool. Only darker, and far, far more permanent. Damn.

Mack jerked away from Deidre, who let out an expletive-laced protest. "Alex."

But Alex was already gone. She'd disappeared down the hall. A bedroom door slammed.

Mack knew for sure it wasn't the door to his room. Clearly, he didn't have to sleep with Alex to screw up their friendship.

* * *

"Joe, let me have a chance."

Joe Crenshaw, the wide, donut-loving managing editor of the *City Times*, didn't even bother to look up from his desk. He just kept on typing into his computer, working on the next day's issue, a cold cup of coffee beside him on one side, a half-empty package of Nicorette on the other. The rest of his desk was a mass of papers so jumbled, it would have sent an organizer into an apoplectic fit. "I don't need another features reporter. They're a dime a dozen. And I got a lot of dimes. Just look around you."

"What if I could bring you something no one else has?" Alex had come in early this morning—leaving before Mack got up, leaving before she'd had to deal with what had happened last night—and after two hours of computer sleuthing, had finally found Willow Clark. Or at least where Willow was working. That was enough to go to Joe with her idea.

"As in, what?" the editor asked. "A one-on-one with Whitey Bulger? An exclusive with Jimmy Hoffa's murderer?"

"How about an interview with Willow Clark?" Alex needed to convince Joe this assignment was perfect. Needed to land the job.

Needed anything that would keep her busy and away from thoughts of Mack Douglas, a man she wanted as little to do with as possible, at least until the image of that Jessica Rabbit clone had gone away. Yeah, like the year 2029.

Joe drummed his fingers on his desk, thinking. "The most reclusive author to come along since Harper Lee and J. D. Salinger. Could be good."

"Could be good? Come on, Joe. You've sent four reporters to do a profile on her and all they've come back with is, 'Willow won't talk.'"

"What makes you think you'll be any better at it?"

Alex drew a tattered paperback out of her bag and slapped it onto Joe's desk. "I read her book."

"So did all the others."

"I read it more than once. This was *the* book of my high school years. I know it better than anyone besides Willow."

Joe picked up the book, flipped it over, read the back. "Was it one of those *Are You There God?* kind of things? You find out about sex in this thing or something?" He started flipping the pages. "Shit. There's no sex in here. Why the hell would you read it more than once?"

The disdain in his voice would have put the entire *Vogue* editorial staff into a permanent cryogenic state. Alex held her ground. She'd land this assignment. There was no way she was going back to fashion. She'd been stuck in that department for three years, and if she had to write one more piece about bangles, she'd hang herself with the next faux-pearl necklace to land on her desk.

She was changing her life, by God. Changing her job. Changing her bad relationship patterns.

Okay, so she hadn't done so well in that category. But she would change the job. Here and now.

Alex jerked the book out of his hands. "Because it's good literature. As in well-written, strong characterization, compelling plot."

Joe let out a snort. "In other words, no sex. I'm not reading it."

"I'm not asking you to. All I want is the assignment."

"You think you can get this Hemingway chick in here to spill her guts, go for it. It'll make a great exclusive. You know how I love to scoop the *Globe.*"

"If I get this, can I be done with pumps and plumping lipsticks? Forever?"

Joe twiddled with a pen and gave her a long, hard stare. His gray eyes were as hard as ice, the kind that took no excuses, short of death or dismemberment, for missing a deadline. "Sure. I'll put Dean in charge of the fashion pages."

"Dean? But he's a guy. What does he know about mascara and panty hose?"

"More than Paris Hilton." Joe's face pinched up. He shifted in his chair. "Trust me. Sometimes I see more than I want to in the men's room. That's what I get for working late."

Alex shuddered. "That's okay. Way more than I wanted to know."

"Yeah, me, too." Joe cleared his throat. "All right, this is yours. Run with it, but bring me something quick. Fall fashions are right around the corner. I hear plaid's coming back, too."

Alex arched a brow in question.

"Hey, I hear Dean blathering all the time." He fluttered fingers in the direction of the door, his gaze back on his work. "Now get the hell out of here."

Alex had her chance. All she had to do was pray she wouldn't blow it.

The incense alone would have killed a cow.

The entrance to Theodora's Tearoom had that suffocating feeling that came from too many flowers and too much kitsch. A cacophony of ceramic figurines posed on every available space, little glassy-eyed faces turned to greet visitors, like a Made in China Noah's Ark. Cats, dogs, elephants, cows, piglets and what looked like a rhino. Silk and dried flowers in unnaturally vibrant oranges, purples and maroons burst from vases tucked around and behind the animals. In the corner by the door, an electric water fountain ran a steady stream of water down a series of fake stones—gurgle, gurgle, gurgle, so fast, Alex had a sudden urge to dash to the restroom. Thin tendrils of scented smoke wended their way above it all, wrapping the space in the spicy scents of patchouli, cinnamon, vanilla.

"I'll be right with you!" a friendly female voice called from the back.

Alex shifted from foot to foot. Tried not to look head-on at any single member of the menagerie of petrified animals. En masse, they gave off a major factor of creepy. "I can wait."

"Goodness, what a day!" The woman who came bustling around the corner was as thin as a birch tree, with thick black hair that hung down to her waist. One streak of white ran down her center part and curled behind her ear, disappearing into the rest of her ebony locks. She wore a V-necked T-shirt that sported baby chickens wearing crowns and said CHICKS RULE, a denim skirt that ended midthigh and black leather boots that nearly met the skirt. "Karma and me had a bit of a disagreement today. Seems she thought I should have paid attention to where my moons were and not been playing the stock market before I came to work. So now, what's Karma go and do?"

Alex didn't respond. She wasn't sure it was a question.

"She not only makes the toilet overflow but breaks the plunger. And on top of that, the Dow is down." The woman shook her head. "That's the last time I try to buy Google before it splits." She thrust out a hand. "I'm Willow Clark, owner of Theodora's Tearoom. And, yes, I realize my name isn't Theodora, but that's a long story. There's a long story behind most things in my life."

She paused for a breath. Alex took that as a signal to introduce herself. "Alex Kenner."

"I know." She grinned. "I mean, I didn't know your name, exactly, but I knew someone with a first name that began with *A* was going to shop here today."

Alex stared at Willow. All her life, she'd imagined what Willow Clark would be like. She'd pictured a bookish, reclusive woman scribbling away on legal pads. Sort of a female John Boy. But this slightly kooky, outrageous woman existed light-years from Walton Mountain.

"So, what can I do for you?" Willow asked.

Alex slid a business card out of her pocket and handed it to the woman. "I'm with the *City Times*—"

"Don't need a subscription. I don't read the paper. Too much bad news in there."

"I'm not selling subscriptions. I'd like to interview you."

The woman's face flipped from sunflower happy to parched-grass droopy. "Oh, you're one of them." She turned away, waving a dismissive hand. "Like I told the last four, I'm not talking."

Okay. So much for this going according to plan. Thus far, not one bit of what Alex had envisioned on her drive over here had happened. Apparently, Lois Lane she was not. "Don't you think the world ought to know, though?"

"Know what? I'm a one-hit wonder. What's so interesting about that?" The woman headed down the hall, disappearing into the bowels of the shop.

Alex followed, ducking amongst fake plants, shelves of décor. Theodora's Tearoom overflowed with lamps, miniature tables, candelabras, every kind and sort of home decoration, as if it were the dumping ground

for every cleaning and organizing team on the HGTV
and DIY networks. The cacophony of items nearly as-
saulted Alex with color and architectural styles, a one-
store war of screaming shabby chic and art deco. "I'm
interested in what you have to say."

The woman snorted. "As a reporter. For the byline."

"I read *The Season of Light*."

Willow paused midstep, then kept walking. "Lots of
people did. That's what made it a best seller."

"I read it eight times. Had to buy a second copy because my first one fell apart."

Willow turned around. "Eight, huh?" She took
three steps back, her gaze narrowing. "What is the
color of Jensine's notebook?"

It was one of those tiny details, buried in the story.
Something a cursory read, even a second read, would
have missed. Alex smiled. "Green, bright green. And
she sits in the second desk, third row. There's a
thumbtack shoved into the bottom of the desk, left
there by the boy who sat there the year before. It
catches on Jensine's tights the first day of school and
tears a hole in them. She covers the hole with the
notebook when she's standing in the lunch line so no
one knows because she's embarrassed and doesn't
want to stick out 'like a bedraggled doll in a sea of perfectly dressed toy soldiers.'"

Willow's mouth curved up into a smile. "You have
read the book."

"I wouldn't lie about that."

"I thought you might. You are a reporter, you know."

"Anything for the story and all that, huh?"

Willow raised one shoulder, let it drop.

"So, will you let me interview you?"

"No."

Alex's spirits fell.

"But I will invite you for tea. And show you some great décor for that house you're renovating."

"How do you know about that?"

Willow's smile widened. "I have more talents than writing. And maybe, my first-letter-*A* visitor, that's where your story really lies."

Chapter Thirteen

"Are you completely insane?" Tony stared at Mack and shook his head. "Why not flowers?"

Mack scowled. "Don't even get me started on flowers and Alex."

Tony laughed. He was sober, and Mack intended to keep him that way, which was why he'd shown up at Wendell and Son's Concrete and Paving at quitting time and dragged Tony out shopping. Tony had grumbled but gone along. In fact, he'd seemed almost glad for something to fill his afternoon.

"Since when do you want to make nice with Alex? She's, like, one of the guys. She's been hanging out with us forever. Listening to your dating horror stories. Hearing you belch and . . ." Tony grinned. "Worse."

"This is different." Mack looked at one box, decided against it and put the item back on the shelf. He'd come into the store with a clear idea of what he wanted—or thought he had. Now that he was here, his mind had gone blank and he'd become as indecisive as an eight-year-old with a full bucket of Halloween candy and no parental supervision.

He knew Alex. Knew what she liked.

Right?

Damn. Maybe he *should* get flowers.

The image of Alex with Steve's white roses in her hand popped into his head and he nearly punched the wall. No. No flowers.

"Whoa. Don't tell me you like her now." Tony leaned in, studied Mack's face, then let out a snort. "Man, you do like her. *Boyfriend* like."

Mack got busy studying the shelves. "No, I don't."

"Mack, this isn't seventh grade. Man up, dude, and tell me the truth."

What was the sense in hiding the truth? Tony would only ferret out the words. The man had an uncanny ability for reading Mack's mind. That's what happened when he knew a man forever.

"All right, yeah, I like her. A lot." He pulled another box off the shelf and turned it around in his hands, reading each of the sides and avoiding Tony's inquisitive gaze. Would Alex like this one better? Or maybe the other one better? He shifted from foot to foot, unable to decide.

When had it gotten this hard? Anything to do with Alex used to be easy. Overnight, things between them seemed to have become as complicated as the *New York Times* crossword puzzle.

That's what happens when you kiss your best friend and take her shirt off, Douglas. Did you think everything would be exactly the same after you threw that *into the mix?*

"Mack, you can't be serious." Tony strolled down the aisle and shook his head. He shoved his hands into his jeans' back pockets, causing his Red Sox jacket to bunch around his waist. "Don't burst my bubble. Don't tell me you're actually thinking about something serious. *Again.* Didn't you learn your lesson the first time?"

Tony had a point. That particular thorn still pricked in Mack's side. "Maybe not. But there's always a chance—"

Tony whirled around. "Are you *insane?* Have you looked at my life? Marriage sucks, Mack. You know that."

"You've had your happy moments."

Tony let out a breath. "Yeah. Like, one."

When had that jaded, defeatist tone crept into Tony's voice? Out of all of them, Tony had been the only one who could put a happy face on marriage, at least every once in a while. Granted, he still hung out like he was one of the guys, but at the end of the night, he'd always made it clear he was going home to a wife. And, truth be told, most nights, Mack had envied Tony that warm body and warm heart.

Mack put back the box, walked down the aisle and joined Tony. "You want to talk about what's going on with you and Renee?"

"No."

"You sure?"

"Yeah."

Mack considered Tony, thought about pushing the issue, then read his friend's face, the shadows dusting the skin under his brown eyes. Tony was in no mood to discuss his life. "All right. Then help me choose." Mack held up two boxes. "Which one of these is more Alex?"

Tony shook his head and vaguely pointed to the box on the right. "That one, I guess. You do realize you're trying to make up to Alex for breaking her heart with another woman, by offering her a *ceiling fan?*"

Mack grinned. "The best way to a girl's heart is through home improvements, don't you know that?"

* * *

"So, are you advising ghosts to wear Egyptian cotton this season? Or are you writing up a piece on stylish capes for vampires?"

Alex grinned and turned to face Renee, glad for the interruption from the study of clairvoyance and the supernatural. "Neither. I just landed my first feature assignment, and it's a little unusual."

"You did? Oh, wow! Congratulations!"

"Don't congratulate me yet." Alex ran a hand through her hair. "It might turn out to be Mission Impossible. And Joe, of course, wants it yesterday."

Renee rolled her eyes. "Joe's a sadist."

"That's why he's the managing editor."

Renee laughed. She pulled up an empty swivel chair and sat down beside Alex. "So, is it a juicy case? Some unsolved murder? One of those sex-for-hire crimes?"

"Nope. Willow Clark."

A blank look filled Renee's features for a second. "Wait. Isn't that the author who has never given anyone an interview?"

Alex nodded. "You know I like a challenge."

"I take it back. Joe's not the sadist, you are. How on earth are you going to get her to talk?"

"Maybe I'll read her mind." Alex turned back to her computer and pointed at the small news article she'd unearthed after an exhaustive search. One of these days, the letters would be erased from the keyboard, the way she was going at it for this story. But she'd be damned if she'd let anything keep her stuck in the hell of hemlines. "Apparently, she dabbles in ESP."

"As in *Sixth Sense,* 'I see dead people' ESP?"

"I think it's more the reading-of-minds kind. I came across this tiny piece in the back of one of those

magazines dedicated to all things supernatural."
Alex held up a printout of the two paragraphs. "You
know, the kind that have a circulation of, like, ten?
After that, I ran down to the library and took out a
bunch of books on that stuff." Alex pointed to the stack
littering her desk, covering the piles of makeup and
shampoo samples. "I've been scanning them for something, *anything*, that would make sense or give me an
edge in the interview, but, frankly, it all sounds crazy."

"Maybe she's crazy. All the fame could have driven
her over the edge. People do a lot of insane things
when they're stressed." Renee reached for a pen and
started toying with the clicker. Click in, click out, click
in, click out. She shifted in the chair, as if she was nervous,
one toe tapping against the carpet, the pen keeping
up its continuous clicking song.

Renee fidgeting? Unusual. Alex shrugged off the
whole thing. Everyone knew the *City Times* had been
under increasing pressure to up revenue lately, and
Renee, as head of the accounting department, was
probably stressing over the bottom line.

"What if Willow Clark is completely loony tunes?"
Alex asked. "I can't go back to Joe and admit failure
on my very first assignment."

Nor did she want to write a story that painted her all-
time favorite author as a few dots short of a full domino.

Renee didn't respond. Alex cast a glance at her. Distant and distracted didn't even begin to describe the
way her friend was acting today. "You okay?"

"Huh? Me? Fine. A little overwhelmed with work.
You know, the job, the kids, the laundry. I won't bore
you with the list." Renee let out a laugh, but the sound
shook like a broken bell. "All that soccer mom crap."

Alex bit her lip and considered again whether to
push Renee. Then she thought of the busy pit, the

congested knot of reporters and editors hustling back and forth in the *City Times*'s offices, and decided this wasn't the time and here wasn't the place. "I have to get started on this story right away. But I should be back by two. Do you want to grab a late lunch? We've barely had any time to talk lately."

"I, uh, have plans."

Alex smiled. "With Tony?"

Renee tossed the pen onto Alex's desk and rose. She smoothed her skirt, avoiding eye contact. "No. With another friend. A friend I haven't seen in a while. That's all. Nothing more."

A friend she wouldn't name? That was unlike Renee, as was the extra protesting. Alex had known Renee for almost a dozen years. Something was up. Foreboding tugged at Alex, persistent and strong, but she pushed it away. What did she have as proof? Renee fidgeting? Meeting a friend for lunch?

Both about as out-of-the-ordinary as a duck in a pond. Alex got to her feet, loading the pile of books into her arms. She added the few articles on Willow Clark, then grabbed her purse. "Okay, well, I'm tackling the impossible first. I'm heading over to where Willow works this morning and I'm going to try to talk to her in person, or via Ouija board, if need be." Alex grinned. "Wish me luck."

Renee gave her a quick hug. "Luck. Not that you need it. You're a great reporter."

"I'm not one yet."

"You will be. When you put your mind to something, you accomplish it. Like you have been with that house, one room at a time." Renee fell into step beside Alex, the two of them heading out of the reporter's pit, around the corner and over to the bank of elevators. Renee pushed the arrow for UP, toward the accounting offices, while Alex pushed the button for DOWN, toward the train station.

"I've been meaning to ask you something." Alex swallowed hard. Should she even broach this subject? What did she have, really, except a nagging suspicion and a couple of odd sightings?

"This elevator is slower than a snail." Renee tapped her toe against the carpet. "I've got a meeting in five minutes."

"What's up with you and Bill Rhinehart?" The words blurted out of Alex's mouth before she could stop them. Had she really said that? God. Where was her tact?

Renee stilled beside Alex, her spine as rigid as a cement pillar. "Damn. Do you think the elevator's broken? Maybe we should call maintenance."

Dean poked his head around the corner. "Hey, Alex, do you mind if I write up a piece on scarves as accessories? We have six inches to fill on page thirty."

"Yeah, whatever." Alex waved him off and turned back to Renee. "You've been having lunch with him every day."

Renee flicked out her wrist and studied her Timex. Her hand trembled. "If I'm late for that meeting, Gerry will kill me. It's our quarterly budget . . . thing."

"Renee."

Renee didn't move.

"Renee," Alex repeated.

Renee pivoted, eyes filling with unshed tears. "I can't talk about it."

Worry weighed on Alex's chest, and she knew what was coming, but still prayed she'd hear Renee say something, anything else. "Why? Renee, tell me."

Tell me it's something innocent. Tell me you and Tony will be okay.

Renee and Tony might not have had a perfect

marriage, but they had always been the ones Alex had seen as proof that if they could work it out, anyone could. If Renee and Tony could have a happily ever after, then maybe Alex could, too.

But if they became yet another divorce statistic, then how sure could Alex be that happily ever after worked out for everyone—including her?

"Alex, hate to bother you one more time, but can I have these as samples?"

Dean again. Alex gritted her teeth and spun toward the reporter. Dean was holding up two pink scarves, one with poufy fringe and the other decorated with light purple polka dots. "Samples for what?"

"Uh . . . research. I've got to see if they block the wind." He pressed a scarf to his cheek and smiled with contentment, then realizing he'd been caught mooning over the froufrou accessories, his face reddened and he yanked away the scarves.

Oh. *Oh.* "Keep them," Alex said.

"Thanks, Alex." He cleared his throat and deepened his voice. "I'll make sure to give them to my, uh, girlfriend when I'm done."

Alex shook her head as Dean left. She turned back to Renee. Just as she did, the elevator arrived with a *ding.* The doors opened, the green lighted triangles above announcing its upstairs destination. "Renee, don't go. I want to talk to you."

"I have a meeting." Renee stepped inside and pressed the button for the twelfth floor. "Don't worry, Alex. Nothing's going on with me. Not . . . yet."

The doors shut before Alex could ask what Renee meant. As the elevator made its journey upward, Alex opted for the stairs, choosing the opposite direction. She'd put this on hold. For now.

But not for long.

Chapter Fourteen

Whatever reaction Mack had expected, it wasn't what he got.

He met Alex in the driveway at the tail end of Tuesday, jumped out of the truck and handed her the box. "Here. My way of saying I'm sorry."

She stared at the fan. Then at him. "Uh, for what?"

"For . . . well, for Deidre."

"You're apologizing for having a date come over? Really, Mack, we're not married. We're not even dating. Or . . . anything close to that. You can do what you want." She bent her gaze to study the pictures on the cardboard container. "But thanks. A ceiling fan, huh?"

What had he expected? Alex to throw a fit of jealousy? To tell him he had no right to a love life? To tell him to never date another woman because he was all hers?

Well . . .

Yeah.

Of course, he didn't say any of that. Clearly, Alex was about as interested in him as she was in the cooling product he'd just bought. Had he completely misread all those signals she'd sent out last night?

Or, worse, had she been faking? Trying to ease his

male ego? Keep their friendship from imploding? Oh, that was the worst. He'd rather she tell him straight out that being with him had sucked.

He covered his disappointment by pointing out the features on the fan. "Don't you like it? It has a remote. This fancy climate control thing, too. You tell it you want the room to be seventy-two degrees, and the fan will keep spinning fast or slow enough to keep the room right at seventy-two. And look at the light kit. It's—"

"I said thank you." Alex gave him a smile. A mannequin could have provided a better one.

"You hate it."

"No, seriously, I don't. It'll look great. Really improve the resale value."

He could have smacked himself in the head. He'd bought her a fan for a house like she intended to stay here when all Alex wanted to do was finish the remodeling, sell this place and get the hell away. "I'm an idiot."

Alex grinned. A much more genuine smile than the first one. "If you want to put a label on yourself . . ."

"Hey, you're supposed to be my friend."

"Yeah," Alex said, and went back to studying the box. "I am."

If anything said it all, those two words did. Mack needed to get that fact straight, and keep it straight. Regardless of what had happened last night. He'd tried marriage before, sucked at it and didn't intend to practice again on Alex. He cleared his throat, took the fan from her and gestured toward the house. "We better get to work."

"Yeah, we better." Alex unlocked the door and entered the house. She flicked on the lights, then let out a gasp. "I have walls."

While she'd been at work today, he'd busted his

butt hanging the drywall. "You do. Granted, only in the living room, but—"

Alex pivoted and dove into his arms, cutting off his words. "Thank you!"

Mack swallowed hard, for a long second unable to say anything at all. He inhaled, and with that breath, caught the scent of raspberries, almonds. Alex's shampoo. Sweet, like home cooking. Even though he knew he shouldn't, even as he told himself to let go, he held her to him a little longer than he had to, then let her go and gave her a grin. "Hey, if I knew that's all it took to get a hug, I'd have hung some Sheetrock a long time ago."

She stepped back, her face red, as if she'd just realized she'd been touching him.

Damn. He *had* screwed everything up last night. Two weeks ago, two months ago, Alex could have hugged him out of the blue and the gesture wouldn't have made her face take on that constipated, regretful look.

She put a little more distance between them. "So, when can we paint?"

"Hold on there, Speed Racer. First we have to tape and mud, then sand the drywall. It'll be a while before we're painting. And, realistically, I'd like to get all the walls put up before we paint any of them, so the dust doesn't get on the paint in here."

"Can't we . . ." Alex entered the living room, then spun around, taking in the whole effect of the drywall. Even Mack could see how much brighter, fresher the room looked. The simple addition of the new walls had changed the entire personality of the space, taking it from dark and depressing to hopeful.

Alex thrust her fists onto her hips, which made her tank top rise a little, exposing a slight expanse of bare skin above her waistband. "Can't we paint one room? And then do it your way?"

She turned back toward him and in her face, he read the reasons why. Because she needed this one visual start-over. Because painting this room would be a way to see the road ahead—one where this house no longer resembled the one where Alex grew up. Already, it had the shape of something different, but it wasn't enough. And even though painting this soon in a renovation project went against conventional wisdom, Mack found himself nodding. Doing whatever it took to keep a smile on her face. Doing, as he always had, what it took to ensure Alex's happiness. Protecting her heart. "Sure. What color do you want?"

"Purple." She smiled, and when she did, Mack's heart turned over.

"Uh . . . purple?"

"Just kidding. I'm thinking a nice, light taupe. Something neutral. Easy to sell later."

"Taupe," he echoed, still watching her smile.

She misinterpreted his dumbstruck staring as idiocy and gave him a light slug in the shoulder, a teasing glance. "It's a gray-tan, you color-challenged male oaf."

He laughed. "Just for that, I'll let you tape the whole first wall." He put the ceiling fan on the floor, then reached over to the makeshift worktable he'd made out of a sheet of plywood and two sawhorses, grabbed a taping knife, a mud pan and a white roll of drywall tape. He opened up a container of joint compound, then, with the knife, slapped a chunk of the white goop into the mud pan and handed it to Alex. "Start putting that master's degree to work. You know, the one you earned sofa surfing on home improvement shows."

"Uh . . ." She held up the taping knife, gave the

mixture in the pan a dubious look, then stared at the tape. "There's no sticky side to this tape."

Mack chuckled, took all of it back out of her hands, then spun Alex toward the wall. "Seems I'm going to need to teach you the finer points of finishing drywall."

Granted, he didn't *need* to be working on this part of the house, or even have Alex learn the picky task of finishing the walls. He had a whole crew he could have called in at any moment. Men he paid to do this exact job. For the rest of the house he'd probably have them take over the tedious job of seaming, sanding and finishing the walls. But with Alex right here, inches before him, he couldn't think of a good reason why the two of them couldn't handle this one room together. "Now, you start with a little joint compound on the wall to set the tape."

"Which isn't tape, if you ask me. No stickiness." She wiggled the long, skinny paper.

"Are you arguing with me?" he asked.

She turned her pert chin toward him, her gaze a tease, one hand on her hip again. The urge to take that chin in the palm of his hand and not let go until she was thoroughly well kissed, soared inside his chest. He watched her lips move, found his heart racing, his blood pounding in his temples. The memory of her breasts in his hands, his mouth, hit him so vividly Mack could almost taste her skin.

Maybe this wasn't such a good idea.

"Of course I'm not arguing, oh wise one," she said. "And since you're so smart, you can be my personal tutor."

"In . . . ?" He let the sentence trail off, watching her pulse tick in her throat, his own accelerating.

"Walls, of course," she said.

"Of course."

Silence ticked between them, Alex's gaze steady on his. Was she thinking what he was? Was she imagining them back in bed? Thinking of his body on hers? In hers?

"The walls, Mack?" Alex asked. "Are we going to work on them or what?"

No. She wasn't imagining any of that.

Mack cleared his throat. *Get back to work.* "Yeah, sure. Now, as I was saying, you apply a thin layer of compound first because that creates a place for the tape to stick." He dipped the knife into the mud pan, smeared it with joint compound, then slid it along the first seam, placing a neat swath of white along the two edges of Sheetrock. Then he followed that with a piece of tape, cutting the end cleanly with the edge of the taping knife.

"Now what?"

"Now you add a little more compound. But carefully, so you don't mess up the tape. Too much and you'll just get cracks in the compound. A thin, even layer. You can always add more, but taking away when it's dry is a lot more work." Using the knife, he again whisked a layer of white down the seam.

"Well, hell, I can do that." She shifted into place in front of him, unwittingly brushing against his pelvis.

Mack swallowed. Resisted the urge to grab her, press her to the wall and finish what they had started last night. Oh, he was not concentrating at all. It'd be a wonder if the wall didn't come out looking like a band of wild kindergartners did it. "This is, uh, not as easy as it looks."

Alex turned and arched a brow. Teasing him, driving him crazy. "Are you saying that because you're a guy? Or because it really is hard?"

"Oh, it's hard," Mack said, watching her, wanting

her, yet all the while her earlier remark about them only being friends beat over and over in his head. "It really is."

"Uh-huh." Alex took the knife from Mack, scooped up some joint compound, then plastered that onto the next seam. Globs of white dropped to the floor and spattered onto the wall, then onto her shirt. "What'd I do wrong?"

"Too much compound, and you pressed too hard. Here, let me show you." He reached out, placed his hand over hers. Acute awareness ran through him as soon as he touched her, shooting into his veins. Mack redoubled his concentration. "Smooth, easy." And he pulled her hand along with one even stroke.

"Smooth, easy," Alex whispered back, shifting against him as she moved, her buttocks sliding along his pelvis with their own smooth and easy movement. "Like that?"

He coughed. "Yeah. Exactly."

She affixed a strip of tape into the seam, then turned back toward him. "Is that good?"

But Mack could hardly see what she had done. All he saw, all he knew, was that Alex stood right in front of him, and it was hot, and he wanted to take off everything he was wearing, everything she was wearing, and throw her into his pool and plunge into her.

But they weren't at his house. His pool was miles from here. And she was staring at him with an expectant look, waiting for an answer. About the damn Sheetrock. Not about them. Not about him taking her to bed and finding out if the rest of her skin tasted as wonderful as her breasts. "Yeah, it's *very* good."

You're very good.

"Great." She beamed at him. "Time for more smooth and easy."

Assuming Mack could take more. He loaded and then handed her the taping knife, then prepared to step back and let Alex take over.

"Uh, Mack? I still don't think I have this part down. Could you help me again?"

"Sure." He moved into position behind her again— did she move closer this time or was that his imagination? —and wrapped his arm around her body, taking her hand in his a second time. It was like they were dancing, a waltz with construction tools Mack could never have imagined in his wildest fantasies. In the background, the radio he kept turned on while he worked played some Top 40 song, a constant fast beat to their work.

Alex shifted, and this time Mack knew she was closer because there was no mistaking the feel of her tight ass against his growing erection, the way her shoulder blades brushed his chest, the feel of her hair tickling against his bare arms, his neck. Oh, God. He bent down, his mouth hovering inches away from the warm, enticing skin of her neck. Mack closed his eyes for a moment, just long enough to inhale the floral notes of her shampoo again. Then he opened them and drew her hand back, nearly gouging the wall as he moved with her arm, because he was looking down her shirt and thinking about the curve of her breasts, wondering how they would feel in his palms. Instead of caring what happened to the damn walls. To anything but him and Alex.

"Did we do it right?" Alex asked.

"We didn't do it at all," Mack said, his voice low, his gaze still on her breasts, the fine sheen of sweat that glistened down her cleavage, dipping beneath her tank top. He reached out his other arm, intending to pull her closer, turn her around, do whatever it took to silence this roaring in his head, when Alex pivoted first.

Out of his grasp.

Mack jerked back. A glob of joint compound fell to the floor with a disappointed thud.

"What are you talking about? We just finished a second seam. Honestly, Mack, it's like you're sleep-walking today."

The wall. The house. The reason he was here in the first place. "Oh, yeah, the wall. It looks great. Perfect job."

"Then let's move on. There's a whole lotta house left to go." She picked up the tools and moved to the next seam, turning back toward him and holding out the taping knife. Expecting him to help.

Oh, no. Not more smooth and easy. He could only take so much.

"Why don't you fill in the screw holes"—damn, even that had him thinking about things he shouldn't— "and I'll do the seams. Filling in the holes is easy." He took a second knife off the table, then showed her how to swipe a little joint compound into the dimple cre-ated by the screw. "See?"

"Sure. Whatever you want." But her face had fallen. With disappointment? Before Mack could tell what it was, Alex had gotten to work, staying a respectable dis-tance away.

For a while, the only sounds in the room were the radio and the scraping of the knives against the wall.

"We need to talk about it sometime, Mack," Alex said.

"Talk about what?" But as the words left Mack's throat, he had a feeling he didn't want to have this conversation.

"What happened last night."

Mack's hand stilled on the wall. The knife's edge carved a skinny canyon in the joint compound. "I told you, I'm sorry about Deidre. She shows up when she feels like it."

"That's not what I meant and you know it." Alex put down her tools and turned toward Mack. "What happened between you and me."

Mack dropped his tools to the bench, then headed to the cooler and grabbed a Coke. He popped the top, then handed it to Alex. He pulled a second one out of the ice, welcoming the cold against his hand and the momentary reprieve. "Not much happened, Alex."

"Maybe in your eyes, but to me . . ." She ran a finger along the rim of the soda can. "What happened changed the dynamics between us. Maybe forever."

So she hadn't been immune to him. She had felt something. Joy roared in his chest, then he looked at her crestfallen face, and the joy plummeted to his gut.

"You're my best friend, Mack," she went on, "and I can't lose that."

"You're my best friend, too." He put down the soda and crossed to her. "But maybe we can have something really good together if we—"

"Mack, be serious. You suck at commitment. Do you want to get married? To settle down?"

"Well, no, but—"

"There. That answers my question. We're not meant for each other. We want different things."

"Did you enjoy yourself last night?"

Her cheeks reddened. Damn. He didn't think he'd ever seen Alex embarrassed.

"Yeah."

"Then what's so wrong with a little more of that?"

"We could get hurt."

He tipped her chin to meet his gaze. "Don't you think we could be smarter than that?"

"Oh, what? Have our cake and eat it, too?"

"Even better." He grinned. "Have our cake and eat it in bed."

Her green eyes darkened and she drew in a breath. "It's a bad idea and you know it. We shouldn't—"

He covered her mouth with his, cutting off her protests with a kiss. Alex groaned and her arms went around him, the cold can in her hand meeting his neck, an ice to the fire erupting in the meeting of their mouths.

She was soft where he was hard, like a ying to his yang, and as much as he told himself he shouldn't do this, should steer clear of her, he couldn't. His tongue plunged into her mouth, and hers surged up to join his. Mack nearly came unglued with desire, every ounce of his body demanding he finish what they'd started once and for all.

But he wouldn't be a jerk with Alex. Wouldn't go from zero to sixty in under thirty seconds.

With reluctance, Mack pulled back. His pulse thudded in his head. "Isn't that enough reason that we should?"

Her face was flushed, her breath short. But her face had slipped into practical, no-nonsense territory. "Should what? Have a few romps in bed?"

Put that way, it all sounded so crass, so awful. He wanted more than that, much more, but the familiar fear raised its ugly head. Alex was right. He'd sucked at marriage. Seen how a well-intentioned relationship could go horribly wrong. The last thing he wanted was to tear down what he had with Alex.

If they became lovers and broke up, then he lost her as a friend, too—

That, Mack knew, would destroy him.

"You and I both know we can't do that," Alex said. Regret filled her delicate features, and a stone sank into Mack's gut. "We couldn't just stop at having sex. Maybe you can, but I can't."

He quirked a grin at her, hoping to defuse the tension between them with a little teasing. "You mean there's more after sex? Something I've been missing all these years?"

"Be serious."

She crossed away from him and refilled her mud pan with more joint compound, even though it was still nearly full. Was she avoiding the subject? Avoiding looking at him?

"And that," she said with a sigh, her back to him, "is the problem with you, Mack. You're never serious."

"I can be."

She turned around. "Are you sure about that?"

"What do you mean?"

"I know you better than anyone. You say you want one thing and you do another. Like last night."

"What did I do wrong last night?"

"If you really wanted me, Mack, *really* wanted me, you would have kicked Deidre out the minute she knocked on the door. You would have told her to go home, told her you were involved with someone else."

"I did get rid of her."

"Twenty minutes later."

"Deidre was determined to get her way, Alex. You don't understand."

She made a face. One he knew well because he'd seen it a hundred times. The one that spelled disappointment in him.

"I do understand. You're a guy. You're ruled by that tiny brain behind your zipper, as you told me the other day. I can't fault you for that. But I'm also not going to be stupid enough to walk into a relationship where I can already see the writing on the wall." She let out a sigh. "Listen, let's be smart about this. We've been friends for a long time. I don't want to ruin that, and neither do you. What we felt last night was loneliness, pure and simple. Leave it at that. I'm looking for Mr. Right, and, let's face it"—her gaze met his, her green eyes soft with truth—"you're not him."

He wanted to tell her he'd be different, that he wouldn't break her heart. But could he make that promise? Could he give Alex an iron-clad guarantee? Given his track record?

"I think we've gotten as far as we can today," Mack said. And this time, he wasn't talking about the job.

Chapter Fifteen

On her second visit to Theodora's Tearoom, Alex had walked out with two lamps and a belly sloshing with too much tea, but no more information about Willow Clark than when she'd walked in. On her third visit, she ended up with a vase, a set of serving dishes and a mirror large enough to reflect the Hancock Tower. And still no inside information from Willow.

This time, Alex left her purse in the car.

"Why hello, Alex," Willow said when the shop door tinkled.

Alex looked around but couldn't see the author anywhere. How could she possibly know who had stepped inside? There had to be some kind of security mirror. "Yep, it's me again."

Bound and determined to get the story. *No escaping me this time, lady.*

"How did the lamps work out? And the mirror?"

Alex wandered down the cramped aisle, still looking for Willow. She fingered a porcelain pig, his gray snout turned toward the ceiling. He looked almost . . . cute. The silly animals were starting to grow on her. "I've only found a place for the vase so far. The house—"

"Isn't ready for the rest," Willow finished. "It will be, don't worry."

Then she swung around the corner, so fast, Alex let out a little squawk of surprise. She'd been right there the whole time? But that was impossible. Alex would have seen her, spied her through the aisle. But she'd seen nothing other than porcelain animals.

Alex shook it off. She was overly distracted today, that was all. She'd tossed and turned all night, trying to wrap her mind around what was going on between her and Mack. They'd made a mistake, shifting the dynamics of their relationship, and she wanted to rewind the clock, send them back into the world of platonic, even as another part of her wanted him to kiss her again.

Insane. Mack was all wrong for her—in a relationship sense. He'd made it clear he wanted nothing more than a good time. She'd been down that path with too many men to want to repeat it with the one man who meant something to her.

Something that tasted an awful lot like disappointment settled in Alex's stomach. She shrugged off the thoughts and refocused on why she was standing in the odd little shop.

"That house will come together in its own good time," Willow continued. She pushed a tendril of her long dark hair behind her ear, and leaned in, studying Alex's face. "It needs . . . healing, doesn't it?"

"It needs something." Alex snorted.

"Healing," Willow repeated. "That's just the right word."

How had the other woman known that? Were those claims of mind reading true? Or was Willow Clark just one more in a long line of kooks? Maybe doing this interview wasn't such a good idea. Thus far, she hadn't gotten much for her efforts. A few garage sale finds and some odd predictions more like horoscopes than reality. She could have gotten both from reading the *City Times* classifieds.

No, Alex decided. If she had to interview Willy Wonka, she'd do it, just to get away from Empire waists. And, a part of her still wanted to know. Know where Jensine had come from. How that character, the girl who had seemed so much like her, had sprung to life in this woman's mind.

Maybe there was something to Willow Clark's madness. Whatever it was, Alex prayed it wasn't contagious.

"Miss Clark," Alex said, "I really want to tell your story."

"Why? I think yours is far more interesting."

Alex scoffed. "Mine is the story everyone else has. Crappy childhood, but I grew up to be a well-adjusted adult."

Willow took a step closer to Alex, her wide brown eyes capturing and studying Alex's. "Did you?"

Heat rushed down Alex's face. The tight, cramped aisle seemed to constrict, the animals that had been friendly before now seeming to stare at her, asking the same question, an army of a hundred all waiting expectantly for an answer.

Of course she had. Her life was on the right path now, or at least close enough to the right path that she could see the happy ending she wanted. She was fine. Just fine. "I'm here to talk about you."

Willow thought about that for a second, then nodded. "Okay."

Finally. Alex pulled the slim reporter's notebook out of her back pocket, along with a pen, then reached for her minirecorder with the other hand.

"But—" Willow said, stopping Alex with a touch of her fingers, "only on one condition."

"What's that?"

"I'll tell you one fact about me for every fact you tell me about you."

"What is this, *Silence of the Lambs*? I don't need to—"

"Then I don't need to do this interview." Willow turned away, her rainbow-colored skirt poufing outward like a bell. "And, in case you forgot, you need me more than I need you. Your job is on the line here, not mine."

And then Willow walked down the aisle, disappearing among the faux ficuses and painted pottery.

Damn. Alex hurried after Willow. No way would she let this story get away. She couldn't go back to fashion. She'd sooner hang herself with the next pair of fishnet stockings to land on her desk than write one more column about what was hot in denim this year. "Miss Clark, wait."

Willow kept going, disappearing into a back room that Alex hadn't seen before.

Alex hesitated. Should she follow? Stay out here? What would Geraldo do?

Alex pushed on the door and slipped inside. "Miss Clark?" Alex rounded a corner and found Willow sitting behind a desk. An old-fashioned typewriter sat before her, a half-filled sheet of paper in the roller. Willow had turned in the chair, arms crossed over her chest, an expectant half smile on her face, as if she'd fully anticipated Alex would follow.

"First thing I'll tell you," she said, resting a loving, protective hand on the round keys of the Smith Corona, "is that I never stopped writing. I just stopped publishing."

Alex's breath caught. She didn't move, afraid Willow would stop talking if she so much as breathed.

"Now it's your turn." Willow gestured to a second chair. "Tell me something about you."

Alex slid into the battered armchair, its worn floral fabric accepting her body in a cushioned hug. "You're a smart woman. Giving me something as enticing as that, and then stopping."

"It's called a hook, my dear. Oldest trick in the author's handbook." Willow grinned. "You want your story, and I want mine."

"Why? Why do you care about me?"

Willow leaned forward, her eyes wide. She clasped her hands together in her lap. "I read something in you, Alex. Something that needs healing as much as your house does."

Unexpected tears stung at the back of Alex's eyes. She shook them off and shifted in the chair. "I'm fine."

"Then why are you tearing out walls at the same time you're building new ones? And I'm not just talking about the ones in that house, but the ones between you and the people who care about you."

"How do you know about the construction I'm doing in the house?" Alex had told her only that she had moved into a new place, not that she was renovating.

A slow, secret smile took over Willow's face. "I know a lot of things. And that, Alex, is also part of my story, so I can't tell you any more."

Alex sat in the chair, chewing on her bottom lip and debating. Willow waited, patience covering her Mona Lisa countenance. What good could come of opening these old wounds? They'd simply rip a hole in her heart, one she didn't want.

But if she didn't open up to Willow—a woman who had an uncanny ability to see through Alex—then she'd never get the story she needed. It'd be eye shadow and nail polish for the next zillion years.

Alex would find more chuckles in the obituary department.

"I'm tearing down the walls in the house because it has too many bad memories, and the place is in bad shape," Alex said finally.

Willow arched a brow in question.

Alex waited. Silence, she had found, was her most powerful tool in an interview. People felt compelled to fill in conversational gaps. Silence made them squirm.

But not Willow. She just sat there, patient as a clam on a beach, the same smile on her face, as if the tables were turned and she was the one doing the interview, not the other way around.

Alex tapped her toe on the vinyl floor, measuring a cadence of impatience.

Willow crossed her hands in her lap with all the serenity of a sensei.

Alex shifted in her seat. She twisted her pen, spinning the cap around and around.

Willow didn't move.

One minute ticked by. Two. Three. Five.

Willow remained as still as the porcelain rhinoceros on the shelf. Alex was tempted to check Willow for a pulse when she leaned forward and peered into Alex's eyes.

"Is that all?"

"Well, no, of course," Alex said. "But that's all I wanted to say about my childhood. Trust me, my life really was that boring."

"I have to say I'm quite disappointed." She rose and crossed to the door. "I really thought you wanted my story more than that, Alex."

Then Willow left the room, letting the door shut

behind her with a finality that told Alex the interview was over.

Nothing bought a kiss like cookies.

"I always knew I loved you, but now I remember why." Carolyn Kenner smiled, then bussed Mack's cheek. "You are the sweetest boy ever."

Mack chuckled. "Grandma, I'm not a boy." He'd been calling Alex's grandmother "Grandma" for as long as he could remember, even though they weren't related. She'd been more family to him than his own grandparents some days, and he couldn't imagine calling her anything else.

"Any man under fifty is a boy to me," she said, then set the box of Windmill Cookies in the center of the table and headed for the stove. "Can I make you some tea?"

He made a face. "Tea?"

She laughed. "Okay, coffee it is. Black, right?"

"Is there another way to drink it?"

Carolyn filled a kettle with water, set it on a burner, then clicked on the stove. She bustled around the kitchen, getting out a teacup and a bag of tea for herself, along with a French press and a container of coffee for Mack. He sat back, enjoying the sunny atmosphere of the room. How he missed this sense of warmth, of home. Ever since his mother had left, the energy seemed to have drained from the Douglas kitchen on Pinewood Street. As for his own kitchen—

Well, the entire time he'd owned the house, it had only been a room, a place to eat cold leftover pizza, grab a cup of coffee in the morning. Until Alex moved in.

Now there were two mugs in the sink. Two plates on the counter. Her purse and shoes dumped carelessly by the back door, a sweatshirt thrown over a chair.

With Samantha, those same things had seemed like an intrusion into his space, his life. But with Alex, it all seemed . . . comfortable.

"So, how's our girl?" Carolyn asked, placing two hot cups and cookies before them both. If Mack didn't know better, he'd swear Alex's grandmother was a mind reader.

"Alex?" Mack sipped at his coffee. "Just fine. She's practically Bob Vila."

Carolyn laughed. "You know Alex. When she puts her mind to something, she's like a little worker bee."

"That she is." He selected a cookie, took a bite. Waited for Carolyn to get to the point, because he could sense one coming as easily as thunderclouds announced an impending storm.

"She told me you fixed her up with one of your friends." Carolyn dunked her tea bag in her cup—up, down, up, down. "A really nice guy, from what Alex said."

"Yeah. Nice guy." Mack chomped off another bite of cookie. The second bite didn't taste nearly as good as the first.

"Do I detect a little jealousy?"

"Me, no way." He fiddled with the cookie. "I want Alex to be happy. If that means she's with Steve . . . well, good."

Carolyn studied him. "Uh-huh. Why don't I believe you?"

"Grandma, Alex and I are friends. Always have been. You know that."

"I know." She removed the tea bag and put it on the saucer, then stirred a teaspoon of sugar into her cup. "But sometimes that comes at a cost to you."

"Maybe in terms of lumber, but, hey, I have that covered. I get a discount at Home Depot." He grinned.

Carolyn folded her hands, one on top of the other,

and gave him that look that told him she knew him well. Too well. "Have you ever told Alex why you married Samantha?"

"Why would I want to bring that up? Samantha and I are divorced now. It's all in the past."

"Is it?"

"You should try these cookies, Grandma. They're really good." He took another bite, giving her a change-the-subject-please grin.

"She doesn't know anything, does she? Nothing about what happened during your marriage? Why you got divorced? You've never said a word."

"I picked these up at a new bakery," Mack said, reaching for a third Windmill, "over in the Back Bay that—"

"Mack." Carolyn laid a hand on his. "Tell her."

"Tell Alex what? That I ran off to Vegas and eloped with a woman and ruined her life?"

"And why did you do that?"

Mack looked away. Studied the sunflowers in the wallpaper. "Thought I was in love," he grumbled.

"Not with Samantha."

"Are you going to eat those cookies?" Mack asked. "Because I'll eat them all before you know it, then I'll leave here feeling bad, because I devoured your gift."

"You are the most exasperating person to have a conversation with." Carolyn selected a cookie, dunked it in her tea, then took a bite of the softened cinnamon- and almond-flavored treat.

"Maybe because this is a conversation I don't want to have." He drew in a breath, let it out. "Alex is looking for something permanent. And if there's one thing my marriage taught me, it's that I have all the sticking power of a cobweb."

"Bullshit."

"Grandma!"

"I call it like I see it, Mack, and you're obviously not seeing what I'm seeing. You're missing the tree because you're too damn busy avoiding the whole forest."

He chuckled. "Are you saying marriage is a forest?"

"The best and most beautiful you'll ever find. I enjoyed nearly fifty years with my Howard before he passed away, God rest his soul." She took a sip of tea, then put the cup back in the saucer, the china chattering together as if joining in the conversation. "Getting married was the most terrifying thing I ever did, but also the most wonderful, believe me. Because I married my best friend."

"You got lucky."

"You could, too."

"Or I could screw up everything with the woman I . . ." His voice trailed off.

"You love more than any other." She smiled at him.

The sunflowers got another close study. "She's my best friend. That's all."

"Uh-huh. That's why you worry so much about breaking her heart. That's why the mere mention of that Steve guy has you ready to break my bone china in half." She wagged a finger at the rose-patterned cup.

Mack pushed his coffee to the side, folded his hands on top of each other and met Carolyn's inquisitive gaze. "What's all this about? You've never tried to shove Alex and me together before."

"Oh, I've always been trying to do that. I've just never been this obvious about it." She turned her cookie around, dunked the other half and gave Mack a grin. "And you are being a big fat chicken, if you ask me."

"Hey. Aren't you supposed to be the loving grandmother?"

"No, I'm supposed to be a crotchety old lady who says exactly what she thinks. And this old lady thinks you're a fool for letting a little fear get in the way of the best woman to come along since Grace Kelly." She shifted in her chair, causing her poufed white hair to bounce a little. "In fact, I happen to think our Alex is even more wonderful, more of a catch than the late princess."

On Mack's scale, Alex ranked light-years ahead of any princess, any woman who had ever adorned a magazine cover, a news story. But that didn't mean she was destined to be with him. If anything, it meant the opposite. "Exactly why she deserves a man who'll give her everything she wants."

"And what does she want? In your opinion?"

"A house. A white picket fence. A dog."

"She has a house. A carpenter who can install a fence. A carpenter who also owns a dog already."

Mack scowled. "That doesn't automatically make me Mr. Right. Steve is better for her. He's . . . stable. Looking to settle down. He said as much to me."

Even if Mack hated the thought of Steve kissing Alex. Taking Alex in his arms. Taking Alex to his bed—

God, no. He couldn't go there. That image was torture.

"I haven't met Steve yet, so I could be wrong, but I think you're a good match. You always have been." Carolyn leaned forward and laid a hand on Mack's. "Not every marriage is like your parents' or yours, you know. You could do even better the second time. You're wiser now."

Alex hadn't introduced Steve to her grandmother? That was a clear sign she wasn't serious. Mack let that fact stew in the back of his mind.

"Rationally, I know not everyone turns out like my mom and dad, Grandma. But in here," Mack said, touching his chest, "in here, it's another story. And I just can't take a chance of hurting Alex. She means too much to me."

"That, in my opinion, is exactly why you should be with her. That's as elementary as daisies blooming in springtime."

He rose and put his empty mug into the sink, the cookies churning in his gut with too much sweetness. "My wife left me, Grandma, not that she was ever happy to begin with. She walked right out the door after less than a month. I broke her heart."

"So you try again. You learned your lessons. You do better the second time."

He swallowed hard, his gaze going out the window to the manicured perfection of Merry Manor's grounds. "Or maybe I do worse."

Carolyn's touch on his shoulder was soft. "You're too hard on yourself. You always were."

"Not as hard as I should be," Mack said. "Not nearly as hard as I should be."

Chapter Sixteen

The picture fluttered to the floor with the grace of a leaf dancing on the wind. It had slipped out from behind the kitchen countertop, a stowaway from years before, dislodged by Mack's crowbar. Alex stared at the grainy color image as it circled and finally landed, trying to make sense of what she saw. Then it came into focus, and she realized it was an image from her past.

She bent and picked it up, the Kodak paper as thick as a postcard. "I remember this."

Mack stopped working and looked over her shoulder. "Is that you?"

They'd been working for hours, sticking to construction only. To business as usual. It was a lot easier for Alex to do that than to come anywhere close to dealing with the simmering sexual tension between her and Mack.

Steve had been calling her, twice a day, and he was exactly the kind of guy she wanted. Pleasant. Dependable. Predictable. He wasn't the kind who would upend her world and drive her crazy.

And if there was one thing Alexandra Kenner wanted, it was predictability. Except, every time she turned around, she got the complete opposite. Like now. A moment from her childhood that had slipped out innocently, and packed a hell of an emotional wallop.

Mack moved in behind her, his tall, solid frame providing a slight shadow. "You look so little."

"Yeah. I was four, I think." A rail-thin Alex with sleep-messed hair and purple feetie pajamas stood in front of a scrawny Christmas tree, holding a new doll and beaming into the camera. A threadbare stuffed white bear sat at her feet, temporarily discarded in favor of the present. Gosh, it seemed a hundred years ago now. How few pictures she had of her early childhood, either because her mother hadn't saved any, or hadn't taken them.

Who had taken this picture? Then she remembered. It had been Grandma Kenner on the other side of the lens. She'd been the one calling out the corny "Say Cheese," grinning at the two younger generations before her.

Mack's fingers clasped the other side of the picture. "You're cute. All cuddly in those pj's."

"Gee, thanks. I look like a big purple Easter Bunny."

"You look happy."

"I was," Alex said, as surprised by the memory as she was by the picture. Christmas morning, of course she would have been happy. But it hadn't been the presents that had brought the smile to her face, it had been the quiet in the house, the three of them together. A family. A *real* family, like the kind Alex had created with her dolls. So she'd flashed that toothy grin at the camera, her joy practically pouring from every pore.

"I guess I never really studied pictures of my mother before. My grandmother has them out, all over the place in the condo, but I haven't looked at them in a long time." Now Alex stared at this one, as if searching for some clue she had missed. Some link to the jigsaw puzzle of her life, the one thread that would knot together this continually unraveling emotional rope in her gut. She thought about what Willow had asked her. About why she was tearing down the walls.

She'd told Willow it was because the house contained only bad memories. But here, in her hands, was evidence of a happy day. Was Alex's memory faulty?

In the photograph, her mother was bundled in a pink terrycloth robe and sitting in a threadbare armchair in the corner. She was leaning forward, her chin in her hands, her hair also still mussed from sleeping, watching everything. And, most of all, smiling at Alex. The smile was unmistakable.

It looked exactly like Alex's. And it was filled with something Alex had never seen before.

Pride.

"Your grandmother must have taken this," Mack said.

Alex nodded, her throat thickening. She traced the outline of her mother's face, the delicate cheekbones, the curve of her jaw. And as her fingertip ran down the last millimeters of the image of her late mother, she realized she was tracing her own features.

"You look just like her," Mack said, reading Alex's mind. His arm slipped around her, a hug she leaned into for one long second, then she pulled away.

"I never thought I did. I never thought I was anything like her."

"Apparently you are. More than you knew."

Alex curled her hand around the photo, pulling it out of Mack's grasp, crumpling it. "No, I'm not. At all."

Then she tossed it into the corner, throwing the picture as far away as she could. What was a picture, but one instant, one second out of a million? She refused to see that second as anything but what it was.

A pose.

"Hey, Alex, don't you want to keep that?"

"No." She shook her head, swiping at her eyes, until the blurriness was gone. Until she couldn't see the resemblance anymore in her mind. Until she'd forgotten the picture, and everything it brought up. "I want to get to work."

Mack opened his mouth, as if he wanted to say something else, then shut it. Before he walked back over to the workbench, he put a hand on her shoulder, and gave her a soft smile. He was there, if she needed him. As always.

For a long time, they kept on working, the only sound between them the whine of the circular saw and the rhythmic pounding of the hammer. They had started replacing the windows that morning, after Mack had showed up with a truckload of them. Alex had asked how much they'd cost and he'd claimed they were "extras" from a job.

She didn't believe him for a second. Once again, Mack was insisting on taking care of her. Irritation rose in her, undoubtedly fostered by finding the picture, but Alex didn't care. She was tired of Mack trying to play hero every five minutes. She couldn't very well rewrite her life if he kept getting in the way.

Alex put down her hammer and pulled a check out of her back pocket. "Here, take this."

Mack stared at the slim piece of paper. "What's this?"

"I went to the bank yesterday and mortgaged the house. It was paid off a long time ago, and I was able to get a loan against it. Not much, because this place apparently isn't worth a whole lot, considering the state it's in. But there's enough to pay you for your work."

He waved off the check. "I don't want your money, Alex. And I won't take it."

She let out a gust. "What *do* you want? Because I won't let you keep on working for free."

He moved closer to her, and everything between them shifted as quickly as the wind. "I want you."

Oh, she knew that. She'd known that for weeks. But sex only complicated things between them, and the last thing Alex needed right now was another complication. Her mind was a whirlpool, spinning with questions and emotions, and every time Mack got close, he launched another boat into the vortex.

"You have me," Alex said, a nervous chuckle escaping her. "Free labor."

The memory of his kiss, of that moment in his bed— that very, very good moment—burst to the surface of her mind. That night they had almost, *almost.*

"That isn't what I'm talking about, and you know it." Mack reached up and cupped her jaw, his thumb tracing a lazy, sensual pattern along her chin, tugging at her bottom lip.

Oh, she wanted to resist. She told herself to resist. But her heart began to race, and her eyes drifted shut, the desire surging through her body of its own volition, like August heat rising from black tar.

She opened her mouth, kissed the tip of his finger. A roaring thunder began to run through her, drowning out any sensible thought. Drowning out anything but Mack, and his touch, and how incredibly hot he made her.

She opened her eyes, pushed one sensible thought to the surface. "Mack, what if . . ."

"What if it was too good to resist?" His voice was

husky, deep, almost a groan. He shifted closer, pressing his body to hers. The heat quadrupled, and desire pooled in Alex's gut.

She'd had a taste of him the other night. A mere appetizer.

What would it be like to have the whole course? What would Mack be like, not as a friend, but as a lover? Would he be as tender and caring as he was when he'd carried her in to the guest bedroom? Or would he tease her like he always had? Would he be selfish like Edward, and leave her wanting at the end? Or would he make sure she'd climaxed, over and over again, before he'd reached his own peak?

Oh, he'd be good. Very good. She knew that as surely as she knew her own name.

"That's what I'm afraid of," she said softly, talking about more than just whether he was too good to resist.

He held her face and lowered his own to within inches. "Oh, Alex, don't be afraid."

Then he kissed her, and she forgot any reason not to kiss him back.

Her cell phone began to ring, loud and insistent, the volume turned up high so she could hear it above the power tools. The sound jerked Alex back to reality and she stumbled out of Mack's arms. She fumbled the phone out of the holster and flipped it open. "Hello?"

"Alex, how are you?"

Steve. "Uh . . . fine. Just-just fine."

"What are doing?"

No way was she going to tell him the truth. She rattled off something about doing an interview, then asked him about his workday, stepping outside as she talked. Lying. Guilt sank like a stone in her stomach.

She turned away from the house, away from Mack. From the disappointment in his eyes. A few minutes later, she and Steve ended the call and she went back inside.

"Prince Charming, huh?" Mack asked.

"He just wanted to see how I was." A month ago, telling Mack about a boyfriend wouldn't have made her as uncomfortable as a bug under a microscope, but now . . .

Now she'd rather talk about getting a colonoscopy than give Mack details about Steve.

"He's a nice guy," Mack said. "Real serious about you, from what he tells me."

"Yeah." She did not want to have this conversation. Especially not after kissing Mack five minutes ago.

She'd set out to straighten out her life, and all she kept doing was making a bigger mess of it. This was exactly why she needed a guy like Steve. Mack was perfect as a friend, and that's where she needed to keep him. Yet, a part of her wondered why Mack kept pursuing her when he knew she wanted the white picket fence package.

And he didn't.

Alex picked up a set of shims for the next windows and fanned them out in her palm. She snuck a glance at Mack, and then decided to test the waters, find out where the hell he was going with what had just happened. "Steve told me the other day that he wants to get married. He didn't say he wants to marry me specifically or anything yet, but I get the feeling he's the kind of guy who wants to settle down right away. He's thirty, and is just as tired of dating as I am. And he's not in-terested in having kids, just like me. I think it's the accountant in him." She let out a nervous laugh. "You know, he ran the numbers and it didn't compute for him."

Mack swallowed hard. His entire body seemed to turn to stone, and an invisible wall went up between them. "Then he's everything you ever wanted, isn't he?"

With a few words, Mack could have said he wanted the same thing. He could have told Alex that he was a man looking to settle down, too. That he wanted to take what had happened between them beyond the bedroom.

But he hadn't.

"Yeah," Alex said. "He's perfect."

Mack hoisted a new window into the opening in the front of the dining room. "Can you get me some nails for this?"

"No."

He turned and looked at her, surprise on his features. "What?"

"Not until you talk to me. All our lives, you and I have been able to talk. About anything. But now, everything's changed. We talk *around* what's going on, but not about it. You need to tell me what you want, Mack."

He put the window down on the floor, leaning it carefully against the wall. Then he dusted his hands together and pivoted, leaning against the framing, his arms crossed over his chest. "I want you to be happy."

"That has to be the lamest thing I have ever heard."

"What do you mean, the lamest thing? I'd say that's nice."

"You're really that self-sacrificing that you'd just let me go, off into the sunset with Steve"—she waved toward the door—"because you want me to be happy?"

He pushed off from the wall and crossed to her. "Is that what you want? Mr. Predictable?"

"I want a man who is honest with me. Who tells me

what he's thinking. Not someone who kisses me, then acts like it doesn't matter."

"It matters, Alex." He shook his head. "It matters more than you know."

"Then what the hell is going on between us?" The volcano in her throat threatened to explode. Mack gave her these circular answers that did nothing but bring them back to where they started. "You have me so confused, I don't know which way is up. You kiss me, you almost make love to me, then Deidre comes over, and you say nothing's going on with her, and then you kiss me again. You're as back and forth as your damn saw."

"How do *you* feel about *me?*" he asked.

She blinked. "What do you mean, how do I feel about you? You're my best friend, Mack."

"Exactly. That's all I am to you. A *friend*. I want more than friendship, Alex. If it hasn't been clear as day, then let me spell it out." He tangled his hand in her hair, his gaze locking with hers, unmistakable heat darkening his blue eyes. "I want to take you to bed, and make love to you until neither one of us can see straight. I want to wake up in the morning with you and then do it all over again. I want to kiss you so badly, it hurts. But what I don't want is for you to look at me and think, 'Damn, that was really good sex with my best friend.'"

"I don't want really good sex with my best friend," Alex said, her heart breaking as the words left her mouth, because for five seconds there, she'd thought—

No, she'd hoped, Mack had wanted more than just that.

"I want forever," she said. "I want a man who wants to get married. Settle down."

He released her and looked away. "I told you, I

won't do that again. Haven't you seen already—from my disaster of a marriage, from my parents, from Renee and Tony—how badly that can go? I'm not going there again. I already ruined one woman's life."

"Then I guess we shouldn't keep kissing." A huge lump of disappointment sank to the bottom of Alex's stomach. She told herself that was crazy. She had what she wanted—Steve, a man who was looking for exactly what she was—and Mack, her best friend, back in that exact role. Her world was righted.

If everything was as it should be, then why did she feel so crappy?

Mack's face was as unreadable as marble. "Yeah, that sounds like a good plan. All kissing has done is mess everything up between us."

"Then we're back to the issue of payment," she said, trying to clear her head, get back to mundane issues. Anything but—

Kissing him again.

Mack slid the window back into the open space, then hammered in several nails to hold it in place, clearly taking the request to return to business as usual to heart. "We'll call it even—if you can figure out a way to get my father out of the damn house. He's become a *Wheel of Fortune* addict. If there was TV rehab, I'd be sending him."

"But your mother walked out over a year ago."

"For my father it's been five minutes." Mack's right hand stilled, a nail propped between two fingers. He cast a glance out the window. "Sometimes I feel the same way. I wish she'd just . . ." He shook his head. "I don't know. What I want doesn't matter. She's not coming back."

Pain had weighed down Mack's shoulders, more than any load of lumber ever could. His eyes glistened, then he swiped at them with the back of his arms. Alex's heart squeezed. She knew how it felt to go without a parent. To feel that sense of betrayal, of loss. That hole in your heart that no one could fill. For her, it was too late, because her mother was gone. But for Mack, his mother was still out there, somewhere.

And then, an idea occurred to Alex. An idea so insane she wasn't sure it could work. But if she could pull it off, maybe, just maybe, she could repay Mack, bring their friendship back onto steady ground and help his father all at once.

Or her plan could completely backfire in her face.

If Alex could bring Emma Douglas home, could she bring home a happy ending, too?

Chapter Seventeen

Emma Douglas lived in a tiny walk-up apartment in Providence. The same address as the one written in the corner of the letters sitting on Mack's desk. The apartment was uncluttered, nearly devoid of the personality Alex used to see back at the house in Boston, other than the easel set up in one corner by the window with the stack of bright, happy landscapes on the floor beside it. She answered the door with her hair in a ponytail, a paint-covered apron over her khaki capris and T-shirt, a crimson-coated brush in one hand. "Alex! What a surprise! I haven't seen you in ages!" She welcomed Alex in, opening the door wide, and her free arm wider, drawing Alex into a hug. "It's so nice to see you."

Alex had always liked Emma Douglas. She and Roy may have fought like crazy, but when it came to hospitality, Emma had always had a cookie ready for the little girl next door. "It's nice to see you, too."

A few minutes later, Emma and Alex were seated at the small, two-person kitchen table in the sunny kitchen, sipping Earl Gray tea and eating biscotti. "I'm sorry I don't have more to offer you," Emma said. "I live pretty simple now. It's just me."

"No more . . ." Alex didn't know the man's name, and let the sentence trail away.

"No. That ended a while ago." Emma toyed with her teaspoon, staring into the silver well, as if studying her distorted reflection. "I realized I needed some time alone. To figure out who I was. What I wanted."

Alex spun her teacup in the saucer. "I can understand that."

"It's been good for me. But I miss Mack." Her gaze went to the window. "He won't talk to me. He won't forgive me."

Alex bit her lip. Why had she thought this was a good idea? Coming here, serving as intermediary for a family with open wounds? She shifted in her seat, not wanting to pour salt into Emma's sore, wishing she could find a polite way to leave.

Then she thought of Mack. Of the hunch in his shoulders. The pain in his eyes. If there was any way to alleviate that, she'd sit here for another twenty hours.

"I think Mack sees how hurt his father is, and that's what has made him so angry."

"I thought . . ." Emma drew in a breath. "I thought Roy would be glad I was gone."

"Roy won't leave the house. He's anything but happy." Alex shook her head. "I'm sorry. I should probably mind my own business. I'm just telling you what Mack has told me."

Emma rose and crossed to the sink. There weren't any dishes to wash. Nothing to do there but prop her hands on either side and stare out the window at the brick wall of the opposite building. "They're hurting. And it's all my fault."

Alex didn't say anything.

"I thought leaving would make it easier. The fighting would stop. They'd . . . find their happiness."

"They didn't." Alex wrapped her hands around the cup and considered whether to say anything else. If her mother was still alive and there was a possibility Josie Kenner could return to close the wounds of the past, would Alex want her to come back? Yes, she would. If only for the closure, the answers. "I think you should go back."

Emma whirled around. "Go back? To Boston?"

"I don't know what happened between you and your husband, but Mack is my best friend, and I'm worried about him. I want to see him happy again." Alex drew in a breath. "I know what it's like not to have a mother. Mine is dead, Emma, so I can't go back and fix anything that went wrong. You're not. You can have a second chance."

"But Mack won't talk to me. I've tried." Tears welled in her eyes. "Believe me, I've tried."

"Try harder." Alex smiled. "You know how stubborn he is."

Emma echoed Alex's smile. "He gets that from his dad. I'll tell you, living with the two of them was like living with two bulls in one pasture."

Alex chuckled. "I can imagine." Then she sobered and met Emma's eyes, so like Mack's. "So, will you do it? Come back to Boston?"

"What if Mack doesn't want to see me?"

"You're his mother, Emma. He'll always love you." As the words left Alex, she wondered if that was true for everyone. She barely remembered her mother. Barely knew her.

How could she love someone like that? Miss someone she didn't know? But she did, didn't she?

Was that what that ache in her chest was? The need to know that persisted, yet triggered the same feelings of resentment and anger that had made her first delight in finding that picture from a long-ago Christmas—and then throw it away. Either way, she had no one waiting in an apartment in Providence to close those gaps in her past. The best she could do was close them for Mack.

"You're right," Emma said, finally. "It's time I went home. In fact, it's past time."

Chapter Eighteen

"You cook like shit."

"Whatever happened to honoring thy father?" Roy settled into the seat opposite his son, popped the top on a beer and drank deeply from the can.

Mack pushed away his plate. "You think this tastes good?"

Roy scowled down at the hamburger-and-noodles mix he'd concocted in a pan earlier. "Well, no. But I'm not your mother. I made do with what I had in the house."

"Next time you invite me to dinner, I'm going grocery shopping first."

Roy laughed. "Yeah, and you'd buy frozen pizzas. Face it. You're no better at being domestic than I am."

"You're right." Mack rose and put his half-eaten plate of food on the counter. Yet another reason he wasn't cut out for marriage. The con list got longer by the minute.

Hell, did he even have a pro list? There was coming home to Alex. To her smile. To knowing she was sleeping in a bed just down the hall. Now *there* was a pro.

Except . . . she was dating another man, and Mack

also had to come home to Alex talking on the phone with Steve. Getting flowers from Steve—the guy seemed to have an unlimited tab at Teleflora, for God's sake—and making plans for everything from lunches to concerts.

Alex wasn't even Mack's, so pretending he was coming home to her was really just that—pretending. Chock yet one more up on the con list.

Besides, he hadn't been a good husband the first time. Hell, he and Samantha hadn't even lasted a month. He'd started out with the best of intentions and ended up driving her away. Which was *exactly* why he shouldn't come within ten feet of a serious relationship with Alex. In the end, Mack knew he'd do the same thing to her.

Some guys were meant to be married. And some were meant for crappy hamburger-and-noodle casseroles. Or at least dinner out. "What do you say we head over to the Drop Inn and grab a bite?" Mack asked.

"Nah." Roy dug into his own dinner, holding back a frown of disgust. "We have food here."

"Come on, Dad. The Drop Inn is your favorite place to eat."

"Was."

Mack let out a gust. "How long are you going to do this?"

"I'm not doing anything. I'm just, uh, watching my finances."

"Then I'll pay."

Roy took another bite. "I don't want to waste all this food."

"Feed it to the neighbor's dog. Fido there might find this palatable because God knows I don't."

His father shot him a glare.

"Sorry, Dad. Just being honest. Come on, let's get a real meal."

"I'm fine."

"You're a *hermit*. And I'm done letting you be one." Just as Roy dipped his fork to scoop up more hamburger, Mack grabbed his father's plate, hurried out of the kitchen, opened the back door and dumped the entire tasteless mess onto the ground by the trash cans.

"What the hell are you doing?"

"Forcing you to leave. Either starve or go to the Drop Inn with me." Mack planted himself in front of his father's chair. Faced Roy's defiant gaze with one of his own. Behind them, the dusty kitchen clock ticked its onward journey, the same one it had made for the past thirty years.

"You're a pain in the ass."

Mack shrugged. "You raised me."

Roy grunted, then got to his feet. "We all make mistakes."

Mack laughed. "Get your coat."

Roy followed Mack out of the house, grumbling about how the trip was a waste of money, waste of time, waste of good food. Nevertheless, he climbed into Mack's truck. When they parked at the Drop Inn, Roy paused before opening his door. "The last time I was here . . ."

"Yeah." Mack didn't need to finish the sentence, either. They both knew that every time Roy had eaten at the Drop Inn, it had been with Emma. At home, their marriage had been as rocky as the shores of Normandy, but this restaurant had been Switzerland. Mack hoped maybe it would be a good place to start, a way for his father to find some good memories again.

Maybe he'd been wrong.

"Are we going to eat or just sit here and look at the

place?" Roy asked. Before Mack could answer, his father got out of the truck, slammed the passenger's side door shut and headed toward the restaurant.

As soon as the two of them walked through the door of the Drop Inn, Holly, the owner, hurried over. The thin redheaded woman extended her arms to Roy. "Lordy-be, it's Roy! There must be pigs flying because I never thought I'd see you 'round here again." She drew him into a tight, quick hug, her bun bopping with the movement.

"A man's gotta eat."

She laughed. "That he does. And I have a table right over here for you. Your regular seat." With a little sashaying walk, something Mack suspected was part and parcel of Holly's nature, she led them toward a booth by a window that faced the sidewalk.

Roy tugged a plastic-covered menu out of the napkin holder and studied the single sheet. "Nothing's changed."

Holly laughed. "You expected the place to go gourmet?"

"I would have liked some new choices." He stuffed the menu back into its slot.

"Who are you kidding? You always loved the food here and you never ordered anything but the meatloaf. Enjoy your meal." Holly toodled a wave, then hipswung her way back to the front.

Roy grunted.

A waitress came over to the table, withdrawing a pad from the black apron at her waist. "What can I get you?" She snapped a piece of gum over and over again while she waited for the answer, shifting her weight with the rest of her nervous energy.

"Meatloaf, mashed potatoes, no gravy, green beans," Roy said. "And make sure Kenny throws in some extra biscuits."

"Kenny don't work here no more. He up and retired," the waitress said. "Phil's in the back now."

Roy scowled. "I don't know Phil."

The waitress shrugged. "He's all right. Food's still good."

"Dad, it'll be fine. I doubt you'll even notice the difference."

"I noticed the difference in the food when your mother left my kitchen. I think I'll know the difference in the food here, too."

Mack rolled his eyes. "Make that two of the same," he told the waitress. "And bring him some biscuits right away. He gets grumpy when his blood sugar's low."

"I'm not grumpy," Roy said.

"When you break out into spontaneous song, I'll believe that," Mack replied.

The waitress took their drink orders, then headed off to the kitchen. Even from their spot in the diner, Roy and Mack could hear her shouting the order to the cook.

"I suppose we'll have to talk to each other now that we're here." Roy drummed his fingers on the table.

"Nope. I'm used to eating alone. I don't need to talk."

"Good. I'm not in the mood for it, now that you've upset my whole evening routine."

"What routine? Pulling out a Hungry Man and eating in front of the TV?"

Roy looked away, letting his gaze stray to the window. He kept up his fingertip dancing while he people-watched. His digit tapping stopped. He sucked in a breath.

Mack glanced at his father, sure he was having a heart attack. Then he followed his father's line of sight, and the bottom dropped out of his stomach. "That isn't—"

"No," Roy said. "Leastways, I don't think so." He turned to look at his son, his light blue eyes filled with hope. "Do you?"

Mack glanced again out the window, leaning closer to the glass, so close his nose bumped against the hard surface. Several blocks away, a familiar-looking figure in an ankle-length black dress stood outside a shop, talking on a cell phone. Long brown hair, held back in a single barrette. Just like his mother had worn her hair. The height, the hair color, the manner of dress, all exactly like Emma's, but from this distance, Mack couldn't be sure, even though a part of him leapt to believe, just as his father had.

Emma, however, was living in Rhode Island. Mack knew because she'd sent him a letter every week for the past year. A card on his birthday, a present at Christmas. All with the same Providence return address.

Yet, standing across the street from the Drop Inn was a woman who looked an awful lot like the one who was supposed to be living in an apartment in another state.

"I don't know, Dad," Mack said, squinting. "I can't see that far. It could be her."

"Nah, it's not." Roy turned away, and started fiddling with the salt and pepper shakers. Then just as quickly, he stopped and looked out the window again. He sighed, the disappointment whistling out of his chest. "Doesn't matter. She's gone. Again."

Chapter Nineteen

Steve only got nicer.

He called twice a day, sent flowers constantly and had stopped by the *City Times* office twice to take Alex to lunch. By the time Saturday rolled around, she found herself actually looking forward to their concert date. She still didn't feel that zing of attraction with Steve, but that was just fine.

Everything about him was even and steady. As foreseeable as mosquitoes in the summer. That was exactly what she needed. No more of these crazy boyfriends with wives on the side for her.

"What the hell are you wearing?" Mack asked when she came downstairs on Saturday night. He sat in one of the armchairs in the living room, his face a stern mask, looking more like an overprotective father than a friend.

Alex glanced down at her denim skirt and flats. "Does it look awful?"

"No."

"Then what's wrong with what I'm wearing?"

"It looks too good, that's what's wrong with it."

Was that jealousy she saw in his eyes? She thought

they'd settled this the other day. Mack had no claim over her. Especially not after he'd made it clear—with that nearly transparent teddy Deidre had been wearing—that Mack was not a one-woman, settling-down kind of man.

Yes, they'd kissed. Come close to making love. And, yes, it had been incredible, mind-blowing. But smart?

No.

Alex swung away from the stairs and headed over to the end table to grab her purse. "I thought the whole point of a date is to make the guy drool."

"No, it's not."

"Since when? Or does that only apply to the men who date me?" Alex peered into his eyes. "Because I've seen you drool over many a babe. You and Boomer could single-handedly fill Boston Harbor."

"Yeah, well, that's different."

Alex crossed her arms over her chest. "Why? Because I'm your friend? You can't have it both ways, Mack. We talked about this. We're not dating, and thus, you have no right to tell me what to wear."

He studied her, his blue eyes dark, intent. "Yeah. I know."

During high school, Mack had always been a guard dog about her dates, but this time, he was like an underfed junkyard dog. Before, that had amused her. This time, it annoyed the hell out of her. "In case you've forgotten, Mack, I am very much a woman. A woman with needs. Specifically the need of a man. A man who wants more than just a quick tumble in and out of bed."

That had stung. She saw him recoil, then he rose and narrowed the gap between them to mere inches, tipping the equation from friendly banter to something more. Something heated. Something that traveled out of the realm of the guy next door and into the very, very available guy right here. "I've noticed."

"Mack—"

The doorbell chimed. Mack scowled and let out a whispered curse. "Prince Charming has arrived. Right on time, damn him." Mack spun on his heel and stalked out of the room.

Alex thought of calling after him, smoothing the waters, but where would that leave them? Right back where they'd started, in a jumbled mess. Instead, she let him go, crossed to the wide oak door and pulled it open. "Hi, Steve."

Every strand of Steve's black hair was perfectly in place, his chin freshly shaven. Steve was as meticulous about his looks as he was about his accounting job, about everything, in fact. He planned every detail of their dates, kept his car white-glove clean, made sure he was ridiculously on time. She'd never met a man as detail oriented as Steve.

"Hi, Alex. It's a pleasure to see you again." His gaze traveled down her frame, lingering on her legs. "Quite a pleasure. You look beautiful."

"Thank you." She thought of inviting him in, then decided Mack's foul mood would put a damper on their date. Besides, she had no desire to add any more complications to her relationship with Mack. What used to be as straightforward as a ruler had become as tangled as a strand of Christmas lights. She needed time and distance from Mack, and more of the kind of quiet certainty a man like Steve offered.

There was no topsy-turvy with him. Nothing unexpected. All calm waters, the kind where she could see miles and predict what was coming over the horizon for the next five years. That was what she needed, not the tumultuous ocean of Mack.

"I'm ready to go if you are," she told Steve.

"Absolutely."

He put out his arm, waited for her to insert hers into the crook—such a gentlemanly thing to do Alex nearly forgot the protocol—then they headed down the stairs and over to Steve's car. A moment later, she was seated in the passenger's seat and Steve was pulling out of the driveway.

"Can I ask you something?"

"Sure."

"Last time I saw you, you were living in an apartment. Now you're living with Mack. I don't mean to pry, but . . ." He glanced over at her. "But what's up with that?"

Alex sighed. "It's a long story."

"We've got a long drive to that outdoor jazz concert. And I'm a good listener."

Steve proved true to his word. Alex told him about the house, leaving out the part about her past. Why, she couldn't have said. Was she embarrassed? Did she think a guy like Steve, all spit and polish and CPA perfection, would find her background pitiful? She shrugged off the analysis. Between Mack and Willow and Renee, she'd shared enough about her past to fill a scrapbook store.

As they drove, she told Steve how she hadn't wanted him to see the dilapidated house, which was why she had pretended to be living at Renee's, then how Mack had insisted she live with him until the house was habitable. "Mack and I have been friends forever. Living together is totally platonic."

Except for that kiss the other day. Except for that time they'd ended up in bed together and rounded the first couple of bases. Not to mention, she'd had an orgasm that had rivaled the Fourth of July. Her face flushed and a *whoosh* of heat ran through her veins.

She didn't mention that, now, did she? There'd been nothing platonic at all about any of that.

An aberration, Alex told herself. Granted, one that had shook her from head to toe, but an aberration all the same. One that wouldn't happen again.

She was looking for a man who believed in commitment. A man who wouldn't break her heart. A good, dependable Clydesdale, not a wild, untamed mustang.

Steve reached across the gearshift and took her hand in his. A warm, solid grip. Nothing sexual about it, but there was a measure of dependability and strength in his touch. She willed her nerves to leap with desire, but they lay as dormant as hibernating bears.

"If you need anything at all," Steve said, "call me. I'm pretty handy myself."

She bit back a smile. She couldn't imagine bookish accountant Steve wielding major power tools, but perhaps this man had a few surprises up his sleeve. She noticed he didn't make a specific offer to help, either, simply one of those vague, call-me kind. "I'll keep that in mind."

"Did you get that assignment you wanted? The one with the reclusive author?"

"You remembered." She clearly had been picking the wrong guys, because she couldn't recall the last time a guy had picked up on the details of her job.

Well, except for Mack. He had always paid attention. Every day, he asked about the Willow Clark saga. He, however, was her friend. Friends were supposed to do that kind of thing. Whereas her dates, on the other hand, had paid attention—but usually only to what was below her brain.

Steve shot her a look of surprise. "Why wouldn't I? That was a pretty big deal for you."

"It will be, if I can get Willow Clark to talk. My editor gave me the assignment, and I went out there to try to get her to talk, but she's a little . . . odd."

As they drove, Steve asked more questions about her off-beat noninterview with Willow. For the first time in a long time, she did most of the talking, with Steve tossing in the occasional comment and question. He had genuine interest in her career, and that, Alex found, was more intoxicating than his late-night kiss.

They pulled into the parking lot of the Tweeter Center. Steve parked the car, then came around to Alex's side and opened her door. "Is this good?" he asked. "If not, I can look for a closer space."

"It's great," she said.

"Let me get the backpack. I've got a blanket, some seat cushions, a couple bottles of—"

Before he could say another word, Alex grabbed Steve and kissed him. Her fingers tangled in his hair, bringing his tall frame closer to her. He hesitated for a fraction of a second, clearly caught off guard, then his arms wrapped around her waist, and he responded, his tongue dipping in to dance with hers, his hands splaying across her back.

After a minute or two, Steve pulled back, a grin on his face. "What was that for?"

"Nothing turns a woman on more than a guy who takes the time to listen."

"Then start talking," Steve said, lowering his mouth to kiss her again, his breath warm against her skin, "because I could listen to you all night."

* * *

Mack suffered like he'd never suffered before.

He paced the floors, back and forth, back and forth, so much, Chester gave up on following him. The mutt trotted over to the corner, and with a sigh, put his head on his paws, content to watch his master wear out his socks. Mack told himself he should have called Deidre. Boomer. Anyone. He should have gone out, gotten good and drunk, so he wouldn't have had hours alone to let his imagination run wild. Finally, a little after midnight, Alex returned, laughing as she entered the house.

"Thanks, Steve. That was an amazing concert."

"We should do this again. Soon. Very, very soon." Steve's voice was low and dark, clearly closer to Alex. Within inches.

Mack knew that voice. He'd used it himself, more than once. It spelled only one thing. Steve was about to go in for a kiss.

Mack stalked out of his kitchen and into the hall, then sputtered to a stop when he realized he had no viable reason for interrupting them. Either way, he was too late. Steve already had his arm around Alex, and his lips on hers.

Jealousy roared to life in Mack's gut, a vicious, untamable beast. He curled his fists at his sides so he wouldn't slam them into Steve's skull. Maybe he should interrupt them. Extract Alex from this horny wolf in gentleman's clothing.

Then he noticed something. Alex was *responding* to Steve. Curving her body into his. Kissing him back with clear desire. Her pelvis had that unmistakable arch of invitation.

Mack swallowed hard, then turned on his heel and went to bed, using the back staircase. He lay on top of his sheets, waiting for what seemed like hours until he finally heard Alex's soft footfalls as she headed down the hall to her room.

He stared at the ceiling and prayed that when her bedroom door shut, she would be climbing into that queen-sized bed alone.

Too late, Mack Douglas realized he'd made the biggest mistake of his life when he'd agreed to introduce Alex to Mr. Right. Because she was clearly falling in love—

And breaking Mack's heart in the process.

Chapter Twenty

"Where have you been?"

Renee stopped short, her hand halfway to the light switch. Even in the ebony darkness of the foyer, she knew that voice. Tony. Waiting for her to come home.

She took in a breath, steadied herself, then flicked on the light and strode forward, depositing her keys into the dish by the door. They jangled an accusatory song. "Out with a friend. Where's the sitter?"

"I sent her home two hours ago." Tony sat in an armchair facing the front door, his lanky frame dwarfing the leather seat. His face was lined, his eyes shadowed. A half-empty beer sat on the end table beside him, but his voice was clear. "It's after midnight, Renee. Where were you?"

"Since when do you care? Ever since we got married, you've gone out almost every night. And God only knows what you were doing when you were living with your brother last week. I have a right to a social life."

"You're a mother. You should be here with your kids."

"And you're a father. The same goes for you."

"I am here."

"Tonight." She stowed her purse in the closet, pausing

to draw in a breath, then ran a hand through her hair. "Can we not have this argument? I'm not in the mood."

"You're never in the mood for anything."

She refused to rise to his bait. Refused to rehash the argument. Renee sidestepped the living room and the heated words on the tip of her tongue, heading instead for the kitchen. She opened the refrigerator door, looking for a snack she didn't want. Willing Tony to follow her, because half of her still hoped.

The crazy half that had yet to give up. The half keeping her from filing for divorce.

For a long time, there was no sound of footsteps behind her. The light and cold from inside the Maytag spilled onto the floor, casting a single shadow. Renee sighed, closed the refrigerator door and turned around to head for bed.

Tony stood in the doorway of the kitchen entrance. "Renee."

Her name escaped his throat in a soft, vulnerable way. Like it had before—before they'd drifted apart. Before they'd stopped talking. Stopped touching.

And for a moment, Renee wanted to believe things hadn't changed.

Tony's gaze met hers. His eyes were clear—he must not have gotten very far with the beer, and for that she was grateful—and filled with the softness she had missed. She found herself falling into those brown depths, getting caught up in the past. The memories.

"Renee," he said again, and he took a step forward.

She found herself moving toward him, hoping, wishing.

Tony reached out, his arms curling around her body, hers fitting into his as familiar as a hand into a well-worn glove, and then he lowered his mouth, slowly and tentatively, unsure. She met him halfway, wanting her husband, the one she had fallen in love with, not the one who abandoned her when the bonds got too tight.

Before his lips met hers, he hesitated. Her heart rate accelerated and she wondered if Tony knew. Knew where she had been tonight. Knew who she had been with. Knew she had been kissed by someone else a half hour earlier.

But wishing all the time her own husband would love her like that.

"I can't do this," Tony said, pulling back and away from her.

Cold air invaded the space between them. Disappointment thudded into Renee's gut. "Can't do what?"

"Can't pretend. We're either doing this or we aren't."

"You mean having sex? Is that all you wanted tonight, Tony?" She turned away from him. Every conversation came back to this. To the basics, instead of to something with meaning. To a conversation that would take them somewhere, move them forward. Instead they always ended up in bed, where they used their bodies as a way to avoid everything else.

"No. I meant we're either going to stay married or break up. I can't live in limbo any longer." His gaze sought hers. "I want more, Renee. I want *us.*"

She pivoted back. "*You're* living in limbo? You never plugged in, Tony, as much as I wanted you to."

"Did you ever let me try?" He threw up his hands. "Or did you just keep on playing the martyr and make it easy for me to check out?"

"I—" She cut off the sentence before the protest finished working its way past her lips. Had she done that? Renee thought back, her mind racing over the eleven years of their marriage, and she realized that from the start, she had held the reins, believing that if she didn't hold on tight, control everything that happened, their marriage, their life, would become some runaway train. "Maybe I did. But you never fought me on it. You . . . let it happen."

"I did. And I'm sorry." A smile curved along his face, slow, reaching into the corners, the dimples she knew so well. He held her gaze, and she saw him want to reach out, to connect. "I guess you could say I'm a marital couch potato, huh?"

Despite everything, Renee laughed. The feeling was so sweet, she could nearly taste it, like a slice of chocolate cake after a very long diet.

"It's good to hear you laugh." He trailed a finger along her jaw, and Renee wanted so badly to lean into that touch, to let all the ugliness between them wash away.

But she'd done that a dozen times before, and where had it gotten her? Right back where she started. Things would get better for a day, a week, then Tony would slip into his old habits, and she would go back to hers, and before she knew it, she was alone in a marriage built for two. "I can't do this again, Tony," she whispered, her voice scraping past her throat. "I can't."

"We can make it work, Renee. Let me try."

She shook her head. Tears welled in her eyes. "We've tried and tried, and every time we come back to the same place. When are you going to grow up and realize you're really married?"

"What's that supposed to mean?"

This was the argument Renee had put off, the words she hadn't spoken, because she knew they would set off the storm she'd been trying to avoid, but she couldn't do that any longer. "Why haven't you taken over the concrete business yet? Your dad wanted to retire five years ago, but you haven't stepped up to the plate to run the business. If you had—"

His face soured, anger flushing his features. "If I had, what? We'd be out of this apartment? Living the life you wanted?"

"The life we all wanted, Tony. And, yes, we'd be out of this place. It's too small. It has been since Kylie was born."

"We're saving for a house."

"No, Tony, we're stuck in limbo," she said, using his word from earlier. "Because if you don't take the big steps, the permanent ones like taking over the business and getting a mortgage, then you can keep on pretending that you're only half-married, and you can keep on letting me shoulder the load for both of us." She let out a breath that seemed to weigh a hundred pounds. "I'm tired, Tony. Tired of all of it. Isn't it about time we got honest?"

"We are being honest. Painfully so, if you ask me."

She moved away, because if she stayed too close to him, her resolve, already thin as a strand of floss, would break. "No, we're not. We keep on lying to ourselves because neither one of us has been brave enough to say what we should have said eleven years ago." She braced her hands on the countertop, took in a deep breath, then let it out. "We rushed into this and got married for all the wrong reasons. We barely knew each other when I got pregnant."

She sensed him behind her, but didn't turn around. Tony didn't touch her, simply stood there.

"Lots of marriages survive after starting out like that."

Renee wheeled around and faced her husband. And a hard reality she'd never spoken aloud. "Tell me the truth, Tony. If you could do it all over again, knowing what you know now, would you have gotten married? Had three kids bang-bang-bang? Sunk ourselves into this never-ending cycle of fighting?"

"We can't undo what's already done, Renee."

"Yeah, but we can stop it from getting any worse." She sucked in another breath, one that seared her lungs. "And file for divorce."

Chapter Twenty-One

The doors were locked. The sign turned to CLOSED. And Willow Clark was nowhere to be found.

Alex sat on the front step of Theodora's Tearoom, blew her bangs out of her face and dropped her head into her arms. She had failed.

She'd be stuck extolling the virtues of waterproof mascara until the day she died. Her epitaph would be written in Revlon Red, for Pete's sake.

"All is not lost. The day is just beginning."

Alex jerked her head up. Willow Clark stood over her, the taller woman's frame casting a thin shadow onto Alex's skin. "I thought you were closed today."

"I am. But that doesn't mean I'm not here. I'm just not here, here."

Of course. That made perfect sense—in Willow's world.

Alex got to her feet, pulling her pad of paper out of the back pocket of her jeans as she did.

"You won't need that," Willow said, laying a hand on Alex's. "Today, I want you to just soak up the words. Let them settle on your heart."

"I want to get the quotes right, Miss Clark. If I misquote you—"

"You won't." Willow smiled and began to walk, strolling around the building, and toward the small patch of woods that ringed the back of the building. Theodora's Tearoom occupied an odd little corner of real estate backing up to suburbia, but with a long rectangle of untouched wooded land that divided the area between the store and the four-bedroom white boxes planted one right after another, a long stretch of nuclear family sameness. "We'll walk today."

"In that little patch of nothing?" Alex scoffed. "It'll take, what, five minutes?"

"A walk can take as long as you want it to, depending on what you need to discover while your feet are moving." Willow lifted a low-hanging branch and swung her head underneath the curtain of leaves, then waited for Alex to follow.

She did. Not just because she needed the story desperately—she'd had to do a piece previewing fall wedding trends this morning to fill next Sunday's fashion section—but also because she needed something else to think about besides the growing soap opera of her life.

A tension headache pounded in Alex's temples, leftover from last night. Who would have thought that a man whispering "I think I'm falling in love with you" would bring on an instant headache?

Alex rubbed at her head, then slipped into the copse of woods. Instantly, the world darkened, became thicker, lusher. Full of greenery and the dense, rich scent of new earth. Birds chirped above, their wings clapping like applause as they flitted from tree to tree, feeding their babies, building nests, eating bugs. Continuing a circle of life in one tiny microcosm.

"It's beautiful back here," Alex said.

"I come here when I need to find peace." Willow let out a little laugh. "Which, in this world, is pretty often."

They walked some more, Alex wanting to get straight to the interview questions. She needed peace—but she needed this piece more. At the rate Willow was sharing information, she'd be lucky to have the story done in a year. "Is this where you got the idea for *The Season of Light*?" Alex asked. "Because the book has a lot of nature analogies in it."

Willow turned to Alex, clearly pleased. "You've picked up quite a bit from the text, and, yes, I was inspired by the great outdoors. But that isn't why I brought you here. I don't want to talk about my career." She waved a hand. "That's old news. Who really cares?"

Alex bit back a scream of frustration. "Lots of people do. It's like an Agatha Christie mystery. You just . . . disappeared. People wonder where you went. Why you stopped writing. If you'll ever publish another book again."

Willow shrugged. "Is that what really matters, in the scheme of things? Really? What matters in your life, Alex?"

Alex tore a maple leaf off a branch, and began to shred off the five sections, tossing them to the ground like strips of green confetti. "My grandmother. My friends."

"You wouldn't be so persistent in getting my story if that was all that mattered."

Alex smiled. "Okay, my job. I want to be more than just a fashion reporter."

"Ah, the ever-elusive quest for fame and fortune. The front page, is it? Well, that comes with a double-edged sword, just remember that. Sometimes, toiling away in obscurity has its merits."

Willow paused to lean against a tree. Alex took a seat on a nearby stump. She noticed the area had been cleared in a small circle, as if made for a place to pause.

"The front page has its merits, too, like a raise in pay," Alex said. "That's something I need right now."

Willow thought a moment, then nodded. "You do, indeed. Great changes are coming your way." She bent forward, her gaze connecting with Alex's. "Are you ready, dear?"

Trepidation snaked down Alex's spine. That was crazy. Willow was crazy. She couldn't possibly predict the future. Still, the desire to know more rose in Alex. "Ready for what?"

"Something's coming that will change everything. All your plans." Willow chuckled softly. "Though planning is just a misnomer, isn't it? Really, we're all at the mercy of Fate."

"Uh . . . yeah." This couldn't go worse if a train derailed right in front of them. Alex could already see the headlines: RECLUSIVE AUTHOR LOSES HER MIND.

And: WANNABE REPORTER LOSES HER JOB.

Willow pushed off from the tree and dusted her hands together. "Fate is how I came to writing in the first place. I was failing school, failing everything, really, and my mother enrolled me in this after-school tutoring program. The woman who ran it, Sister Angela, believed in making us write. She said the written word was the key to everything you wanted in life."

Thank God. Willow was finally telling Alex something she could use, and understand.

Alex rose, and began to walk beside Willow again. "Now that's a concept I can get behind."

"Sister Angela brought out this side of me I never knew I had, and all of a sudden, I realized I could be something. Somebody. I started carrying a notebook everywhere I went, and, well"—she put up her hands—

"that's how Jensine's story was born. It took a lot of drafts before it became the book you read, but that's where it all started. In a tiny classroom at St. Mary's Catholic School."

"But why didn't you ever write another book? If you loved it so much?"

Willow tick-tocked a finger at Alex. "Remember our deal? An answer for an answer. You have to tell me what Fate brought you to."

"You. And the front page. Hopefully." Alex grinned.

"Is that all Fate has done for you?" Willow circled around a tree, bringing them through the patch of woods and back toward the shop. Alex could just see the outline of the building through the trees.

"No. It gave me a crappy childhood, too. But I already mentioned that." Alex yanked another maple leaf off a branch and tossed it to the side. "Can we talk about something else? Like what city I'd most like to visit? My favorite food?"

"Fate would only give you the crappy childhood as a learning experience. There's a reason behind everything." Willow ran her hand over a burst of bright yellow daylilies, the blooms brushing their soft petals against her palm as if in greeting. "What was your reason?"

"To make me appreciate eating three square meals a day."

Willow's lips pursed in disappointment, but she said nothing. She continued strolling through the woods, as calm as ever, and silent.

That game again. The one where she said nothing. And waited.

Alex tried a second time to wait her out, letting the birds, the cracking of branches, the sound of their footfalls, fill the silence. But all it did was seem to multiply the absence of conversation.

Willow stopped walking and pivoted toward Alex. "We're at the end of our walk. I think we've gotten all we can out of this path, don't you?"

"But we've just gotten started," Alex said. "It's been a great conversation so far."

Willow reached out and patted Alex's hand. "It has been, but you need to leave. You have much bigger things coming your way and you need to go get your house in order."

Then Willow was gone, leaving Alex once again wondering where her real story lay. In the crazy author—or in how crazy the author was driving her.

Chapter Twenty-Two

If someone had told Mack that his life would change inside the aisles of True Value, he would have laughed them off. After all, the chances of having a major life moment while buying a drill bit were pretty damn slim.

But apparently Slim had ridden on into town, and dropped right into Mack's lap, because as he rounded the corner of the aisle, he walked straight into the last person he expected to see.

His mother.

"Mack!" she exclaimed, her voice soft but high with surprise.

He stopped, unsure of how to respond. Hug her? Yell at her? Walk away? In the end, he simply stood there and said, "Mom."

She took a half step forward, as if she, too, didn't know how to approach him. "How have you been? Have you gotten my cards? My letters?"

He searched her face, looking for . . . what? Nothing had changed, that he could see. The same soft blue eyes, the same long light brown hair with a touch of gray. She seemed a little thinner, looked a little more tired than usual, but otherwise, Emma was the mother he knew and remembered.

He thought of her letters, the chatty, breezy pages talking about the classes she'd taken, the people she'd met. He'd answered some but not all of them, needing that paper connection as much as he wanted to sever it, because it hurt just as much to maintain the lines of communication as it did to lose them.

His gaze met hers and an ache spread through his chest, deep and sharp. "Yes, I got them. And I'm fine," he said. "Just fine."

"That's good. I'm glad."

"What are you doing here?"

She smiled, the same soft smile as always, as if he'd just come home from school or popped in for dinner. "Buying some wiper fluid for my car and a . . . a gardening trowel."

"No, I meant here, in town. Why are you back?"

His mother swallowed and looked away, her gaze going past Mack's shoulder and down the aisle of drill bits. "I missed it here."

Not "I missed your father." Not "I missed you." But "I missed it here." The ache in Mack's chest became a stabbing sensation and suddenly, he couldn't stand there one more second.

"Well, I hope you find a good trowel," Mack said, then he slid past her and headed toward the cash register.

"Mack." She reached for him, her touch landing on his bare arm. He halted midstep, as if he'd had been caught by a rope. "Don't go, not yet."

"I have to get back to the job site."

"I want to talk to you. I haven't seen you in a year."

He wheeled around, the sharp pain so severe he nearly couldn't breathe. "And whose fault is that? *You* walked away from *us*, Mom. And now you want to walk back in, as if nothing happened. This wasn't a party you left, it was our lives."

Then he spun on his heel and walked out of the store, dropping the drill bit onto the checkout counter as he left. He didn't need anything bad enough that he would linger in that place one minute longer.

The scents of pepperoni and cheese filled the kitchen, drawing an ever-hopeful Chester to the table, but not Mack. Alex popped her head into the den. "I made dinner. Meaning, I stopped by Papa Gino's and placed an order for two large pizzas with extra pepperoni. It was a lot of work." She grinned.

"I'm not hungry." He sat on the sofa, his feet on the ottoman, and flicked through the channels on the television, scrolling past one sporting event after another.

"You didn't come back to the house this afternoon. Did you get tied up at another job site?"

"No." Mack sighed, then clicked off the television and put the remote on the coffee table. "I saw my mother today."

Alex slipped into the room and settled into the chair opposite Mack. For a second, she considered not telling him she'd been the one to contact Emma. But in all the years she'd known Mack, she'd never lied to him and she wasn't about to start now. "I went and saw her the other day."

"You . . ." He blinked. "You saw my mother?"

"I knew you missed her, and your father does, too. So I talked to her, told her maybe she should visit you."

Mack's feet dropped to the floor with a loud plop.

Then he rose, slowly, fury filling his features. "You were the one that told my mother to come back? Why the hell would you do that?"

"I thought I was helping, Mack. I thought I was doing you a favor."

"You didn't do anyone a favor, Alex. All you did was interfere in my life. I didn't need you to do that." He stalked away to the bay window that faced the wooded backyard. His shoulders hunched. He stared out at the trees.

She went to Mack and placed a hand on his back, but his muscles were taut. Almost cold. "I'm just trying to be your friend. You were in pain, and I wanted to help."

"How did that help, Alex? My father already saw her when we were out at dinner. Inevitably, if she's stays in town, they're going to run into each other. I can see it coming. They'll end up getting back together. In a week, they'll be fighting again. And she'll leave." He shook his head. "I don't have the energy to pull him out of this depression the next time she walks away."

"What if she doesn't? She really seemed like she wants things to be different. She missed both of you as much as you miss her. Why can't you let her back into your life?"

He didn't say anything for a long time. The silence stretched between them until it became a taut thread, ready to snap with the slightest pressure. "I don't want my father to get hurt again."

"Maybe he won't. He's a big boy, Mack. He can make that decision for himself."

"Either way, Alex," Mack said, turning to her, "I don't need you trying to create a happy ending for my parents. You're so damn determined to make a fairy tale come true for everyone." He walked to the door, then turned back. "You need to realize not all stories end in happily ever after."

Chapter Twenty-Three

Alex couldn't sleep. The humidity hung in the air like weights on her shoulders, driving her from bed. Mack's air-conditioning system was pumping cool air into the house, but it didn't seem to be enough. She wandered down to the kitchen, got a glass of ice water, but still felt sticky, hot.

Ever since her conversation with Mack, she'd been restless. Maybe he was right . . . maybe not all stories ended in happily ever after. But damn it, she was tired of seeing her own story be like one of Grimms' Fairy Tales. It seemed, though, that she couldn't have it all.

She had found a man who wanted the life she did. A man who had every quality she'd ever looked for. And yet, when he kissed her, she felt . . .

Nothing.

What was wrong with her? Was she somehow undermining her relationship with Steve by turning off her libido? Or could he be Mr. Wrong?

Alex ran a hand through her hair. If she could just clear her head, get out of this heat, then maybe she'd find the answers she needed. She paused in the great room. Beyond the French doors, the reflection of the stars twinkled in the pool's water. The filter gurgled softly, almost like a siren's song, calling to her, whispering coolness. Escape.

Her muscles ached. Her entire body seemed to ache, from the hard work, the stress of the last week, the odd feelings awakened by Mack, the one man she *shouldn't* want. Emotions and questions still churned inside her, unanswered despite their conversation about keeping everything strictly friends the other day.

He wanted her. But he didn't want anything permanent.

How could that be? Mack had married once before, though no one knew why, or why he'd gotten divorced almost as quickly as he'd run off to Vegas. It was a part of himself he'd kept quiet. Had his marriage to Samantha been that bad that it had soured him forever on settling down?

The trouble was, Alex wanted him, too. She wanted Mack in a way that ran so deep, she couldn't even begin to describe the desire that coursed through her veins. She wanted it all—the man who lit her on fire, and a man who wanted to settle down.

Alex paced the living room, questions running through her at warp speed. At this rate, she'd never find peace, or sleep. What would it hurt to slip into that pool, for just a little while, and surrender to the bliss of the water?

Her swimsuit was all the way upstairs. Alex didn't feel like making that trek, not when the water was mere feet away. She crossed to the doors and unlatched them quietly. Chester popped his head up, then went back to sleep, nonplussed.

Mack's yard was surrounded by thick pine trees, and backed up to protected wetlands, offering the perfect private retreat. No one would see her. No one would know if she just—

Slipped off her T-shirt and slid into the water in her panties.

Instantly, the luscious coolness met her skin like a kiss, peaking her nipples, waking her pulse. She dove to the bottom, delighting in the slightly illicit feeling of being half-naked and outdoors in the middle of the night. She swam slowly, enjoying the caress of the water, her eyes closed, drifting to one end and upward, until she reached the top, then floated back to the shallow end, water sluicing over her breasts, tickling at her nipples, reminding her of Mack. Of Mack's tongue. Of climaxing beneath his touch.

Who was she kidding? She wanted to sleep with him, wanted to go to bed with him, wanted to know exactly what it felt like to have him inside her. She slid a hand down her chest, wishing it was his hand, his much bigger, rougher, more powerful hand, a hand that could engulf her breast. She kneaded at the nipple, wanting release, wanting that fantasy again, wanting—

"You could drown doing that."

Alex jerked upright, sucking in a great gulp of water as she did. She spun toward Mack's voice, spitting out the chlorinated drink. She covered her chest with one arm, grateful she was in shallow enough water to stand. "What are you doing out here?"

"Watching you." He stood on the edge of the pool, clad in nothing but a pair of light blue boxers. A single light burned inside the house, but it was enough to outline him through the thin cotton. The hard, muscular definition of his legs. Firm thighs. And an unmistakable erection. "I wanted to apologize for getting so angry earlier, but I'm having a little trouble remembering what we were talking about."

He let out a low laugh. "Hell, right now I can't even remember my own name."

She couldn't remember much, either, except why she was here. "Sorry. I . . . I was hot."

"You are *very* hot."

They stared at each other for one long, taut second. Then Mack stepped into the pool and crossed to Alex. Her gaze locked with his, his eyes so dark in the moonlight, they seemed almost black. Her heart rate accelerated, thudding so loud in her chest she was sure it was going to explode.

Mack approached her, and slowly, as if both of them knew this moment was going to come at some point or another no matter what either of them had said, her arm came down, exposing her breasts to his view. His mouth dropped open, then he smiled. He looked up, at her, and she nodded.

Yes, she wanted him. Damn the consequences.

That was all it took.

Mack closed the distance between them, then slid his hands down her back, around her ass and into her panties. He cupped her cheeks, his palms warm where the water had cooled her skin. He began to slide the wet fabric down, an inch at a time, and as he did, he trailed kisses along her throat. Alex tipped her head back, exposing the valleys of her skin. Wherever Mack touched, he ignited fire, and she wanted more. So much more.

He licked, he nibbled, he sucked, he teased, as he drew a torturous, slow map down her body, between her breasts, ending at her belly button, teasing where the water's edge met his chin. He slipped her panties down to the bottom of the pool and she stepped out of them, not caring if she ever saw them again.

Then he came back up, holding his kisses just outside her lips. "We shouldn't do this," he murmured.

"No," she said back. "We shouldn't."

"It could ruin everything."

Or it could be so good. So very, very good. She pressed her mound against his erection. Barely anything separated them now, just the scrap of wet fabric of his boxers. She didn't give a damn what was smart or stupid. She only knew that Mack lit a fire in her like no other man, and she wanted that fire quenched, wanted to have this aching need finally met.

"I need to know," she whispered.

"What?" He moved to kiss her neck, suck on her earlobe, and she almost screamed.

"Everything." Then Alex reached forward, grabbed Mack's boxers, and brought them down, freeing his penis. She grabbed it in one hand, curling her grip tightly around his stiffness. The water provided natural lubrication and she slid her hand up and down, as Mack's hand came up to cup her breast, his thumb teasing at the nipple, sending her into a sweet, incredible agony.

He groaned and leaned into her touch, kissing her deeply now, his tongue doing a wild dance with hers, so hot she was sure he'd explode in her palm, and she would climax beneath his hand. Then he released her breasts, both hands coming around to grasp her ass again. She let go of him, reaching for his shoulders as he hoisted her onto him and, finally, finally, plunged deep inside her.

Alex cried out and arched her back, her slick breasts sliding against his chest, as he rocked her up and down, a hot and sweet fire that drove her insane, sending her spiraling into a dizzying abyss. His hands grasped tighter, and she clenched around him, sliding back and forth faster and faster until finally everything in her body exploded in a dazzling fireworks of heart-stopping sensations. Mack called out her name, then came with her. She felt the last pulses of his climax before his hold on her eased and she opened her eyes.

"That was . . . incredible," Mack said.

She nodded, her vocabulary pretty much gone right now.

"They didn't have that in the brochure for the pool," Mack said, grinning. "If they did, I bet they'd sell a lot more."

She laughed. "Maybe I should put one in at my house."

Mack trailed a finger down her cheek. "If you do, I'll help you christen it."

"Does that mean we'll be doing this again?" she asked. Where were they going with this? She hadn't thought about that before she'd gotten naked with Mack. Maybe she should have.

He dipped his head to kiss her neck. Desire rose within her, and she was oh so aware of her body against his, the way the water made everything so much more slippery and sexy.

"I already want to do this again."

Alex pulled back and looked into Mack's eyes. He didn't want anything more than this. He didn't want the picket fence life that she did.

But right now, she really didn't give a damn.

"So do I," Alex said, then kissed him.

Chapter Twenty-Four

No.

Alex stared at the stick.

Stared some more.

Shook it.

Stared again.

Walked out of the bathroom. Shut the door. Paced Mack's bedroom three times, then opened the bathroom door slowly. The sunlight from the bedroom sliced across the bathroom, landing squarely on the sink and the long white stick. Illuminating the two pink stripes clearly.

Pregnant.

Impossible.

"Alex?" A knock on the bedroom door. "You okay?"

Mack. The last person she needed right now, and yet the very person she would have turned to—for anything but this. Especially after what had happened two nights ago. And last night. And early this morning.

Yeah, it's all fun and games until someone gets nauseous, isn't it?

Oh, God. What had she done? How could she have been this stupid?

"Alex?"

"I'm fine, Mack. Fine."

Her life was falling apart and she was just fine. Thanks.

Just forty-eight hours ago, everything had been wonderful. Okay, a little messy, considering she was dating Steve and sleeping with Mack, but the sex part had been absolutely incredible. And now—this.

All those weeks of being nauseous, and she'd thought it was nothing. Apparently nothing had turned out to be a very big something. Or would be, by March.

Oh, God.

Alex strode over to the stick, picked it up, then yanked up the directions and read them three more times. Read them in Spanish, just to be sure there hadn't been some moron on crack in the marketing department. But, no, in two languages, it said if there were two pink lines, "*Congratulations! You're pregnant!*"

Exclamation points everywhere. Happy faces. Yippee skippy.

Alex crumpled up the directions and stuffed them into the bottom of Mack's trash. Maybe the test was faulty. That's what she got for buying the one on sale.

After they'd left the home improvement store at the end of another day of working on the house, she'd made Mack stop at a drugstore, telling him she hadn't been able to kick that food poisoning from the Chinese food. She'd insisted on running in herself to buy some Pepto-Bismol—best-case scenario—and a pregnancy test: worst-case scenario.

Because the more she'd thought about it on the drive home, the more she'd begun to realize what one answer could explain everything. The raging hormones. The nausea. The growing exhaustion.

So she'd bought a two-pack, just in case she screwed

up, considering this was the first one she'd ever used. Yeah, she'd just take it again. The first one was a dud.

But five minutes later, the second stick gave her the same happy, double–exclamation point answer.

Impossible.

Alex sank onto the cool marble floor and buried her head in her hands. The nausea that had been growing increasingly worse each day suddenly quadrupled. "Oh, God. Oh, God. What am I going to do?"

"Alex? Are you in there?"

"Go away, Mack."

She totally didn't need him right now.

"You don't sound good. You sound sick."

"I'm not sick."

"You almost puked twice. On the ride home and in my kitchen. Not to mention you didn't look so good earlier. That's sick, Alex. Let me in. I don't mind taking care of you. Just try not to puke on me. Friend-ship only goes so far before I have to *pay* somebody to be your friend."

She tried to laugh. But it didn't work. Nothing about this was funny. "Just leave me alone, Mack. I'll be fine."

In nine months.

"Are you naked?"

"No."

"Then I'm coming in." She heard the doorknob rattle and panicked, shoved the pregnancy tests deep into the trash, stuffing a thick wad of tissues on top of them. Not a moment too soon—because Mack opened the door and entered the bathroom. He bent down, his face a mask of concern. "Let me get you some flu medicine or a cold cloth or—"

Then he cut off the sentence as he took in the sight

before him. Alex, curled against the wall. Clutching her stomach. Tears streaming down her face.

Mack opened his mouth. Closed it. Opened it again. "Are you okay?"

She sniffled, tried to nod and ended up shaking her head. "Yeah."

No.

"You look horrible."

"I'm . . . sick." She drew her knees up to her chest and laid her head over her arms. "I just want to go back to bed."

Wake me up in nine months.

Without a word, Mack scooped her up, carried her out of the bathroom and deposited her on the bed. He pulled the thick comforter over her body and tucked it around her like she was a child. "You stay here. I'll bring you some toast and flat soda. This isn't exactly Mercy Hospital, so I don't have much else to offer, sorry."

Alex began to push up on her elbows. "Mack, I'm—" She cut herself off before she told him the truth, because she didn't know what to tell him, not yet. "I'm not dying. I can get my own breakfast."

"You never get sick, Alex. You can afford a day in bed, with me taking care of you. Besides, I don't want to clean up after you all over my house." He tossed her a teasing grin before he left the room.

Leaving Alex to absorb the news alone.

She ran a hand over her stomach. It was still as flat as it had been five minutes, five days before. If she hadn't seen the evidence, she could believe nothing had changed. But something had. Something huge.

The one thing she, of all people, should have known better than to have happen. She'd tried the Depo shot for a while, and hadn't liked the side effects, so while she'd been in the process of switching to the pill, the doctor had recommended a backup method. Which had been Edward's department. Apparently he'd missed a raincoat or two. Or had a faulty one.

For a man who'd made it clear from the minute they'd met that he didn't want children, he should have doubled up. But maybe, as with everything else that she was now seeing as Edward's pattern of self-centeredness, he'd figured that should have been her job.

And forgot to tell her. Kind of like the forgetting the wife part. Bastard.

Alex slid her palm beneath her T-shirt and splayed her fingers against her skin. A life beat within her now, a life she could not quite believe existed.

And now she had to decide what to do about it.

"Room service," Mack said, entering the room. He had a plate in one hand, a glass in the other.

Alex worked a smile to her face. "What, no tray? No flower?"

"No tip?" He handed her the plate.

"Touché." She chuckled. "Really, Mack, I'm not an invalid. I can get up. There's a ton of work to do at the house today—"

He put out a hand to cut her off. "You're done there. I'm not letting a sick woman, who could puke at any moment, swing a sledgehammer."

"This isn't the Dark Ages. I can still work on the house."

"No. You can do your job right here from bed, which doesn't involve tools that can raise your blood pressure into dangerous levels or leave you completely exhausted at the end of the day. Work at home until you're better. You need to take care of yourself, Alex. Let me handle the construction."

"There's too much work for one person." She took a bite of toast.

"I own a construction company, remember? I do have resources."

"You won't take my check and you know I don't want you to work on my house for free. I especially don't want you to pay your guys to do the job out of your own pocket." She eyed him. "There's no way I'm going to let you do this without giving you anything in return. So tell me . . . what can I give you? Name your price, Mack Douglas. Anything at all."

"I thought we worked that out the other night." His voice was low and dark, his grin teasing, tempting.

"That wasn't part of the bargain, either."

"Then what was it, Alex?"

"A . . . distraction. One I really can't afford, not right now." Especially not now, but she wouldn't tell him why. "We've got a house to fix and I've got a story to work on, and on top of all that, I'm . . . sick." She still couldn't get that word out. Sometime over the next nine months she'd have to say it, she figured. "Either way, Mack, I'm serious. I'm either working on that house or you're taking that check I offered."

His gaze darkened. "Then I'll make it simple. Take care of me."

For a split second, she thought he meant in a sexual way. The memory of the night in the pool stirred inside her. That exquisite, oh-my-God, do-it-again time in the water. She would repeat that willingly. And often.

And that was the problem. She had much bigger concerns right now, and sleeping with Mack would only make matters worse.

"Me, take care of you? I can barely take care of myself." She laughed. "Come on, Mack. For five seconds, be serious."

"No, I mean it. I have a housekeeper who comes in once a week and cleans up after me because I'm not exactly domestic. And didn't you just bring home pizza the other night? That's more than I can do." He grinned.

"I can't—"

He put a finger over her mouth. "That's all I want, until you get better. Take care of you . . . so you can take care of me. Think of it as practice for when you get married and have a family of your own."

Panic gripped Alex. She'd found out she was pregnant only a few minutes ago and already here was Mack, throwing out words that implied she might keep it.

He didn't know, did he?

No. He couldn't.

He, of everyone who knew her, should know she wasn't suited to be a mother. Alex swung her feet over the bed and sat up. "No, Mack. You've been taking care of me almost all my life. I can't keep letting you do that."

"This time, I don't think you have any choice," Mack said, tucking the blanket around her. He pressed a palm to her forehead before he rose. "Mother Nature is dictating this one, Alex."

Then he left the room, leaving her even more frustrated than she was five minutes earlier. And with a monkey wrench thrown into her life that she hadn't asked for.

For once, Willow Clark had been right. Something that would change everything *had* just arrived on her doorstep, via a stork with a bad sense of humor.

Chapter Twenty-Five

It took only about five seconds for Mack's crew to realize they should steer clear of him if they wanted to keep their jobs. His temper was shorter than a fuse on a stick of dynamite and twice as ready to blow. He buried himself in work, putting his back into the house, until he was exhausted and the entire crew had left for the day.

And the only thing left to do was go home to Alex. Go home to her.

That was as foreign a concept to him as living on the moon. He didn't do relationships. Didn't do women living in his home. Hell, he didn't even do sleepovers. But for over a week now, Alex had been living with him, and he'd been getting kind of used to the idea. That alone told him it was time to get her house finished up and get her out of his. Before he started getting bad ideas like thinking he could make this a permanent arrangement.

The trouble? Her house was so far from being done, it would take his crew the next three weeks of constant work to finish up. The place was a dump. Like one of those homes they featured on *Flip This House* just for kicks where the homeowner got sucked into a nightmare that dragged on and on in an ever-widening pile of debt and problems.

And the other problem? He wanted Alex.

He wanted her so much, he thought of nothing else but her all day. Every day.

And especially every time he looked at his pool. Especially that.

Either way, he wasn't going to do anything about it. Alex was sick, with a summer flu or something. She wanted him to bring her chicken soup and crackers, with no side of hanky-panky.

Karma had had some serious good timing with that. Ever since that night in the pool, Mack and Alex had pretty much gotten into bed and not gotten out. He would have stayed there with her, too, if not for her getting sick. And only tangled himself in deeper in a relationship that wasn't going to go beyond the bedroom.

Except . . .

Mack had started enjoying having her there. Being with Alex wasn't like being with other women. It hadn't been about the sex. It had been something more, something intangible.

He laughed. Wasn't that what Alex had told him not long ago? That there was more than just sex?

And for the first time in a long time, Mack found himself wanting that more. The trouble was, he knew for a fact he wasn't cut out to have it. Mack hammered a nail into a stud, slamming the metal on metal, driving the slim nail into the wood until it disappeared, then hitting the wood again, just for good measure, leaving a round dent with a basket weave print on the stud.

"Where'd you learn to hammer? The circus?"

Mack turned around at the sound of his father's voice. "Dad. What are you doing here?"

"You invited me out, remember?" He held up a cooler. "I brought some refreshments."

Mack grinned, then gestured toward a couple of overturned five-gallon buckets. "You read my mind."

Roy handed his son a soda, then took one for himself. The two of them drank for a minute before talking. "Remind me again why you are working on this place. Because it's a total piece of crap, from what I can see."

"It's for Alex."

His father nodded, looked around. "It's still a piece of crap."

"I know."

"She making you do it?"

"No."

"You in love with her or something?"

"Hell, no. She's a friend."

His father harrumphed. "You help a friend install a garage door. Help a friend change out a trannie. You don't help a friend rebuild the money pit from hell."

Mack toyed with the flip tab to the can, crushing it in two before flinging it across the room. It bounced off the rim of a trash can and spiraled into the gray bucket. "She needs me. Needs some help."

His father glanced sharply at him. "You've got it bad, Son."

"No, I don't. You know me. I don't get serious about women. I learned my lesson."

"Good idea." His father sucked long and hard on the soda. "Women are nothing but trouble."

"Yeah." Mack took a long sip, too. They weren't guys that exchanged a lot of words. At least, not about personal things. When he was talking to his father about laying tile or fixing a plumbing leak, they could go on for hours. But when it came to talking about anything resembling feelings, the two of them ran like animals from a fire.

Probably explained why they'd barely touched the subject of his mother's leaving.

"So, you want to help me with this place?" Mack asked. His father had come this far, had ventured out of the house long enough to go to the store and drive over here. Dare Mack hope for more? "I sure could use an extra pair of hands. And it'd be good for you to—"

Roy rose. Put the soda he'd had only a sip of on the floor and left the cooler beside Mack's feet. "No. I've got stuff to do at home."

Mack bit back a sigh. "What stuff, Dad?"

"The landscaping. Your mother will get mad if I don't get those spring flowers planted. You know how she always likes to have her impatiens in the ground by the first week of June, and here it is nearly July. I want her to see them when she—" He cut off the sentence. Just let it go like a child releasing a balloon into the air.

Mack's heart broke. He stood, too, and reached forward, but let his hand drop. His father wouldn't want the sympathy. He'd brush off any attempt at connection.

Even though Mack knew that had been his mother outside the Drop Inn, that didn't mean anything had changed, that she was going to return and want to see her impatiens. She had left his father a year ago, with another man. Walked out on their marriage, given him the clearest sign a woman could that it was over. She hadn't made any promises in the True Value, and Mack wasn't about to raise any false hopes.

The sooner Roy accepted Emma was gone for good, the sooner he could move on. Mack thought of arguing with his father, of reminding Roy that Emma wasn't coming back to their marriage, but he didn't have the stomach to do that. Not when he could see the puddle of tears in his father's eyes, the whispers of hope that lingered there still, that little part of him that believed a ring of pink and white flowers could be enough to bring his true love back. "Yeah, Dad, you do that. If you want any help . . ."

"I'll call you." Roy cleared his throat, then nodded and turned away. "You should give up on this place. Tell that girl to let you build her a place. Sometimes you just got to know when to give up on a lost cause."

"Yeah, Dad, you do."

But his father had already walked out the door.

Work. She'd work. And somewhere, she'd come up with an answer. Uh-huh. Like they popped out of the trees, like cherry blossoms.

Alex's hand strayed to her stomach, then away. She shook her head. No, she wouldn't think about that. Not now. It was way too much. Besides, she was feeling better. Not nauseous at all. Maybe the tests had been wrong. Both of those cheap store-brand things had been faulty. Yeah, that was it. "Inspected by No. 121"—some assembly line flunky.

Alex drummed her fingers on her desk, trying to concentrate on her assignment. She flipped through the file again. Still no ideas came to mind on how to get Willow Clark to talk, without having to do this painful trading-one-question-at-a-time thing. She reached forward, fingered the petals of the white roses Steve had sent her that morning—he'd sent her a second dozen after she'd told him she'd brought the first dozen to the house—and kept on brainstorming.

And kept coming up empty.

Joe's shadow loomed over her. "How's that thing with the writer who lives in a cave going?"

She turned and gave him a smile. "Getting warmer by the second."

"So's my bullshit meter." Joe scowled. "Get me something concrete quick or you'll be back to boleros and bandanas faster than the Victoria's Secret models can change their panties."

Alex sighed, then picked up the phone and made two appointments. One with Willow Clark. And one with a doctor.

Chapter Twenty-Six

Willow Clark was humming.

Alex had learned she didn't like to be interrupted when she did that, so Alex sat in the chair across from Willow's and waited. There was no way she was leaving without what she needed. Joe's deadline freak-out at the editorial meeting later that morning had made it clear Alex had to put up or get back to plumping lipsticks. She hadn't known the human face was capable of that many shades of red.

Short of sticking Willow with an electric cattle prod, Alex saw no way of moving this thing along and getting her story done. She had two pages of interview notes, but they were a jumble. Fits and starts of questions and answers, not enough to pull together a whole story.

She picked up one of the porcelain pigs from the shelf beside her and ran a hand over his smooth back, her fingers slipping down the chinalike surface, sliding along the curves, then up and over the curlicue of a tail.

Dread pooled in Alex's stomach, along with the saltines and flat soda she'd had for breakfast. Undoubtedly, Willow was going to have some more of those my-question-for-your-question games today. Was it writer's curiosity? Some weird interest in Alex's personal life? Or was Willow mining Alex's past for her next book?

Either way, Alex kept coming back. Partly because she wanted to know more about Willow Clark. Alex was hooked—like a reader of a suspense novel. Partly because she needed the story. And partly because, now, she needed the additional income, not just to pay for the house repairs, but also for the extra expenses if she—

No, she hadn't decided that yet. Hadn't decided yet what to do.

She couldn't even call this pregnancy her child. Not yet. It was too surreal.

Once she knew for sure how she felt about the whole thing, then she could decide whether to—

"Hold on or let it go," Willow said.

"What?" Alex jerked her head up. "What did you just say?"

"The pig. Hold on or let go." Willow smiled.

Alex shoved the pig back onto the shelf so fast, he clattered against his porcine partners. "Are you ready for our interview?"

"Certainly. I feel much better now." Willow waved at the tendrils of incense, wafting the smoke over herself. "Everything has been cleansed."

"Great," Alex said.

This was her childhood idol? The woman who had written the book that had defined her teen years? How could that be? How could such a loony also be such an insightful author?

"Now, where were we?"

"Today? We, uh, didn't talk about anything. You've been humming since I walked in."

"I meant on Thursday. You asked me a question. I didn't answer it. If you could ask it again, I could give you a response."

Alex flipped through her notepad, down the long list of questions. Only thirteen had been answered so far, so she could start anywhere. "Who was your biggest influence as an author?"

"Nope, that wasn't it. Try another one."

Alex asked a second question, a third, getting the same response both times. She sighed, put the pad in her lap. "I don't remember what I asked you on Thursday."

"Oh, well, you should have said something then. I could have told you." Willow smiled. "You asked me how I thought Jensine's story related to yours."

Alex racked her brain. Ran down every mental recollection of the last two conversations with Willow. "I don't remember asking that."

"It's not like you used words, my dear. But I heard the question, all the same." Willow leaned forward in her chair, propping her elbows on her lap. "And now I'll tell you. Jensine keeps searching for herself throughout *The Season of Light*, first in other people, then in the journal that she keeps, then finally in the relationship she begins with the old woman down the street who becomes her mentor. She finally realizes that the only way she can find out who she really is, is to look deep inside. And she does that—"

"With painting."

Willow beamed like a proud parent. "Exactly. She gets all her feelings out on the page in that art class. It's a breakthrough for her. She breaks down and weeps right in the middle of her first art show at school, it's such a big moment."

"The light, that's what she sees," Alex said. "It's in

the paintings she does. They show her the way out of the darkness she has felt all that time. The darkness that has kept her from feeling happy, because she never knew who she was."

Willow nodded, excited now, waving her hands as she talked. "Well, being an orphan, adopted from another country, with no record of who her parents were, she literally had no heritage. She had to build one."

Alex jerked to attention. "I should have been writing this down. I just missed a bunch of great quotes. Damn." She flipped open the pad, got to a blank page, then started scribbling. "Can you repeat some of that?"

"No."

Alex paused and looked up. "Why not?"

"I'd rather you capture the essence of it, when you put yourself into the story. Sort of like when Jensine put herself into her art."

"Miss Clark, this is a feature story for the newspaper. I'm supposed to be impartial. And accurate."

Willow rolled her eyes. "Save me from the middle-of-the-roaders who never have an opinion. Life is all about taking a stand, Alex. Having feelings. When you do, that's when you really live."

Alex snorted. "That's when you get hurt, if you ask me." She turned back a page, to her other questions. "Do you see Jensine as a role model for young girls?"

Willow cocked her head and studied Alex. "When did you get hurt?"

Back to that again. Alex barreled forward, refusing to get detoured. "Because I see Jensine as providing a great example of strength for girls in those pivotal tween years. That's when they have a hard time standing up for themselves. Being true to who they are."

"It must have been someone you really loved. Those

are the ones who have the longest knives. Even if they don't mean to."

Alex shifted in her chair. "Jensine's best friend. She's not drawn as strong in this book. Did you have a reason for making her a weaker character?"

"Was it . . . your mother?" Willow's voice was soft, almost like a song, floating across the room, the words curling around Alex, reaching out their syllabic tendrils just as the incense did.

"I think Jensine has a . . ." Alex cleared her throat. "I think she, uh, has . . ." The words on her pad swam before her eyes. She blinked twice, but they kept on swimming. "I wanted to know if she . . ."

"It was, wasn't it?"

She didn't want to answer. Didn't want to dip into this. Wanted to avoid the subject, let it die, make it go away. She tried to press her lips together, to force the word back into her throat, but it slipped out all the same. "Yes."

"My mother was the same," Willow said. "That's why Jensine was so easy to write. And so hard. She was . . . me."

Alex's gaze met Willow's. The kookiness was gone from her eyes, and in its place Alex saw honesty, and the kind of connection that came from a shared past. For the first time since she had met Willow Clark, she realized she was seeing the real woman, the true person behind all the karma and the incense. "You?"

Willow nodded. "I was given up for adoption when I was three. My mother was a single mother, and in those days, well, raising a child on your own just wasn't done. She tried, I know she did, but she couldn't raise me and go to work. She had no support system because her parents didn't approve and my father, well, he was doing whatever he wanted to do, which wasn't being a parent. So she let me go." She got up and motioned for Alex to follow her out of the back room and into the shop. They began to meander down the aisles, going nowhere in particular.

"At three? But you were so . . . old."

"And she was still so young. She had a life to live, and I wasn't part of it." Willow tried on a smile, but it didn't fit. "I found her again, years later, and she had her regrets, but it was late. Too late."

Alex toyed with her pen. Twirled it over and over, the *City Times* logo spinning by so fast, she couldn't read it. "I never knew my father, either, but mostly because my mother dated . . . a lot . . . and wasn't sure who my father was. My mother was a party girl, and she had a lot of boyfriends. She got pregnant, thought she could keep me and make it work, and still keep on living the way she had before."

"The parties? The staying out late?"

Alex nodded. "Not a way to raise a kid."

"Not a way to raise so much as a puppy."

Alex laughed, and the sound scraped her throat. "Yeah, well, no one could tell her that. She had a falling out with my grandmother, and wouldn't talk to her. I think that hurt my grandma a lot."

She drew in a breath, let it go. As the air left her chest, everything hurt a little less. Had Willow been right? That talking would make this easier?

She never had talked about it, not really. Not to Mack, not to Grandma, not to anyone. She'd just kept it all inside, in this little mental box, and left it there, as if leaving it locked away would make her forget what had happened. Forget how hurt she had felt. Forget everything from the first five years of her life.

"What happened to your mother?" Willow asked.

"She died. In a drunk driving accident." Alex fingered

a fake plant, running her fingers down the silky flowers, dyed an unnatural bright blue.

"I'm sorry," Willow said, reaching out, her touch lighting on Alex's knee. "What was your mother like?"

Alex ran a hand through her hair and prayed for the bell over the door to ring. For the phone to jangle, for anything to interrupt this quid pro quo game. What was it with this store? It seemed that whenever Alex was in here with Willow, no customers came in. No one to rescue her from this torturous line of questioning. "Can we pick another *Jeopardy!* topic?"

Willow smiled. "How about that man you're falling in love with?"

"Steve? Oh, well, I don't know . . ."

"Not that one."

Alex blinked. "I'm not in love with anyone else."

Willow didn't say anything. That Mona Lisa smile took over her face again.

"I've answered tons of questions, so now it's your turn," Alex said. "Who were some of your inspirations for writing?"

"Oh, that's an easy question," Willow said. "All the greats, of course. Dickens. Shakespeare. Twain. But then there were the little, unknown authors. The one-hit wonders who have those books no one has heard of, the kind you find in the back of used bookstores, dusty little volumes that have hardly been read. I call them treasures, because I feel like I've discovered a secret no one else knows about."

"Was that what you thought you'd be? A one-hit wonder?"

"I wanted more," Willow said softly, drifting over to a display of porcelain floral vases. She picked up one and traced its rose pattern, her fingertip outlining the delicate red flower. "I dreamed of publishing dozens of books. Of becoming a Joyce Carol Oates. Going on speaking tours. Teaching at colleges."

"What happened?"

"The fame hit me harder than I expected. Reporters started delving into my past. And it brought a lot of things up that I wasn't ready to talk about then."

Alex ventured the question, even as she was afraid it might trigger the end of the interview. "Why are you talking to me now?"

"Because it's time. And because I'm getting too old to keep on hiding in this little shop. I've written a lot of words since *The Season of Light,* words that should"— Willow looked up and smiled—"see the light."

"Good. Because you're a great writer."

"If not a little odd?"

Alex laughed. "Just a little."

"That comes from spending too much time alone, I'm afraid. I had only me and my imagination when I was growing up, so I cultivated my sixth sense." She shrugged. "Anyway, that's a lot of questions and answers from me. You still owe me one. So choose one. You can either tell me what your mother was like . . . or about the man you're falling in love with."

Willow's ESP radar was definitely off regarding Alex's love life, but Alex let the subject drop. Arguing the point would only lead to more questions, and Alex didn't need that. What she needed were more answers. The sooner she gave Willow what she wanted, the sooner she could get what she needed. She'd gone through her notes last night, and she was halfway to a story. Maybe after today she'd have enough to write the piece.

She sucked in another dose of patience. "My mother was beautiful," Alex said, the words surprising her as they escaped her mouth. Of all the things that she could have said, that would have been the last sentence Alex would have expected to hear out of herself. She thought of the picture, of her mother's smile, and realized it was true. "She was young and pretty and she laughed a lot."

Was that really what she remembered the most? For years, Alex thought she'd remembered only the bad. The days when her mother had been gone, leaving her with one friend or another, or the times her mother had forgotten to buy groceries, leaving Alex with nothing of substance to eat. The parties that lasted long into the night, the strangers sleeping on the floors, sometimes even on Alex's bedroom floor—

But no. When she closed her eyes and reached into her mind, she heard—

Laughter.

"Then what made her so bad?"

"She forgot what was important. Like me. And my sister." But had she always? Every single day? Alex reached again into her memory, striving to find more, more clues, more images, but her mind drew a blank. She felt as if she was missing a key somewhere, to a door she hadn't opened.

"I know how you feel. There was good among the bad, light among the shadows," Willow said softly. "And you saw that in my book, didn't you?"

Alex nodded. "Probably why I read it so many times."

"And probably why I can read you so well. Sometimes, people's auras are fuzzy. But yours, it's clear as a bell." She laid a hand on Alex's reporter's pad. "I think, if you look over your pages, you'll find that you have what you need."

"I still have a lot of questions—"

"I didn't mean for your story about me. I'm willing

to talk the rest of the afternoon and give you the inside scoop on Willow Clark." She smiled. "I meant for *your* story. You came here, whether you knew it or not, seeking answers for yourself, too. You've already got what you need inside your heart. Now all you have to do is finish writing the tale in your heart."

She had what she needed? All those keys were there? Yet, it all still felt like a confusing jumble, especially now that Alex was following down the same path as her mother had, with a baby on the way, no husband and a house that was a mess.

"How?" Alex asked. "How do I do that?"

"Easy. Do what authors do. Start at the beginning. Then just go from Once Upon a Time to The End." Willow reached for a bright-red heart-shaped vase on the shelf. She picked it up and put it into Alex's hands. "Your happy ending is just waiting for you to find it."

Chapter Twenty-Seven

Renee's jaw nearly hit the restaurant table. "Oh, my God, Alex."

"I know. That's what I said, too." Alex sipped at an iced tea—about the only thing she could stomach—and then fiddled with the straw. It had been a full twenty-four hours since she'd seen the pink lines, and still she couldn't believe they were real. She'd managed to avoid Mack, by going in early to work, because his mother-hen concern had started to get on her nerves. Then the appointment with Willow Clark, followed by an after-work doctor's appointment and, finally, an emergency dinner with Renee. Somewhere in there, she hoped to come up with an answer, because despite everything that Willow had said, she'd yet to find any ending to her personal story. "I suppose I should be happy."

"And are you?"

"Are you kidding me? This is the *last* thing I want in my life right now. The whole time I'm sitting in the gynecologist's office, I kept thinking they'd come back and tell me that their test would be negative, that those stupid store-brand tests would be wrong, but no, they weren't. And here's everyone congratulating me like this is a great thing."

"Most people *do* think babies are a great thing."

"Not Edward. I called him and told him about the baby."

"What did he say?"

"That he and his wife got back together, and that he'd send me some money, but that's all he'd do." Alex shook her head, anger and frustration mingling with hot tears. What had she ever seen in him? "He didn't want his own child. He didn't even want me, Renee."

Renee reached out and clasped Alex's hand. "He was an idiot. A complete and total idiot. You are better off without him."

"True."

"And you don't need an idiot raising your kid. It'll only turn your kid into an idiot." Renee smiled. "See? A bright side."

"You're reaching."

"Okay, I was. *The baby* is the bright side, Alex."

"Renee, I'm totally not mother material." She couldn't repeat her mother's mistakes, couldn't step into those same shoes. She fiddled with her silverware. "It's not a great thing at all," she repeated.

"I'm sure you'll work it out. And whatever you decide, I'll be right behind you."

"Thanks." Alex worked a smile to her face, forced herself to feign happiness so that Renee would quit trying to cheer her up. "Now, can we order, and change the subject? Like, to your life?"

Renee picked up her menu. "I thought you wanted to stay away from nauseating topics."

"Things still not better with Tony?"

"Do you mean is he still living with his brother? Still

acting like he's single? No and yes. He moved back home, but things still suck." Renee let out a sigh and put her menu to the side. Tears pooled in her eyes, and she drew in a deep breath. "I wasn't going to tell you. I wasn't going to tell anyone. But I'm filing for divorce."

The seven-letter word hit Alex like a blast of ice. Divorced? Renee and Tony?

"Oh, God, Renee, I'm so sorry." Now it was Alex's turn to give Renee a little mano a mano support. "Things are that bad? I thought . . ."

"Thought we were getting back together? We've done that, Alex. It never works. I'm tired. I don't want to try anymore." She sat back in her chair and ran a hand through her hair. Exhaustion shaded the space beneath her eyes, sadness drooped her face.

"You're giving up?"

"I'm not giving up. I'm accepting the inevitable." Renee dabbed her eyes with her napkin. "And I think it's time Tony and I just stopped beating this dead horse."

Alex had known Renee and Tony for almost twelve years. Been their maid of honor, for God's sake. Stood right across from Tony and seen him pledge forever to Renee, a huge, goofy grin on his face. The last thing she'd ever imagined was the two of them splitting up. Ending the fairy tale.

Sure, they'd fought, but they'd always made up. They'd seemed to have the typical American marriage. What chance did Alex—whose only long-term relationship had been with a bigamist—have of making a relationship work if Renee and Tony couldn't? They had kids, a life together. Everything to stay together for. And still, it had all fallen apart.

Alex signaled to the waiter for two more drinks. Already she envied Renee her margarita, and wished her empty glass of tea had a splash or two of rum. But until she made up her mind about what to do about her . . . situation, she'd do the right thing and avoid alcohol. "You can't give up so easily."

"Marriage is harder than it looks. Add in kids and credit cards, and you might as well be pushing a train up Mount Everest." Renee shook her head. "Let's not dwell on all the ways that my life went down the wrong path. Let's celebrate your news instead."

A burst of nearly manic laughter escaped Alex. She covered her mouth and bit it back. "What's to celebrate? I'm single, pregnant, up to my eyeballs trying to fix the house from hell, and I have yet to finish the one story I promised my boss was a sure thing. I don't think there are any other ways left to screw up my life."

Renee tipped her margarita toward Alex. "You didn't marry a bigamist, remember?"

"There is that." Alex laughed.

Renee reached into the bread basket, withdrew a cheddar biscuit and slathered it with butter. "So, have you decided what you're going to do?"

"No." She sighed. "I have time, though."

"How did Mack take the news?"

"I didn't tell him."

"What?" Renee arched a brow. "Why?"

"Because he'd want to rush in and do something to make it right. You know how he is. And I don't need that right now. I need time to . . ." She drew in a breath, let it out. "Think. Mack makes it very hard to do that."

Renee popped a piece of biscuit into her mouth, chewed, then fiddled with her knife. "I can imagine he would. If only he was the settling-down kind, you could solve all your problems at once."

"Or maybe Prince Charming will come along

tomorrow and sweep me off my feet and we'll go live in a castle on a hill." Alex grinned.

"Don't go holding your breath." Renee took another sip of her margarita and chuckled. "That's why they call them fairy tales. Because they're make-believe."

Alex's hand strayed to her stomach, then to her empty left hand. "Maybe you and I need to start reading different books."

Renee took a long sip of her drink, the disappointment of her marriage clear in her face. "Either that, or start expecting a different ending than happily ever after. Because that only seems to happen when there are dwarves or mice involved."

Chapter Twenty-Eight

Alex had never been courted with such determination before. The vases of roses multiplied. Cards piled up on her doorstep. Text messages appeared on her cell phone at all hours. And then there were the dinners at fancy restaurants, the dancing at intimate jazz clubs in Boston.

Steve exhausted her with all his attention. She should have been glad, but instead she found herself wishing for a break.

What was wrong with her? She finally had what she thought she wanted—the perfect gentleman, one who made it clear he was falling in love—but all she wanted was for him to leave her alone.

Nor had she managed to tell him yet that she was pregnant. Every time she opened her mouth to say the words, they got lodged in her throat. Maybe Willow Clark had been right. She was building walls between herself and other people faster than she could tear them down.

"Steve, you really don't have to go to all this trouble," Alex said, staring at two tickets to a Broadway show at the Wang Center that she'd mentioned in passing she wanted to see.

He grinned. "It's no trouble at all. Really."

"Honest, I'm content to sit at home, pop some pop-corn and rent a movie. I don't need all this . . ." She waved a hand over her dress, his suit, the bouquet of roses sitting on her lap.

Steve glanced over at her, then back at the road as he drove toward yet another restaurant, this one newly opened by a former television actor. Steve had worked for a week solid to get reservations for open-ing night, something he'd surprised Alex with that af-ternoon.

She'd called Mack to tell him she wouldn't be home for dinner that night, but her call had gone straight to voice mail. Lately, he'd been more and more unavailable, almost as if he was avoiding her. She saw him at the house, of course, but there he talked only about the construction and very little about their personal lives. Ever since that night in the pool, Mack had gone grumpy and silent, which was completely not like him.

There'd been no more flirting, no kissing, no sexual contact whatsoever. Exactly what she wanted—except . . .

She missed him.

The distance stung, but Alex had no idea what to do to close the gap. In all the years she'd known Mack, they'd never exchanged a cross word. When-ever she tried to get him to talk to her, he clammed up and went back to work.

Could he be avoiding her? Did he regret that night in the pool, as she did?

But did she *really* regret it? A part of her, a very vocal part, especially late at night, wanted to go back and make love to Mack all over again. And again. Every time she looked at him or thought about him, she pictured that heated encounter. It had to be the pregnancy hormones. Yeah, that was it.

"You might not need all these things," Steve said, drawing her back to their conversation, "but a woman like you deserves it."

She shifted in her seat. "But don't you want to do something casual?"

"Like . . . what?"

"Just hang out. Walk on the beach. Play some basketball." The kinds of things she and Mack always did. Of course, that was because he usually treated her more like one of his buddies than like a girlfriend, but still, she found those days fun.

And even better, none of those activities required panty hose.

Was Mack doing any of those things with Deidre right now? Was he taking her to dinner? Kissing her? Or was he . . . taking her to bed, sliding his hands down her—

"That's not a date," Steve said, laughing and interrupting her torturous thoughts. "I don't know what kind of guys have been taking you out, Alex, but they have seriously undertreated you." He leaned over and placed a quick kiss on her cheek. "Let me spoil you."

She sat back in her seat and watched the I-93 traffic whiz by in a blur of white lights. A light rain began to fall, the droplets blurring her view like a melted painting. Alex traced a finger in the condensation on her window and told herself she should be delighted. Steve was everything any woman would want. Attentive, charming, devoted. Whatever she wanted, she got—to the nth degree.

But over the last few dates, it had all become too much. To the point where his eagerness to please her had begun to grate on her nerves.

Maybe Grandma was right, maybe the problem lay not with the men she was dating, but with herself. She glanced over at Steve. He was exactly what she had asked Mack to find for her, as if she'd placed a cosmic order and it had been delivered on a silver platter.

She reached out and clasped Steve's free hand, resting on the gearshift. He shot her a smile, the kind that broke like sunshine on the horizon, and made guilt rocket through Alex. She should be happy to have a guy like him catering to her.

But instead she found her mind wandering again back to Mack. What had gotten into him lately? Why was her best friend avoiding her as if she'd picked up some contagious fatal disease?

And why, when she had everything she had ever wanted within her grasp, did she suddenly stop wanting it?

"This is too much commitment, Mack." Alex backed away, shaking her head.

They'd been standing in the store for an hour, debating one choice after another. Mack had dreaded the trip with Alex. The thought of spending all this time alone with her, especially after last week, had made him as antsy as the last lobster in the tank at an all-you-can-eat seafood festival.

But after sixty minutes of forced proximity, they had eased back into their usual closeness. The tension eased from Mack's shoulders for the first time in days.

"I don't know," Alex said, tapping her lip with a finger.

"Alex, you're not cementing anything for a lifetime here. Just pick a pattern and we can go home."

Back to my house. To a night alone.

Even if it would be another mistake, it was one he was

willing to make. He knew she had no plans tonight, and he'd already canceled his date with Deidre. Going out with Deidre was like inhaling helium when he really craved oxygen.

"Yeah, but what if my choice isn't what anybody else wants?" Alex asked. "What if the next person hates it?"

He came up behind her, his tall frame nearly dwarfing Alex. He caught the sweet scent of her shampoo. "Quit worrying about what the next person wants. Tell me which cabinets you'd put in your kitchen if this was going to be your house. If you were staying there. If you were going to be making me pancakes in the morning—"

She turned in his arms. "Making *you* pancakes?"

He'd done it again. Stepped into territory he'd had no intention of treading on, moving down the path he'd meant to avoid. So he turned on a grin and forced a joke into his voice. "Hey, I might as well get something out of the deal, if I'm doing all this work."

But did he really want just one breakfast in Alex's kitchen? A couple buttermilk pancakes with a side of bacon?

No. He didn't. Ever since they'd made love, and he'd awakened with her beside him, he'd had this constant pang in his chest, an aching that ran deep into his veins, his gut. The feeling was so foreign, so new, something he hadn't felt even when he'd married Samantha, but now, as he looked at Alex and the ache rose anew, Mack realized the feeling.

He wanted more. What that more was, Mack wasn't sure, but it definitely wasn't just sex. Every time she left with Steve, or talked to him on the phone, Mack wanted to rip out a wall or tear apart a concrete patio with his bare hands. Yet, he kept silent, because Steve was offering Alex what Mack couldn't—

Forever, on a golden platter, and with a white picket fence. So Mack kept doing what he had always done, and put Alex's needs ahead of his own.

"The maple cabinets," Alex said, drawing Mack back to reality. "I like the simplicity of them. And," she laughed, "the price."

"Maple's . . . perfect," Mack said. "And the counter-tops?"

She turned and tipped her face toward him. Her cheeks were flushed, her lips full and lush. Her breath seemed to come a little faster, and Mack had to wonder if it was because he was close—if it was because she was thinking, as he was, about everything but the building project. Was she thinking instead about what was building between them?

"What do you think?" Alex asked. "Laminate? Granite? That . . . what is it called . . . ? Solid surface stuff?"

"The last two choices have permanence. Durability."

"That's good. Right?"

He ached to trace the line of her jaw, to capture her mouth with his. To bring her body against his own, and feel her heat imprint its hourglass pattern. The desire coiled even tighter this time, because he'd already tasted her skin, already felt her body beneath his. He shook off the thoughts. A home improvement store wasn't exactly the best place to get cozy. "Yes, that's good."

Alex nibbled on her bottom lip. Mack bit back a groan. "Those options are probably really expensive."

"Sometimes the benefits outweigh the price you'll pay." Was he even still talking about cabinets? Countertops?

She hesitated, her green eyes wide, luminous. She exhaled a long, slow breath. "I don't know if I can make this decision, Mack. I had no idea it would be this difficult."

"There are a lot of colors and stones to choose between, so if you want to take some samples with you—"

"That's not it." She shook her head and stepped back, dropping into a nearby chair. Alex pressed the back of her hand against her forehead. Beads of sweat had broken out on her skin.

"Are you okay?"

"Actually, no." She brushed her hand against her temples again, then pressed her palms against her cheeks. "I don't feel well. Can we go home?"

"Sure, sure." He put out his hand and helped her to her feet. They headed out of the store, Alex's face paling more with every step.

Way to go, Romeo. Disappointment whistled through Mack with the bitter cold of a winter wind. Here he'd been thinking she'd had some hot and heavy thoughts for him, when actually she'd been sick. Talk about crossed signals. He couldn't have been more off base if he'd been running Fenway Park backward.

Just when he thought he had this all figured out—

He didn't.

Chapter Twenty-Nine

"When were you going to tell me?"

Alex sat across from Grandma Kenner on Friday afternoon, in the sunny kitchen of Grandma's condo, and gave her an update on the progress of the Dorchester house. She'd spread out a fan of paint chips on the laminate kitchen table. "Tell you what, Grandma? That I secretly loved the color seafoam green?" Alex grinned.

"That you're pregnant."

The word hung in the air between them, so heavy, Alex was sure it weighed a hundred pounds. She shuffled through the paint chips some more. "How about this butter cream? I think it would be great in the kitchen. I also like the melted vanilla, even though the name makes me hungry."

Grandma ignored the color palette. She poked her face in front of Alex's, her light blue eyes missing nothing. "I've had a child of my own, you know. Seen my own child have kids. Worked as a nurse for ten years before I quit to be a mother. I can tell these things."

If Alex acknowledged the words, she'd have to acknowledge the situation. Maybe if she just let the subject drop, Grandma would, too. For now. Until she could clear her head, get her mind around it, because right now everything was still whirling and spinning inside there with disbelief.

"Cinnamon would be good in the dining room. Or maybe hot tamale. I thought it might be dramatic. You know, make a statement. But I'm worried the orange-red tones might clash with the taupe in the living room. Either way," Alex said, folding up the color wheel, "we don't need to make a decision today. There's still plenty of work to be done before we paint. I'll come back later."

"Not so fast." Grandma clamped a vise grip hand onto Alex's arm. "How far along?"

Alex sighed. Denying would get her nowhere. She knew her grandmother. If she didn't get the answers she wanted, she'd probably trot on down to Alex's doctor's office and wheedle the information out of the gynecologist herself. "Six weeks. Maybe seven."

"Oh, Alex!" Her grandmother put a hand over her mouth, then got to her feet and drew her grand-daughter into her arms. "I'm so happy!"

Alex wriggled out of the hug. "I'm not sure I want to keep it." She still couldn't quantify this as a baby. Or a pregnancy. She kept thinking of the whole thing as an "it" and an "event." Doing that kept her from having to come to a decision. She knew she couldn't put it off forever, but another day or two wasn't going to change anything.

A stricken look took over Grandma's face, and guilt twisted in Alex's gut. She'd disappointed Grandma Kenner, something she hated to do. "Why?"

Alex swung her purse over her shoulder. Beads of sweat broke out on her forehead, and suddenly the room felt tight, stuffy, closed in. "I have to go, Grandma. I have to go meet Mack and place the order for the light fixtures. If I don't get there in time, he'll pick out something awful. Some guy kind of thing."

Her grandmother pursed her lips. "That is not the Kenner way."

"Since when?"

"Since I made all new rules. And being the oldest surviving Kenner, and the one who raised you, I make the rules. So that means you have to go at this head-on, face your problems straight into the wind."

"And how exactly am I supposed to go at this"—Alex still couldn't get the words out—"head-on?"

Grandma picked up the paint chips and waved them at Alex. "By picking either a pink or blue room."

Alex pressed a hand to her face and shuddered. She wanted to cry, scream and run out of the room. Why had she gotten into this situation? And how was she going to get out of it? The suffocating feeling began to climb up her throat, and she plucked at her T-shirt, pulling the collar away from her neck. "Grandma, don't get ten steps ahead of me."

"Well, you have to make at least one step, granddaughter. Or before you know it, that little booger inside you will be making them all."

"Grandma, please let it go. I need to think about this, and pressuring me isn't helping. At all. It's just making it worse." Alex rose, crossed to the refrigerator, pulled out a water bottle and unscrewed the top. She drank deeply, then put the bottle on the counter. Anything to avoid the questions in her grandmother's eyes, questions she couldn't answer, not right now. Not while she was still asking them herself. She reached into her handbag, pulled out the catalog of lighting fixtures and flipped through them, the pages going by fast and furious, and not doing much to quell the quick racing of her pulse. "So, do you want to pick out one of these or let Mack go with his disco strobe idea?"

"Did you tell Mack?"

Clearly, Grandma Kenner wasn't going to let the subject drop. "No."

"Why not?"

"He's not the father. He doesn't need to know."

"He cares about you. He'd want to know."

Alex turned the page of the catalog. She pointed at a picture of something, she didn't even care what. "This one's nice. I like the polished bronze finish. It's kind of antiquey." Her voice shook. She needed to sit down.

"He'd want to help you, Alex."

"I don't need him to help me. I'm a big girl." Alex flipped several pages forward and pointed at another item, all of them a blur, just a diversion, but they weren't working. Alex sank into the chair, willing her grandmother to change the subject, to just let her forget that she'd made this incredible stupid mistake. "They have matching ceiling fans, and there are even outdoor lights that coordinate. See? Aren't they great? It's like Garanimals for homeowners."

"Alex." Grandma laid a hand on her granddaughter's and waited until she looked up. "What's the matter?"

"I have to . . ." She pointed vaguely at the catalog. "I can't . . ."

"Tell me, sweetheart."

"I can't . . . do this," she said finally, the words breaking with a sob. "I can't make this decision right now."

"Nobody said you had to do it right now. You've got time."

Alex closed her eyes, and finally pushed out the

doubts that had been sitting in her gut for days. "I don't want to make the same mistakes she did."

"Who says you will?"

"And who says I won't?" She shook her head. "I can't talk about this right now. I have lighting fixtures to choose." Concentrate on that, not the bigger problem. She'd deal with one thing at a time. Tackle the little problems first, the ones she could manage. Yeah, like dome lighting or chandeliers. Now *there* was a life-changing decision.

"You're in no state to make any decisions right now. You need some time to think."

Alex pushed the lighting pictures aside. "Fine. Then let's talk about something else. Like . . . what the doom-and-gloomers are up to now. What is it today? Predicting tornadoes?"

Grandma ignored the temporary attempt at levity. She reached out and ran a hand down Alex's hair, her touch tender and full of years of love. "I love you, Alex, and your mother did, too. From the minute she found out she was pregnant, she loved you. In fact, she bought a stuffed animal that very first day. A little bear."

The bear. Alex remembered it. Her constant companion, a tagalong everywhere she'd gone. And now, the only picture she had of it, she'd thrown away. Regret pooled in her chest.

Alex had heard that story before—but never really heard it. Could her mother have been excited, not panicked, the first time she heard she was having a baby? Or did she change her mind after the baby arrived?

"If that was so," Alex said, "then why did she ditch me every chance she got?"

Grandma sighed. "She was young, honey. Fool-hardy, and stubborn as all hell. And scared. Scared that she would be a terrible mother."

That was one emotion Alex understood now. But not how being scared could make someone put their children in second place.

Alex concentrated her attention on the vase of orange daylilies on Grandma's kitchen. They blurred in her line of sight until they were one big circle, like a watery sun. "She was terrible."

"All the time?" Grandma asked, her voice soft.

Alex didn't answer. Just kept watching that orange flower sun.

"You need to let go of the resentment. So you can open your heart to what's good, like a garden that's finally planted with the right crops for its soil. And then you can heal."

"I am healed."

"About everything?"

Alex looked away and sucked in a breath. A long moment passed, then she let the air out of her lungs. "No, not everything."

"You still think what happened to Brittany is your fault?"

As if Grandma had flipped a switch, a tear ran down Alex's face. Her breath hitched in her chest, so hard it hurt. The pink room flooded back into her mind, as clear as if it was yesterday. The stuffed bunny in the crib. The clowns dancing on the mobile. Soft yellow light from the Winnie the Pooh nightlight bathing everything in a golden glow, making her believe for several minutes that nothing was wrong, even as the babysitter continued to scream. Alex had told herself it was all a trick of the light, a cruel trick. "My mother should have been there that night. *She* should have been there, not a babysitter. But where was she? Out at a party. And if I had gone up there sooner, I could have—"

"You were five, honey. What did you think you were going to do? You were a little kid."

"I was the big sister, Grandma. I was supposed to protect her. When she was born, I *promised* her I'd protect her."

Grandma cupped Alex's face in her soft palms, as tears slid down Alex's cheeks and over her grandmother's fingers. Her lighter eyes held Alex's, held them tight, and in Grandma's shattered gaze, Alex saw the shared grief of a broken heart who had lost a loved one, too. "You were not responsible for what happened to Brittany. It was no one's fault. It was SIDS, honey. A terrible tragedy that happens sometimes to babies whether their mothers are there or their big sisters or their babysitters. It was no one's fault," she repeated.

Alex still wanted to blame someone. She *needed* to blame someone. Anger was so much easier to hold on to than grief.

The orange circle blurred until Alex couldn't see anything at all. She closed her eyes and wished the memories away, but they wouldn't stay back this time. They came rushing at her like a truckload of linebackers, colliding into her chest, pummeling her heart, taking away her breath. That history played over and over in Alex's head like a movie with only one repeating scene. She twined her fingers together so tight, the knuckles turned white.

And still the images came. Her mother, running into the house, crying and collapsing as she hurried up the stairs, calling out Brittany's name again and again. All these years, Alex had blamed Josie for being gone, for putting herself ahead of her child, but now, with a life beating inside her own body, she began to see that past with new eyes.

The anger slowly gave way to empathy, to realizing how deep Josie's anguish, pain and overwhelming guilt had gone. She hadn't been there—and her child had died.

No wonder she had turned and run from the house, racked with an unspeakable agony. She'd gotten in her car, probably trying to outrun the image of her lifeless child, and found no amount of speed could close that gap. Blinded by grief, she'd run off the road, not knowing the mess she'd be leaving behind.

"What if it happens again? What if it happens to me? To my . . ." Alex let out a breath. "My baby?"

Understanding and empathy crested in Grandma's smile. "And what if it doesn't, sweetheart? You'll be a wonderful mother. I know you will."

She shook her head. "I don't think I can raise a child, Grandma. What if I turn out to be just like her?"

"And what if you don't?"

Alex shook her head harder this time, cementing her resolve. "I can't take that chance."

Her grandmother opened her mouth, as if she wanted to argue, then closed it again. She paused a moment, watching Alex's face, as if trying to accept Alex's decision. "What are you going to do?"

"I have an appointment at an adoption agency later this week. I thought I'd look at all my options."

Grandma grasped Alex's hand with comfort and support. "Are you sure you want to give your baby away? That's a forever thing, honey."

Give her baby away. Abandon her child, essentially.

The words sliced through Alex with a sharpness that nearly took her breath away. She hadn't, until that moment, realized that she had, indeed, been contemplating exactly that. And would it leave her child feeling the same way she had felt as a kid? Alone? Rejected?

Her eyes misted, and she turned away, fingering the edge of the table, not seeing the wood, but needing the hardness of the oak for something sturdy to hold on to. "I don't know. I don't know what I want."

Her grandmother's arm went around her and she drew Alex into a White Linen–scented hug, one that reminded her of her childhood, of safety, security, and of someone who had been there no matter what. "I just want you to be happy, sweetheart, and to do what will be best for you. And for your baby."

"I'm trying, Grandma, I'm trying."

Her grandmother pressed a kiss to her forehead, and for a moment, Alex felt six again. "I know you are. I know you are."

Chapter Thirty

The fliers littered the floor at Alex's feet, pictures of happy families spread around her like a montage of what could be for other people. The words on the covers of the brochures seemed to leap off the pages and scream back at her.

Adoption.

A Chosen Child.

The Gift of Family.

A Forever Home.

Queasiness rose in Alex's stomach, rolling like an ocean on a stormy day. She pressed her hand against her gut, trying to quell the nausea, but it continued to grow. She scrambled to her feet and dashed to the only working bathroom in the house, the one upstairs, upchucking what was left of the small lunch she'd had earlier.

After rinsing out her mouth and wiping her face with a damp paper towel, Alex leaned against the sink and stared at her reflection. "What are you going to do?"

The other, paler version of herself didn't provide an answer. She had no idea what to do. When she'd walked into the adoption agency earlier this morning and picked up the brochures, the answer had seemed so clear. But now, not so much.

She couldn't raise a child. She could barely take care of herself, for God's sake.

The work waiting for her downstairs—work Mack didn't want her doing because he thought she had the flu, but work that served as a blessed distraction from the one growing in her belly—suddenly seemed too overwhelming. Alex didn't want to go back down there and face the unfinished walls, the piles of construction debris. Instead, she exited the bathroom and wandered aimlessly down the hall.

She'd avoided the upstairs, except to use the bathroom, ever since she'd realized whose house this was. Mack had tried to convince her to do the construction on all the rooms at the same time—and he was right, it was the most practical way to tackle a renovation—but she hadn't been able to make any decisions about these bedrooms. Not right away. So she'd put him off, and put him off, telling him they'd do those rooms later, once the new downstairs walls were in place.

Save for that one time, she hadn't stepped foot in the other bedrooms, hadn't looked in a single closet. Hadn't opened any other doors, except the one to the pink room. Resurrecting those ghosts had been enough.

But now, something pulled Alex down the hall, past her old bedroom, to the master at the back of the house. The door opened to a view of a wide picture window that looked out over the yard—or what was essentially a weed factory now.

Alex pushed open the door. The hinges creaked in protest. She crossed the threshold, stepping onto brown shag carpeting that had long ago faded from the sunlight and matted like a mangy dog's fur. A double bed frame sat squarely in the middle of the room, an eerie metal skeleton. On either side of the window hung the remnants of lacy white curtains, more tatters than fabric now, yellowed to the color of butter.

An old dresser sat against the wall, the drawers opened, half-spilled onto the floor, the contents long gone. The wood—maple, maybe—was scratched and stained. A hand-me-down, she thought, or a side-of-the-road find. In the corner of the room, a pile of clothes sat in a dusty bundle. Whether they were her mother's or some teenager's who had broken in at some point over the years, Alex didn't know.

The rest of the room was stripped as bare as the walls. Her mother hadn't owned much. Whatever she'd had of value had been sold or pawned to support the never-ending party.

Alex crossed the room to the closet. The cheap particleboard door stood open, the walls falling apart, damaged from a leak in the roof. Mack had mentioned that they should open up this closet space, expand it into the room and create a walk-in.

She pressed a hand to her stomach and looked around at the room, so empty it nearly echoed. What was she doing here, in this situation? Weeks ago, she'd set out to change her life, to change this house.

She scoffed. All she'd ended up doing was repeating the very past she'd tried so hard to leave behind. What an idiot. How stupid could she be?

Anger roared inside her gut, fast, a tidal wave bursting with frustration at herself, her mother, everything. Here she was, twenty-seven years down the road, making the same mistakes all over again. Had she learned nothing from her childhood?

The closet was empty. No clothes. As if no one had ever lived there, ever made their mark on this space.

For some reason, that only fanned the flames of Alex's temper.

"Where were you?" she shouted into the room, spinning back toward the closet, the closet that no longer held even one memento from her mother. It was as if she'd never existed, as if she'd simply evaporated, leaving Alex alone, to handle everything in her life—and now, this, this pregnancy—all by herself. "Where were you when I needed you? You weren't here. You weren't with me, with my sister, with anyone. You aren't even here now, goddamn you." Tears escaped her, hot and furious. She let out a shriek of frustration, along with a fist that landed square in the middle of the Sheetrock. "Where were you? I needed you, damn it! I needed you!"

Long-ago softened by water damage, the wall crumbled beneath the force of the blow and fell onto the floor. Something skittered behind the wall and Alex jumped back, thinking it was a mouse, until she heard a thud.

She swiped at her face, her lungs heaving with the spent energy. She thought of leaving, but curiosity nudged her forward and she peeled away more of the wall. Beneath it she found a large white box, lodged to the side of the bruised walls, just out of the reach of the water. It must have fallen down when the shelf and walls caved in, and gotten wedged in the nook between the framing and the drywall.

A box? Where had that come from? She didn't remember ever having seen that before.

Alex hesitated, simply staring at it for a solid minute. Then she reached out, grasped the fragile cardboard and tugged it out, along with a generous pile of dust that scattered in a cloud. Coughing, she stumbled back, waving away the dust from her face with one hand, clutching the container to her chest.

When she could see again, Alex sat down on the floor, crossing her legs. The box was nothing out of the ordinary, an oversized one department stores handed out at Christmas for wrapping robes or coats. When Alex tugged off the lid the old glue gave way and the sides popped outward.

Inside, the contents appeared nearly the same as the day they had been tucked away, except for one corner that had mildewed, turning the edges of the papers green. At first, Alex didn't recognize what she was seeing, then the images before her and the ones in her memory began to connect, linking like Tinkertoys.

The construction paper might have faded, but the crude crayon drawings had kept their color. On the first paper, a black and yellow scribbled oval with two little black lines drawn on the top. Alex flipped over the paper, and in her mother's loopy scrawl were the words ALEX'S DRAWING OF A BEE, AGE 3.

"She kept my drawings," Alex said aloud. To the room, to herself, her voice filled with wonder. "She kept my drawings."

Beneath that picture, another of a pumpkin with a toothy smile and two triangular eyes. Alex turned over the page, and again found her mother's handwriting. ALEX, A JACK-O-LANTERN, AGE 4½.

And so it went, all through the box, every drawing Alex could remember making, from the first scribbles that she must have told her mother were a dragon—but looked more like a squiggle—to the last one she'd made in this house: a picture of another house, not this one.

Alex put a hand to her mouth and closed her eyes for a moment, remembering. That day. The crayons in her hand. The images she'd wanted so badly to translate from her mind to the paper. A child's means of communicating everything she was feeling.

The house was big, with ten windows in the front. In one of the windows, a stick figure of herself. In another, a tinier stick figure of her baby sister. A long driveway, several trees and a dog. Alex chuckled. She remembered drawing that dog, because that had been the one thing she'd always wanted so badly, had asked Santa for a hundred times, but never received. Not until she'd gone to live at Grandma Kenner's house, because her grandmother had a fenced-in yard and the time to take care of a puppy. There were flowers in front of this perfect house, little pink and yellow dots. And over all of it, a big orange sun shining with its drawn-on smile.

A Utopia, far removed from the one she sat in now.

Alex flipped over the thick paper, her hand shaking. The handwriting had faded—this time, her mother had written in pencil instead of pen—but the letters were still legible. "What Alex wants most of all. Lord, help me be a good enough mother to give it to her and Brittany."

Her mother had noticed. Her mother had cared.

A single tear ran down Alex's cheek and dropped onto the picture, puddling in the green of the grass. Alex swiped at her face, then started digging through the box, pulling out picture after picture. Something bulged beneath the pile. Alex shoved the papers aside, her hand lighting on four leather items. Two pairs of white baby shoes. Hers, and her sister's.

She clutched them to her chest. They were so small, so tiny. One pair nearly worn through, the other still pristine. Little sneakers, their laces fragile now after so many years of being tucked away. But she could still imagine them on her feet, on Brittany's feet.

And someday, maybe, on her own baby's feet. If she decided to do this, to keep the baby.

She thought of the fliers she'd been looking at, all of them covered with images of happy, smiling two-parent families, in front of perfectly manicured homes, playing catch with the dog, or swinging in the backyard. Just like the picture she'd drawn. Always two kids, clean, well dressed, well fed. Everyone living the perfect life. Not a single mom in sight.

Would she be giving this child the best life if she raised it alone? Or would this be a better option? A two-parent family, something she had never had.

"You lied to me."

Alex spun around, and found Mack standing in the doorway, his face filled with hurt. In one hand, he held the papers from downstairs, the stark evidence of her pregnancy in bright multicolored pamphlets.

"I . . . I didn't want to involve you," she said.

He crossed the room in three short strides and knelt down beside her. "Involve me? Alex, if you're pregnant with our—"

"It's not yours. It's Edward's."

The information hit him slowly, filtering into his features a little at a time. He opened his mouth, shut it again, then she could have sworn she saw disappointment flicker in his eyes. "What's he going to do about it?"

Alex let out a bitter laugh. "What he does best. Send me some money and hope I go away. Leave him and his wife alone."

"That bastard." Mack muttered a few other unflattering curses under his breath. "I'll kill him."

"Don't." She placed a hand on his arm. "I can handle this on my own."

"Handle it, how? Alex, this is a huge deal. I mean . . ." He ran a hand through his hair. "I don't understand why you didn't say anything. How could you keep this from me?"

"How could I keep it from you? It's my body, not yours. I'm the one who would be raising this child, if I keep it."

"What do you mean, *if*? Are you . . ." Mack swallowed. Then he realized what she was implying and knew he had to ask the question, even as saying it seemed to take something from him. "Are you thinking of getting rid of the baby?"

Alex got to her feet and crossed to the window, her arms wrapped around her midsection, every ounce of her body language telling him to stay away. "Mack, this isn't a question about installing cabinets or rerouting the plumbing. I don't need you to make this decision with me. I can handle it alone."

He wanted to shake her. Scream at her. Tell her she was crazy, that no woman should go through something like this alone. Instead, he reached out and drew her into his arms. "I'm not letting you push me away."

She wriggled out of his grasp. "And I'm not letting you take care of me this time. You've done it all my life. You're not doing it now. I'm a big girl."

"Alex—"

She shook her head and backed up, putting distance between them that seemed like miles. What had happened to them? How had their relationship fallen into this crevice that he couldn't seem to close? "No, Mack. Don't."

"Don't what? Don't support you? Don't be your friend?

Because I'm telling you, Alex, lately it's getting pretty damn hard to read you."

"And what about you? Every time I turn around, we end up in bed, or somewhere close to it. What do you want from me?"

He caught her hand. "Isn't it obvious? I want *you*."

"For what, Mack? For a night? A week? A month?"

He took in a deep breath. God, he missed her. Missed having Alex close to him, having her to talk to, to be with, to laugh with. Maybe if he could find a way to recoup that, they'd be able to rebuild what they had lost. Because if there was one person he couldn't stand to lose, it was Alex. "What if I said . . . forever?"

"Don't do that. Don't rescue me again just because I'm pregnant."

"Is that what you think this is?" He scooped her into his arms and kissed her, hard and sure. One fast, searing kiss that rushed heat through his veins and ignited sparks in every ounce of his body. Enough to remind her of what had happened that night in the pool, but not so much to distract them from what was important right now.

Mack broke away from her. Alex's green eyes had darkened, her breathing had roughened. "Do you think that's about rescuing you?" he asked. "Or wanting you so badly I can't even see straight every time you walk into a room?"

"Mack, don't play with me—" She shook her head, turning away, tears welling in those eyes that seemed to want him just five seconds ago. What was he doing wrong?

"Is it that hard to believe someone would love you, Alex, really love you?"

"No, Mack. It's just hard to believe anyone would love me . . . and be there tomorrow."

He took her hands again in his, clasping them tight, his thumbs tracing a pattern over the backs. "Alex, if anyone would be there tomorrow, it would be me. I've loved you since first grade."

"You've never committed to a long-term relationship in your life, Mack Douglas. Why should I think it would be different this time?"

He let out a gust of frustration. Why did she keep pushing him away? "Is it really that, Alex? Or are you just coming up with a convenient reason to avoid making a commitment? Because I wouldn't be calling this kettle black, until you've taken a look at the color of your own." He tipped her chin, and peered deeply into her eyes. "You've never settled down with anyone, not really. And here I am, offering a lifelong commitment, and you're running like a jackrabbit on the first day of hunting season."

"Because you don't love me that way, Mack. You just think you do." She touched his face, her hand gentle against his cheek. "You love me as a friend, not as a man really loves a woman. I don't want a man who marries me because he wants to take care of me. I want a man who marries me because he can't live without me, because he is head over heels in love. Because he can't imagine anything better than spending the rest of our lives together."

"What if I said I wanted that, too?"

"Did you want to marry me five minutes before you walked into this room?"

"What does that matter? I want to marry you now."

She let out a long breath, and her eyes filled with a sad wisdom. "Thank you for wanting to play Prince Charming," she said, drawing her hands out of his grasp and pulling away in ways that went far beyond physical distance, "but I'm holding out for the real thing."

Chapter Thirty-One

Renee stood in the motel room, her shirt on the floor, her mouth on a man's mouth, his hand kneading her breast through the lace of her bra—

And hated herself.

She kept waiting for that spark to light. For the fire of desire she had felt a hundred times with Bill Rhinehart to roar to life, but her gut remained as cold as a ball of ice, and no matter how much she kissed him back, no matter how many times his hands roamed over her body, she felt . . .

Nothing.

She broke away from Bill and backed up two steps. "I can't."

He let out a huff of impatience. "Renee, what's wrong?"

The implied words he left off: *this time.*

"I can't do this. I can't sleep with you."

His mouth worked, as if he was chewing his impatience. "Why?"

Renee grabbed her sweater off the floor and pressed it to her chest. She suddenly felt more naked than she had five seconds earlier. "I thought I wanted you, Bill.

I really did. But what I wanted . . ." She inhaled, trying to find the words, to capture the last three months in a single sentence. "Was simply to feel wanted."

He moved closer, smiling, and for the first time, Renee noticed how big his teeth were. Almost bucktoothed.

"I want you, Renee. Believe me, *I want you.*"

One glimpse at the bulge in his trousers proved that. All Renee would have to do was put her hand on that and she could have a man making love to her. But she didn't want just any man making love to her. She wanted a man who loved her. A man who knew her, faults and all.

She wanted, quite simply, her husband.

The problem was, she'd already ended things with Tony. Either way, she wasn't going to make a bad situation worse.

"Thank you, Bill," Renee said, sliding her sweater over her head. She took one last look around the room. Bill hadn't even splurged on this. The place was cheesy, cheap, just two double beds with scratchy comforters, cheap art deco paintings and threadbare carpet. *This* was what she'd considered choosing over her marriage? Why? What had she been thinking? Renee grabbed her purse off the nightstand and picked up her high heels.

"Thanks for what?" Bill nearly spat out the words, his face red with anger. "We didn't even do anything."

She smiled, then grasped the door handle. "Exactly."

Before fixing him up with Alex, Mack had liked Steve. Considered him a good friend. The kind he'd grab a couple of beers with, hang out at a game with.

But now that Steve was dating Alex, and was, at this very moment out somewhere alone with her, doing God only knew what, Mack hated Steve's guts with the kind of passion normally reserved for vermin.

"If you don't mind me saying, you look like shit."

"Gee, thanks, Dad." Mack sailed the paper plate with the slice of pepperoni across the piece of plywood they were using as a makeshift kitchen table. Their usual Tuesday night dinner, this time served in Alex's house, with the two of them sitting on overturned five-gallon buckets. Chester lay at their feet, nibbling on the crusts. Not exactly gourmet fare, but considering both of them had all the cooking skills of a monkey, takeout was the safest and tastiest option. The pizza reminded him of the night Alex had brought him two large pepperonis. The same night they had made love for the first time.

Mack pushed away his plate. Damn. At this rate, he was never going to eat again.

"I mean it," Roy said. "Are you getting any sleep at night?"

"Not much."

"You could kick her out, you know."

"And you could mind your own business." He drew the plate back and took a few bites, if only to avoid the subject.

"I'm your father. I'm supposed to tell you what to do."

"Until I'm eighteen."

"That assumes you were a grown-up at eighteen." Roy gave him a grin, then reached for another piece of pizza.

Mack toyed with his can of soda, weighing whether he should tell his father that he had seen Emma in the True Value. What good could come of that, really? Emma hadn't come by to see her husband, and telling him that his wife was in town would only reopen a wound that had barely healed. His father would likely retreat to the seclusion of the basement again.

"So, are you ever going to finish this house, or what? It's the project that never ends." He gestured at the piles of construction supplies and tools stacked up around the room.

"You could help. Then I'd have a second pair of experienced hands."

Roy waved him off. "You have a crew. Let them help you."

"I can't pull them off a paying job to put them on Alex's house."

"Because she isn't paying you, is she?" His father wagged a finger at him. "I told you, it's a losing proposition. You shouldn't get involved. Trouble all around."

"She offered, but I wouldn't take the money." Mack shrugged. "I owe her."

"For what?"

Mack didn't answer. Just kept eating his dinner.

"Boy, aren't you Mister Talkative?"

Mack arched a brow. "Since when did you become interested in conversation? Usually I can't get more than three words out of you when I see you. And I visit you a lot." He reached for another piece of pizza. "Hey, where'd all the pizza go?"

Roy patted his stomach. "Gut National Bank, that's where. You should have bought two. And as for conversation, well, it's too damn quiet around my house. A man can only watch Pat Sajak so many times before he starts shouting vowels in his sleep."

That was as close to an admission that his son had been right that Roy would make, but Mack would take it. "Then get out more. Go on a date or something."

Roy pushed off from the table and crossed to the coffeepot. He started slamming the pieces together, dropping the grounds into the holder with all the finesse of a bulldozer. "I don't need a date."

Okay. Wrong thing to suggest. "Dad, you gotta do something with yourself. This is the second time you've been here, so I'm taking that as a sign that you actually do want to pitch in, whether you grumble and moan or not. I've got to tile the downstairs bathroom tonight. So, you want to help or just eat all my dinner?"

"I'll help you." Roy gave his son a half grin. "Gotta make sure you remember which side goes down."

"Are you ever going to let me forget that?" The first time his father had left him alone to work on a tile floor—and Mack had screwed it up within five minutes.

"Hey, you lay a floor upside down and it's a memorable experience."

"Dad, I was twelve. Cut me some slack."

Roy grinned, flicked on the coffeepot, then clapped his son on the shoulder. "I'll do better than that. I'll cut the tiles for you."

As they headed off to the bathroom, Chester staying behind to polish off any pizza crumbs, Mack counted his blessings. Finally, his father was smiling. Excited about something. Granted, it was just a box of ceramic tiles, but it was a start.

A few minutes later, they had drawn the chalk lines for the first few tiles, mixed up the mortar and begun the job. Roy had laid enough tile in his career that he no longer used spacers and could fit in the squares entirely by eye. Mack had offered to do the grunt work, the bending over and laying of the ceramic floor, but once Roy got his hands on the materials, he'd seemed anxious to do the work.

"Do you think that was her?" Roy asked as he slid a twelve-by-twelve tan tile into place.

There was no need to ask who he meant. Or what he was talking about. Mack considered lying, then decided it wouldn't do any good. If his mother did see his father while she was in Boston, the truth would come out eventually. "Yes, Dad, I do."

"Think she's back for good?" Roy reached for a few more tiles, acting like he didn't care, but the tension in his shoulders, the set of his jaw, said he did. Very much.

"I don't know." Working ahead of his father, Mack took the trowel and spread some adhesive in a semi-circle.

"Well, if I see her, I suppose I'll have some apologizing to do."

Mack scooped up more mortar and smeared it against the floor. "Mom walked out on *us,* Dad. I don't know why you keep on acting like she's the injured party."

Roy sat back on his heels and let out a long sigh. "Because I was a shitty husband. I would have walked out on me if I could have."

Mack stopped troweling. He stared at his father, speechless.

"Don't look at me like I've got two heads," Roy said. "You lived in that house. I never treated her like I should have. Women deserve to be treated like gold, and your mother, hell, I never even gave her the bronze treatment. I took her for granted, acted like she was one of the guys when I was home. Forgot she was a lady. Let me tell you the secret to women, son, learned by a man who is too old to apply it."

"You're not too old, Dad."

"Well, then a man who met the only great love of

his life and was too much of an idiot to figure that out until she was gone." Roy let out a gust filled with regret. "I'm never going to love another woman like I loved your mother. So I'm not even going to try. I had it great, and I didn't realize it, so I screwed it up. She left me. Smartest thing she could have ever done." He shook his head, his eyes glistening, then laid another tile, wiggling it into place with exact precision.

Mack had never considered the other side of the coin, he'd simply automatically taken his father's side, because his father had been the one left behind. All this time, Mack's judgment had been clouded, his perceptions skewed.

Roy stopped working and looked up. "What? You think she just walked out because she wanted to? I *drove* her out, Mack. I was a friggin' moron. She didn't want to go, and I could have stopped her with one word, but I had my pride." He scoffed. "Yeah, that shit don't keep your bed warm at night, now, does it?"

"But you two fought all the time. It was like World War Three in our house."

Roy grinned. "Yeah, we did, but boy could we make up."

Mack put up his hands. "Dad!"

"There's fighting, Mack, and there's *fighting*. Your mother and I . . . we had the first kind. We were like two roosters in the same henhouse, and half the time, we were both too pigheaded to back down. But when one of us got smart and apologized, oh, the making up . . ." His father smiled. "It was worth it all. It was worth it all."

"You were . . . *happy* being married?"

"Well, hell, yes. Why do you think I stayed married so damn long? I'm miserable now. Can't you tell?"

"Gee, with all the smiles and laughter, it never showed," Mack deadpanned.

"You know, what people see through the windows of a house ain't what's really going on inside. You keep that in mind." Roy emphasized the point with a tile. "Marriage is a hell of a lot better than you think it is. It's also harder than it seems. I wish someone had told me that before I walked down the aisle. My father's only bit of wisdom was, 'Don't go home with whiskey on your breath or your wife will think you're running around.'"

"Grandpa Douglas wasn't much of a talker."

"Nope. Probably why he stayed married so long, too." Roy grinned. "Now, let's get these tiles in. I'm done yammering about what can't be fixed. Let's work on something that can."

As Mack handed his father the squares that would finish off another room in Alex's house, he wondered whether he could fix that part of himself. The part that had always been so afraid of settling down.

He knew one thing for sure: he didn't want to repeat his father's mistake of meeting the one great love of his life and not realizing it until she was gone.

But he was afraid he had already done that—and lost her before he ever really had her.

Chapter Thirty-Two

"Marry me."

The words rang in Alex's ears like off-key chimes. "Marry you?"

Steve grinned. "I know it's sudden, and I know we hardly know each other, but, Alex, I've fallen head over heels in love with you, and at my age, I simply don't see the point in waiting forever."

Alex's pulse began to hammer in her chest. She sat in Steve's Toyota, staring at the marquise cut diamond he held toward her. They'd had dinner at an intimate little restaurant in Boston earlier, then he'd brought her out to the car, saying he had something important to tell her. Now she felt the little car closing in on her. This was what she'd wanted, exactly what she'd told Mack she'd been hoping for, but now that the moment had arrived, it was as terrifying as a Wes Craven movie.

"You're only thirty, Steve."

"Exactly. And it's high time I started living the life I was meant to live. Buying a condo instead of renting one. We won't need a house, since we won't be having kids. We can start making a retirement plan, and settling on a coinvestment strategy." He waved at the world at large, the one passing by them on bustling Tremont Street, people hurrying toward dinners and plays, loved ones and homes. "Traveling the world with my life partner." He grinned. "You."

"But . . ."

"I know, I know. But I feel something when I'm with you," Steve went on, clasping Alex's hand in his and pressing her palm to his chest, "and I know you feel it, too."

"I want all those things, Steve," she said, but as the words left her mouth and she thought about what Steve had proposed for their life ahead—a condo, a life of two people, working, traveling and then retiring in a tight little nest of just them—the sentence soured on her tongue. "Or, I used to."

He cocked his head. "What are you talking about?"

"I . . ." She met his gaze, and knew in that moment that no amount of fliers, doctor's visits, conversations with social workers or anyone else was going to hold as much weight with her decision as the voice inside her heart. The one that now surged in volume, pressing to be heard above all others. "I'm going to have a baby."

A smile covered her face, the kind of goofy smile she could feel all the way to her toes. She was going to have a baby.

A baby.

Right then, Alex knew. She was keeping this child. There'd be no giving up the child. Her hand strayed to her abdomen, pressing against the flat expanse of skin beneath her skirt. Soon it would round and grow, and she would feel life begin kicking there. The life of her baby.

Across from her, Steve wasn't taking the news with the same joy. His eyes widened. His Adam's apple bobbed up and down like a sixth-grader in a dunk tank. "But we . . . we never . . ."

"I know. It's not yours, obviously."

She watched him run some mental math, then start adding a few two and twos. "*Mack*. Is it his? You've been living with him. Has something else been going on? I knew he had feelings for you. He gets angry every time I talk to him. I thought it was just being overprotective, but—" Steve shook his head and spun away, his voice a low rumble of jealous thunder.

"It's not Mack's, either."

"Wait a minute. You're not seriously going to have this child, are you? Out of wedlock?"

She laughed. "You make it sound like the nineteenth century, Steve. Women have babies all the time, with and without husbands."

He shook his head. "I thought we were agreed."

"*We* didn't agree on anything." The traits Alex had once liked about Steve—his attention to detail, his insistence on making everything perfect, his quest for quiet and intimate dates—now became major annoyances. So much quiet, there'd be no room for fun. The kind of fun she'd had with Mack when they were growing up, the kind of fun that was essential for bringing up a child. "Steve, I just don't think we'd work out together. You're a nice guy and all, but not my type."

"Who is? Mack?" Again, the jealous thunder roared in his voice.

"I don't know, I mean . . ." She put up her hands, vague.

"You do care about him."

"He's my best friend, of course I care about him."

Silence ticked between them. Steve clicked the velvet box shut and shoved it into the Toyota's center console. The anger drained from his face, dimming his features into something paler, filled with disappointment, as the reality of what she'd just said hit him, and he began to fit the pieces together in his mind. "You care about him . . . in a way you don't care about me?"

"Steve . . ."

He moved closer, his hand touching her hair in a gesture so gentle, it was almost like a breeze. "I think I have made how I feel about you as clear as a 1090-EZ form, Alex. I want you. I want to marry you, be with you in every way." His fingers ran through her hair and his eyes sought hers, reaching deep into her gaze. "But you don't want any of that with me, do you?"

"I . . ." Then she sighed. Better to tell him the truth now than to tangle him deeper in a relationship built on a lie, one where she kept on forcing herself to feel something that wasn't there. "I tried to love you, Steve. You're a nice guy."

His face fell, and she wanted to take it back, to repair the damage she had inflicted on him. "At least you were honest. Better to know now than after I've claimed you on my taxes." Then he put the car in gear and drove her back to Mack's.

Tony had been an idiot most of his life.

He played the part of the fool well. He'd been voted Class Clown. Could be counted on to be the cutup at everyone's party, the one to provide the jokes, the gag gifts, the pranks. No one called on him to be the responsible driver, to be a witness to a will, or anything that even smacked at grown-up and reliable.

Not even his wife.

And that, he knew, had been half the problem in

his marriage. But over the years, it had simply gotten easier to go on playing his role and letting Renee play hers than to step up to the plate and become something else. Now, his marriage was in a ditch, his wife was filing for divorce, and he was about to lose everything that mattered.

It was time for the court jester to become the king. Except he had no idea how.

He balanced three-year-old Anthony on one hip, and a basket of laundry on the other, while some half-Spanish, half-English show screamed in the background. Anthony chattered along with the TV, saying something about some girl named Dora and her boots. "Yeah, boots are good, Anthony," Tony said. "They keep your feet dry."

Anthony stared at him like he had three heads. "Daddy. Boots is Dora monkey."

"Oh, the monkey has boots? Yeah, well, how's he tie them?"

Anthony stared at his father some more, then went back to singing with the show. Now it was something about a map. What the hell were these kids watching? No wonder half of America failed the damn SAT.

"Let's switch it to Big Bird," Tony said. "You know, the Count? He's at least got some math going for you."

"I like Dora, Daddy. Dora!" Anthony bounced on Tony's hip, nearly dislodging a bone. "Dora!"

"All right, all right. Dora it is." How did Renee do this all day? He'd been at it only for an hour, and he already wanted to run away from home.

"Dad! Kylie took my MP3 player. She's in my room! Get out, Kylie! Get out!"

The twelve-year-old. Again. Tony put the laundry basket on the couch, left Anthony there, too, then headed around the corner. "You guys share a room."

"Not my problem," Melanie said. "Get her to leave before I kill her. She's always in my face."

"It's my room!" Kylie screamed. "Dad, tell her to leave me alone. I *hate* sharing a room. This place is too small!"

"It wouldn't be so small if you left," Melanie threw back.

"Dad! Do something!" Before he could, Kylie stomped off to the bathroom and slammed the door.

Tony walked out of the girls' bedroom, leaned against the wall and let out a sigh. Sixty-two minutes into this parenting-alone thing and he already had a raging headache. This was why Renee so rarely left him in charge. He missed his wife. Where the hell was she?

Oh, yeah. Off on a girls' thing. Getting her nails done or something.

Staying away from him, in other words.

He supposed he deserved this, for all the nights he'd left her alone to go out with the guys. All the weekends he'd gone on hunting and fishing trips. All these years he'd avoided being the husband and father he should have.

Leaving them crammed in a too-small apartment with a mountain of bills and short tempers. No wonder Renee was stressed. No wonder she hated his guts. No wonder she wanted to run away from him and their marriage. Because he sure as hell did now, too.

He dug in his back pocket for his cell phone and flipped it open, just as the two girls started their verbal sniping again from behind closed doors. Tony plugged his free ear and prayed that Mack would answer. "Mack? Thank God you're there. I need a favor. I need you to rescue me."

Chapter Thirty-Three

The door swung open and the blonde on the other side stared at Mack, her mouth open in a wide, surprised *O*. "Mack."

"Hi, Samantha."

"What are you doing here?"

"I wanted to talk to you."

The *O* pressed into a thin line, but nevertheless, she stepped back and opened her front door, letting Mack enter the spacious Colonial. Mack had seen the wedding announcement in the *Globe* last month, telling him that Samantha had moved on—and found a doctor with a booming Chestnut Hill practice.

Samantha led Mack into the front parlor, and gestured to him to take a seat on a rose-patterned loveseat that looked about as comfortable as a box of rocks. He lowered his large frame gingerly onto the delicate piece of furniture.

"Can I get you anything to drink?"

A glass of bourbon would be good, but considering the clock had yet to hit noon, Mack kept that to himself. He shifted his weight, and knew he couldn't put this off. It was a conversation long overdue. Still, he hesitated. "I'm fine. Thanks."

~~Samantha perched in~~ a matching armchair, crossing her legs primly at the ankles. She laid her hands on the arms of the chair, then in her lap. "What did you want to talk about?"

"Us." He put up his hands, warding off the shock in Samantha's features. Way to get to the point, Douglas. "No, not getting back together or anything like that. I meant, what went wrong. I, well, I wanted to apologize."

"Apologize? For what?"

"For . . ." He was already regretting not asking for the bourbon. "For being a horrible husband."

"You? You were a great husband."

He let out a gust. "Samantha, you don't need to stroke my ego, trust me. I want to know what went wrong. So I don't do it again."

She leaned forward, resting her temples on her fists. For a long time, Samantha didn't say anything. When she looked up, her green eyes were misty with unshed tears. "It wasn't you, Mack, it was me. I never loved you like I should have. I thought I did, I really did, but . . . I got all wrapped up in the . . . well, the fantasy of being rescued."

"Rescued? How did I rescue you?" Alex had accused him of the same thing. What was he, some kind of Coast Guard swimmer? For God's sake, all he did was try to help his friends.

Samantha let out a little laugh. "Mack, that's what you *do*. You take care of people. Your friends. Your father. Your dog, for Pete's sake. And me. I was a mess when I met you, and you rescued me from myself, took me out of that dive of a bar in Vegas, convinced me I could be something better than a glorified stripper."

She waved a hand around the fancy room. "Now look at me. Married to a doctor. Living in the suburbs."

He shook his head. She gave him too much credit. "All I did was talk to you, Samantha, you did all the rest."

"Oh, Mack," she said, a generous smile taking over her face, "you did so much more than that. You do this stuff, and you don't even realize it when you do. It was so easy for me to just sit back and let you make all the decisions, to take the reins. To lead me through all those changes I needed to make and hold my hand while I did it."

"I helped you because I cared about you. How could that be wrong?"

"It wasn't." She let out a breath. "Every woman dreams of being rescued. It's that Rapunzel-in-the-castle, Snow White-in-the-bed fantasy. But sometimes, we fall in love with the idea of the hero, and not the man himself. That's what happened with us. I thought I should automatically love the prince who took me out of the dungeon. That we would live happily ever after."

"That this frog would turn into a prince?" He grinned. Had that been what he'd been doing, too, with Samantha? Thinking that he could save her and then creating a fantasy that didn't really exist? Or creating the fantasy he couldn't have?

He'd met Samantha a week after Alex had moved in with Edward. He'd been hurting. And he'd gone looking for something to fill that hole. He'd thought he could manufacture the happy ending he wanted. Clearly, it didn't work that way.

Samantha straightened a picture on the end table. "You were already a prince, Mack. But the problem was"—she exhaled, and her eyes deepened with sorrow— "I was never in love with you. Only the idea of what I thought love should be."

"You were never in love with me?" The surprise hit him hard, like a punch to the chest.

"I should have told you, should have said something right in the beginning. I should have been more honest about a lot of things." Samantha rose and crossed to the window, staring out at the manicured expanse of lawn. "Instead I cheated."

The words no longer hurt. It had been over a year, and Mack had gotten over the divorce. But he still had regrets. Wished he could get a giant do-over, for Samantha's sake.

He stood and went to Samantha, standing just behind her, not touching her, but close enough that he could catch whispers of her perfume. It wasn't the same scent she'd worn when they'd been married. This one was richer, deeper. Maybe chosen by the new husband. "I blamed myself, Samantha, not you. If I'd been better—"

She wheeled around. "See? That's exactly what I was talking about. You can't fix the world, Mack, no matter how many tools you use. We weren't meant for each other, and I was too chicken to tell you that. Instead, I went looking elsewhere for what I wanted. I was the one who was wrong, Mack, not you."

"You can't take all the blame, Samantha. I wasn't exactly Mr. Communication."

She smiled. "Yeah, you could have been better at the emotions thing. But all the heart-to-hearts in the world can't create love where there isn't any to begin with."

He turned away and went back to the loveseat, gripping the cherry wood that curved along the back. "What if there is love? How do I keep it from going into the ditch?"

"Like we did?"

"Yeah." He turned back toward her. "You're happy now, aren't you?"

The soft contentment that filled her face slammed into Mack with a bullet of envy, not because he wanted Samantha, but because he wanted what Samantha had. "Very."

"Good. I'm glad." And he was. He and Samantha might be divorced, but he had never wished her ill. They had, as she'd said, made a mistake, and at least been smart enough to undo it before they'd brought children into the mix.

"Mack, I'm no expert at this marriage thing, God knows, but I know you well enough to say this." Samantha laid a hand on his shoulder and met his gaze. "You're so busy fixing things for the people you care about that you don't take time to get involved. To be vulnerable. You don't need to rescue anyone, Mack. You just have to do the one thing that's hardest."

"What's that?"

She smiled. "Let someone into your heart."

Chapter Thirty-Four

Renee stood in her empty apartment and cried. She was too late. Tony was gone.

"How many boxes did he take with him?" she asked the sitter for the third time.

The poor teenager shook her head, causing a quiver in her spiky pink-tipped blond hair. "I dunno, Mrs. Wendell. Maybe three? Four? It was kinda busy, with the kids and all."

Renee paced the living room floor, navigating past toys and Game Boys, in the quick-stepping dance of a mother long-used to children's clutter on the carpet. Two of the kids were wrapped up in *Dora the Explorer*, their eyes glued to the television, the third was chatting on the telephone, but all three had their hands busy in separate cans of Pringles.

"Did he say when he was coming back?" Renee asked, keeping her voice beneath the range of Dora's.

The babysitter did a one-shoulder shrug.

"Did he say where he was going? Who he was going with?"

A double pump of the single shoulder. Renee was half-tempted to break the girl's clavicle. "I dunno.

Like I said, Mrs. Wendell, the kids kept me kinda busy. Good thing I've got the TV, or I'd never catch a break."

"Yeah, good thing." Renee vowed to find another babysitter with the memory of an elephant and the child-entertaining skills of Bozo the Clown. For ten bucks an hour, she should get more than a *Dora*-watching buddy.

"Mommy?" Anthony asked. "Where's Daddy?"

"Is he going to be here for dinner?" Kylie piped in. "I have to do a science project and I need his help. It's a model. He's good at that. If he's not going to be here, I need to know." She glanced at her mother, waiting for an answer, a solution to this limbo.

All three kids stared at Renee, their small faces looking like giant question marks. Would their father ever be home and stay there for good? Would their lives ever stay on an even keel? In that trio of the blend of her genes and Tony's, Renee knew one thing: she would do whatever it took to save her marriage.

Because those three kids were counting on her and Tony to be the heroes, to be the ones who stepped up and played adult. And lately, she'd been acting like a kid who hadn't gotten dessert.

Renee grabbed her purse from the hall table. "Sarah, can you watch the kids for a little while longer? I'm going to"—she cut herself off before she said "find Tony" because she didn't want to alarm the kids—"run an errand."

This time, the babysitter shrugged both shoulders. "Whatever. What do you want me to feed them?"

Love and attention, Renee thought of shouting back, but instead she just said, "Order in some pizza. There's money on the kitchen table. I'll be back. And so will Daddy," she told the kids. "I promise."

* * *

"Everything's different now, isn't it?" Alex asked.

"Yeah, it is." Mack stood beside her, wishing he could disagree. In the days since their conversation in the upstairs bedroom, Alex had managed to avoid him by staying late at work and leaving early in the morning. He had poured himself into his own work, collapsing into bed every night, hoping that enough physical labor would help him sleep. And forget. And try like hell to figure out how to put Samantha's advice into action.

It didn't. He'd lain awake, staring at the Spanish lace pattern of his ceiling and seeing Alex's face in every swirl. Hearing her voice in the whispers of the wind, the calls of the night birds, the gurgles of the pool filter.

"I can't thank you enough," she said, turning toward him, her arms opening, as if she meant to hug him. Then they dropped to her sides, and she looked away. Uncomfortable silence filled the gap between them.

Yeah, everything was different. Different in a way that sucked. Royally.

"The house is beautiful, Mack." Alex stepped away and began circling the rooms, taking in the finished woodwork, paint, flooring. In a matter of days, Mack and his crew had taken the Dorchester Cape from a disaster to a dream. He'd used his own guys, putting the work schedule on hyperdrive because he couldn't stand to spend one more minute working on a place Alex was probably going to live in with Steve. Now the fresh, clean scent of new paint and carpet hung in the air, coupled with the sweet summer breeze blowing in through the opened windows. It was as if spring had exploded inside the walls, bursting into colors of cinnamon, cranberry and vanilla.

Except for answering the occasional question about a lighting fixture or paint color, Alex had barely talked to Mack in the last few days. The two of them had gone from being best friends to near strangers in a matter of weeks. And Mack was miserable.

"Thank you," Alex said again. "I don't know how I can ever repay you."

"You could start talking to me again."

"I am talking to you."

"I meant really talking to me." He picked up an empty paint can and stacked it on top of the others in the corner. "You've done nothing but avoid me for days."

"I'm just trying to work through a few things in my mind. I had a lot going on."

"Yeah, I bet," Mack grumbled. The paint cans toppled over, and he let out a curse.

"What's that supposed to mean?"

He restacked the paint, avoided looking at Alex. "Steve told me he bought you a ring."

"I didn't accept it."

The four words seemed to echo off the empty rooms, bouncing from wall to wall, until they hit Mack square in the chest. He turned around, slowly, and met her gaze. "You aren't marrying Steve?"

"No." Alex's green eyes were clear, direct with honesty. "I couldn't because . . . I don't love him."

Mack waited for her to say she loved him instead, that she'd broken up with Steve because she couldn't imagine marrying another man when she had Mack in her life. "Is that all?"

She held his gaze a moment longer, then swallowed and moved toward the pile of leftover cleaning supplies, reaching for the glass cleaner and a rag. "Yes.

That's it." She went to work on one of the windows, even though the new surfaces already gleamed.

"What about the baby?"

"I'm fine, Mack. We'll be fine."

He let out a gust. "Damn it, Alex, you are the most infuriating woman I know."

She wheeled around. "And you butt into my life way too much. I told you, I can handle this on my own. I don't need you to play the knight on the white horse."

He advanced on her, closing the distance between them, his frustration with this entire game they'd been playing for the past week at a Mount Everest peak. "Is that what you think I'm trying to do?"

She looked away. "Let it go, Mack. Please."

"What the hell is the matter with you? I don't get it. I am trying here, trying my damnedest, to get you to understand that—"

"That you want to marry me to take care of the baby? That you want to start us off on the wrong foot? And do what? End up like Renee and Tony? Why don't we just skip straight to divorce court right now? We can join them down there and maybe get a two-for-one deal." She shook her head and moved over to the next window. "No thanks. I'm not signing up for that."

"What about you wanting a guy you could settle down with? A one-woman man?"

"I still want that."

"As long as he's not me, you mean."

She stilled, her hand in the middle of swiping a circle of sprayed ammonia. "It's not that I don't care about you, Mack. Or that I don't think you'd make a wonderful husband. But you're my best friend. And I can't . . ." She bit her lip. "I can't lose that."

Mack realized then, as he looked at her, that he had fallen in love, and that there was no way he could turn back the clock and go back to where they had been before. He had moved forward with their relationship and now he wanted more.

But she didn't.

He couldn't do this, not anymore. If he couldn't have all of Alex, he'd rather not have anything. And knowing that made his heart ache, the pain so deep, Mack hadn't thought his chest could ever recover. "You already did, Alex."

Chapter Thirty-Five

"I know what you're going to say." Tony put up his hands, warding off Renee's objections before she could voice them. "But hear me out first. I've got a really good reason for being here."

Renee's throat tightened. The pile of boxes on the front stoop of the house, marked LIVING ROOM, KITCHEN, HOME OFFICE, said everything she needed to know. Tony had moved into one of the houses built by Mack's company, leaving her and the kids for good. She'd gone too far, and lost everything. Lost her husband, lost her marriage. She strode forward and pressed a finger to Tony's lips. "Don't. Don't say anything. Please, let me talk first."

"Renee, I have to tell you something."

She shook her head, insistent. "No, Tony. Please. I . . ." She took in a breath, let it out. "I can't let it end this way."

"End? But, Renee—"

"I was wrong, Tony," she said, barreling on before he could say what she knew he was about to. Before he could explain the boxes. The move he'd already made. "It wasn't just you. I kept saying you checked out of the marriage, but you were right, I let it happen. When I got pregnant, and we had to get married, I felt"—she threw up her hands, searching for the words, a sentence that could sum up the past eleven years of their lives—"trapped, and I blamed you. So I closed myself off. I took control of the family, and did everything I was supposed to do as a mom, as a wife, but I didn't let you in here."

She pressed a fist to her heart. Tears welled and burned in her eyes. She held them back, her gut twisting in agony. She prayed she wasn't too late, that those boxes hadn't been unpacked, that she and Tony could still fix this, if only she could find the right words to reach him. "I didn't let you in, into my heart, into what mattered to me, into what I cared about. I'm sorry. I'm so sorry."

Renee held her breath. Was it too late? Were they over? Were there too many cracks in their union to repair?

And then Tony took her face in his work-calloused hands. The tender connection pushed her tears to the surface, and they trickled down her cheeks. "Oh, God, Renee, you weren't the one at fault here. Ever. I'm the man in the family, the one who's supposed to be the head of the household, and I never stepped up to that role. I was eighteen when you got pregnant, and, hell, I didn't want to grow up yet. I know, that sounds selfish and it was. But I was just a kid. Barely out of high school. I had plans, dreams. I was . . . angry. With you, with myself."

And there it was, finally. The thorn in the side of their marriage. The words both of them had left unsaid, as if speaking them aloud would fracture the delicate balance they had created. Puncture a hole in the belief that they were happy. That they were both okay with

giving up their entire world—friends, college, parties—
to become instant grown-ups. But now that the worst
had been voiced, it hadn't pushed them apart. Instead,
their connection tightened.

Renee curved into Tony's embrace. "Me, too," she
said. The tears kept coming, but she didn't brush
them away. "I love the kids, but if I could do it all over
again—"

"I know. I know." He swallowed hard, and his eyes
welled. "We made a lot of mistakes. No, *I* made a lot
of mistakes." He traced the outline of her jaw with his
thumbs, and she leaned into that touch, the one she
knew so well, the only one she wanted to know. "I
don't want to lose you. I don't want to lose my family.
Ever. It would kill me."

"You don't?" The words choked out of her, caught on
a sob of disbelief. "But the boxes . . . the house . . . ?"

Tony cut off her questions with a kiss, the gesture
sweet and gentle. It was the kiss of a man who was still
in love with his wife. A man who wanted nothing in
return, only to show her he loved her. "I've been too
selfish for too long. Not thinking of what we really
need, only of how much I missed out on. And you
know what? If I lost you, if I lost the kids, I'd be missing out on everything that ever mattered. I'd lose my
life." He pressed a kiss to her forehead, another to her
lips, a third to her cheek. "I want us to move forward.
To start fresh. Do you want to try, too?"

She nodded, crying now, so damn grateful she
hadn't thrown away her marriage for a temporary fix.
She had everything she wanted here, in Tony's arms,
and always had. All it took was trying harder. Being
plugged in to him, as much as she'd been with Bill.
She'd gone outside looking for what she already had
right in front of her. What if she had invested as much

effort in her marriage over the past three months as she had in getting to know Bill? What if she had talked to Tony that way? Spent three days a week having lunch alone with her husband, sharing her thoughts, her dreams, her feelings? Snuck off to a hotel room in the middle of the day with Tony instead?

How would that have shifted the dynamics between them?

Her arms stole around his waist and she pressed her cheek to his chest. She listened to his heart beat, the steady thump-thump that had beat beside her own for more than three thousand nights. "Will you move back home, Tony?"

"We are home, Renee."

She lifted her head from his chest and looked up at him. "What?"

"I wanted to prove to you that I'm in this for the long haul. First, I called my dad and told him I'm ready to take charge when he's ready to retire. Then"—he pivoted and waved a hand toward the Colonial behind him—"I bought that house, the one you loved. Remember? You came out and visited me when I was laying the driveway a few months ago, and thought it was gorgeous."

"Yeah, I do, but . . ." She gaped, not quite putting all the pieces together. "How? Why?"

"Mack hadn't sold it yet. He finished construction and it just sat on the market." Tony looked back at the house and grinned. "I don't know why. Maybe nobody liked the concrete job."

She laughed. "I think the concrete's the best part."

"Yeah, me, too." He slipped his hand into hers and together, they walked up the stamped concrete walk. "There are four bedrooms, you know. And a big kitchen. A home office. And a fenced-in yard for the kids."

"We can't afford this, Tony."

"I called in a favor with Mack. I'm going to work it out with him. I'll be laying concrete for free for the rest of my natural life," he laughed, "but we'll make it work, Renee. We'll make it work."

She looked up at her husband, and saw in his eyes a determination and strength that hadn't been there before. For the first time since they'd gotten married, Tony had fully filled the shoes of husband and father. They'd undoubtedly have rocky days ahead—no marriage ran smoothly every day—but she'd never feel alone again. The partner she'd been seeking had been right here, all along.

"I love you, Renee," Tony said.

"I love you, too." She leaned her head on Tony's chest. His arm stole around her waist and drew her tighter into his embrace.

"Are you ready to move in?"

"Not yet." She smiled up at him. "I have to bring you home first. I made a promise to the kids. This time, Mommy found the backpack, and it had Daddy in it."

Tony's laughter echoed hers. "Thank God. I never thought the monkey had it in him to track it down to begin with."

By the time Mack got home, she was gone. The house stood empty, as sterile as a hospital. He checked the guestroom and found it just as devoid of Alex's personality, her things.

He sank onto the double bed and dropped his head into his hands. He'd hoped against hope that maybe Alex would still be in his house, that some miracle would occur and everything he'd ever wanted would be waiting for him inside these walls.

Chester nosed at him. "Yeah, I thought she'd be here, too, boy," Mack said.

Chester whined.

"Guess I don't know women very well at all. Especially Alex."

And Alex's heart.

Chapter Thirty-Six

"How long do think it'll be before someone realizes you're not collecting Social Security?"

Alex sat on her grandmother's back patio, in one of the two cushioned chairs that faced the grassy grounds of Merry Manor. Twin pots of geraniums decorated the corners of the brick space, with a small terra-cotta–colored chiminea in the center. "It's only for a few days, Grandma. Until I find my own place."

Grandma handed Alex a glass of lemonade, then settled in the opposite chair with her own glass. "You already have your own place."

Alex rolled her eyes. She refused to talk about that subject again. She'd arrived at Grandma's condo with her boxes of possessions just that morning and already, her grandmother had brought up the topic three times.

Alex pointed to that day's *City Times*. "Did you see where they placed my article on Willow Clark? It's above the fold. That's a big deal."

She'd written the story as Willow had wanted, sure Joe would have a heart attack. Just in case, Alex had prepared a backup, plain old objective feature piece.

But to her surprise, Joe had loved the personal spin
Alex had put on her article about Willow Clark and already assigned her two more similar articles.

Grandma gave the newspaper on the small table between them a glance. She'd read the piece earlier and
already proclaimed it worthy of a Pulitzer. "I'm proud
of you, honey, don't get me wrong, and down the
road, we'll celebrate your new job. But right now, I
want to know exactly what the hell you're thinking.
Because I happen to think you are completely off
your gourd."

"Grandma!"

"Well, you are. You've run away from home. Literally. Run away from Mack. Literally. And now you're
hiding out in a senior citizen's community. If that's
not crazy, I don't know what is."

Alex sipped at her drink. The ice clinked together,
like soft music. "I have my reasons."

Grandma put down her own drink, then steepled
her fingers and stared at Alex, waiting.

"You wouldn't understand."

"Alexandra, I am eighty-one years old. I didn't get
to this age by not learning a thing or two about life.
Try me."

"I'm pregnant."

"Uh-huh. So tell me something I didn't know."

"And Mack's in love with me."

Grandma rubbed at her ear. "Did I just hear you
right? Oh, Alex, that's wonderful! Mack will make
such a wonderful—"

"No. I don't want him to marry me. He offered and
I turned him down." Alex curled her hands around
the icy glass, the condensation a cool relief from the
warm day.

"Why? Just because the baby is Edward's? Do you

think Mack's going to care that the baby isn't his? If that man loves you, which I know he does—he always has, you know—then he'll treat this child just like his own." Grandma smiled. "And, believe me, he'll marry you before you can blink."

"Exactly. And keep on taking care of me, just like always."

"Maybe I'm going senile, but I don't really see the problem with that."

Alex leaned forward, drawing her knees to her chest. She wished this was easier, that she could suddenly have some lightbulb turn on in her heart and illuminate the right answer, because every time she came to the subject of Mack, she couldn't figure out which way to go. "There's a huge problem. All Mack has ever done is take care of me. I don't want him marrying me—or loving me—because he feels like he *has* to." Alex put little air quotes around the last few words.

"Do you truly think that little of Mack?"

"You know how he is. He's like a German shepherd when it comes to me." Alex shook her head. "It's better this way. He won't marry me out of some misguided sense of what's right, and get stuck in another dead-end marriage."

"Better for who? Better for you? Because then" —Grandma reached out and laid a hand on Alex's, her paper-thin skin marked with a roadmap of her life— "you don't have to get at what's really scaring you?"

Alex bit her lip. "Nothing's really scaring me."

"Sweetheart, you have more abandonment issues than the ugly duckling."

Alex laughed, but the sound got caught in her throat with a sob. Oh, Lord, this was exactly why she hadn't wanted to bring up this subject. "Aw, Grandma, you're right. And every time I think I've dealt with this crap, it keeps coming back, like mooching relatives."

Grandma chuckled softly. "Before you drive that man away, maybe you better come to terms with whether you're running from him or you."

Alex toyed with her lemonade glass. Slices of lemon danced with the ice. "I don't want to make a mistake."

"If you love him, it's not a mistake."

"Ah, Grandma, that's where I think you're wrong. If I love him and hold on to him for all the wrong reasons, it's the biggest mistake I could ever make."

Because she'd break Mack's heart. Lose him as a friend. Destroy the man she loved most. How could she do that to him? How could she let him tie himself to her for a lifetime, knowing they'd end up unhappy down the road?

She'd done the right thing, turning down his proposal. Except it hurt like hell, and no matter how much time or distance she put between them, the hurt only seemed to multiply. Alex got up and went into the condo, done with the subject of things she couldn't change.

Grandma followed a few minutes later, and found Alex poring over the box of memorabilia and drawings that she had pulled from the house. She'd spread them out on the kitchen table, as if assembling the jigsaw puzzle of her life. Alex had brought them over because she knew her grandmother would want to see these pictures, and fill in the blanks of her daughter's last few years.

"Oh, my. What's this?" Grandma asked.

"They were my mother's. She saved all these."

Grandma slipped into a chair beside Alex and picked up a crayoned image of a fish. She smoothed her palm over the picture, as if simply touching it could bring Josie back. "She did?"

Alex nodded, and scooted closer to Grandma. Going through these items this time would be a more joyful experience because she'd have Grandma to share it with. "There was this box, in the back of a closet, and it was filled with stuff. It's like . . . a gold mine of my childhood." Soon, Grandma got out the photo albums and together they laid out the photographs, one after another, a Technicolor brick road of Alex's first five years. Moments she'd forgotten, or never remembered happening. Alex and her mother at the park, with Alex on a swing. Alex sitting in front of a huge birthday cake and a tiny candle shaped like a number three.

The two of them flipped through the dozens of photographs, and with each one, Grandma had a story to tell, a memory to share. As she talked, sprinkles of images filtered into Alex's mind and she began to fill in those first five years, with a new set of memories, ones that were sweeter.

The final photo they came to was one from the day Alex was born, her tiny form cradled in her mother's arms, an exhausted Josie looking down at her daughter with one clear and obvious emotion: love.

Grandma Kenner picked up the picture and held it tight in her hand, her eyes misting, her smile trembling on her lips. "Oh, how she loved you."

"But if she did," Alex asked, her throat raw, the questions stuck there for so long, "what went wrong after this day? How did everything change?"

"When it came to you, Josie started out with the best of intentions." Grandma sighed. "She just . . . didn't know how to put them into practice. It's like wanting to be a gardener and not knowing a thing at all about how to make a plant grow."

Alex considered that, and this time, her grandmother's nature analogy made sense. Inside her own body, a seed was growing into a person. And right now, she didn't know the first thing about how to nurture this child and help it grow. But she had an ally beside her, one she intended to call on. Probably every day. "I don't understand why she wouldn't ask you for help. You were such a great parent to me."

Grandma sighed. "I think you do better the second time around. I learned my lessons, realized my mistakes. Lord knows I made more than enough of them." Grief pooled in her eyes, lined her face. "When I lost Josie, it nearly killed me, Alex." Her voice cracked, and she shook her head, her eyes closed, her mind reaching back two decades. "We're three generations of hardheaded women, us Kenner girls, and your mother and I, we would just dig our heels in like two bulls. If I'd been easier with her, more flexible, less judgmental, maybe she would have come around sooner. Talked to me more. Instead of feeling like she had to do this all alone."

Grandma rose, using the arms of the chair to help her up, as if the conversation had weakened her. She trailed her fingers along the photographs, taking a tangible memory walk, her gaze misty, her voice soft with regret. "I drove her away. I was so tough on her, so quick to criticize, and that just made her go in the opposite direction. And when she needed me most—"

Grandma shook her head and looked away. She went to the window, her frail hands grasping the sill, pale skin looking so much lighter against the white painted wood. She hung her head, face pressed to the clear pane of glass.

Alex went to Grandma, wrapping her arms around her grandmother's waist and pressing her chin to the soft comfort of the light cardigan. "Oh, Grandma, don't blame yourself. You did your best."

"I didn't." Grandma heaved a sigh that became a sob, and she pressed a trembling fist to her lips. "I didn't."

"How can you say that? You kept trying. What more could you do?"

"I never told you this, but . . ." Grandma stilled, and drew in a breath, her entire face filled with sorrow. "She came to see me earlier that night. The night that Brittany died. And I wouldn't talk to her. I was mad at her for something. Something stupid. I couldn't tell you what it was five minutes after Josie left, but at the time, it was enough to keep me from answering the door. So she got mad and she went to a party, instead of staying home. I know it probably wouldn't have made a difference, but still, I wish . . . Oh, God, how I wish I had opened that door. She died, not knowing how much I loved her. How proud I was of her." Grandma shook her head, and the shake continued down her body, a tremble of repentance and grief. "I would have given anything to turn back the clock and do it all over again. To open that door. To open my heart, my stubborn heart, to my little girl."

She broke down, her face dropping into her hands, and sobbed. Alex wrapped her arms tight around her grandmother's body, two generations of Kenner women, holding each other up like bookends, a link for the one they both missed.

"She knew, Grandma," Alex whispered. "She knew."

She released her grandmother and crossed to the box. Alex dug deep inside, pushing aside drawing after drawing, until she found what she was looking for, something she had found that day at the very bottom. A single photo. She fished it out, then slid the image into Grandma's hands. "Look, Grandma."

Grandma Kenner ran a finger over the partly faded

Polaroid image, a soft smile spreading across her face. It was just mother and daughter, outside the little house in Dorchester, on a sunny day, both of them smiling and holding sodas. Their foreheads hadn't quite made it into the frame, which meant a young Alex had probably been the one behind the lens. None of them could have ever imagined that a month later Josie's car would veer off the side of the road and she'd leave her daughter without a mother, her own mother without a daughter. A family fractured.

"She was so beautiful," Grandma whispered. "Oh, God. I miss her so much."

"Look on the back." Alex nudged at the edge of the photo. "She wrote on the back of all the drawings, and on this picture. It was kind of like a diary."

Grandma flipped to the back, and read aloud the words written in her daughter's familiar script. "Mom, my hero. I love you."

Grandma bit her lip, then looked at Alex, tears welling in her eyes. "She really wrote this?"

Alex nodded. Just a few words, but they seemed to turn a tide, offer a bandage of healing to Carolyn Kenner, and bridge more than two decades of guilt. Grandma pressed the picture to her chest and held it there for one long moment, tears welling in her eyes, but this time, they weren't filled with grief, only joy.

Alex sank into a chair. She tugged out the drawing of her perfect house, the one she'd colored twenty-two years ago and realized she may not have the dog, or the flowers, but she had so much she hadn't expected inside the walls of the house she already had. "Thank you."

"For what?"

"For forcing me into working on that house." Alex

grinned. "I never would have done it if I didn't think you needed a place to live."

"Oh." Crimson filled Grandma's cheeks. "About that . . ."

"You have no intentions of moving, do you? Doom-and-gloomers, or not." Alex laughed. "That's okay. I figured that out a long time ago. I figured out why you did it. Like you said, us Kenner girls are stubborn."

"Are you saying all that work was worth it?" Grandma asked.

"It was. But not just the physical part." She paused, thinking over the past few weeks, not just what it had cost her, but also how much more she had gained. "As I was peeling back the walls, I guess I started to peel back layers of myself, too. I saw so much more of what was underneath." She pressed a hand to her abdomen, to the life living inside her. "I understand me better now, and my mother. I'm still afraid I'll screw up as a parent, but I already love this baby, as crazy as that sounds."

Grandma brushed a tendril of hair off Alex's forehead. "That doesn't sound crazy at all."

"I can see, now, how terrifying it had to be for my mother. And I . . ." She picked up a picture of her mother, this one a head shot of Josie alone, a soft smile on her face, as if the camera had caught her unawares. Alex traced the outline of her mother's face, the wide green eyes, the long brown hair, the delicate line of her jaw. Holding the image caused a sense of peace to settle over Alex. There were no answers left to seek. She'd found them all. "I forgive her. It's like finishing the house finished all of this for me, too." She sighed. "I wonder what she was like."

Grandma smiled. "Just like you."

Suddenly, that comparison didn't seem so bad. For

the first time in her life, Alex was proud to be associated with her mother. A woman who may not have done the best job, but who had, nevertheless, loved her children, and left a legacy in this box that had given Alex a peek into her past, the keys she had been looking for, for so long. "I've been thinking, Grandma," Alex said, as she returned the scattered photographs and drawings to the box. "Maybe I won't sell the house. Not just yet."

Grandma beamed. "That's a good plan. You'll need a place to start your family."

"Yeah. A house will come in—" Alex halted, as her hands lighted on the one photograph she'd thought was gone forever. How had it gotten in the box?

She picked up the Kodak image and cradled it in her palm. The Christmas tree. The purple pajamas. The little teddy bear. And her mother, leaning forward, smiling. The picture now smoothed, the wrinkles nearly gone from when she'd crumpled it and tossed it away. And attached to the bottom, a Post-it note with Mack's distinctive handwriting. Mack. Of course.

> *Building a home is a lot more work than building a house, but not if you start with the right tools.*
> *Come home, Alex.*
>
> > *Love,*
> > *Mack*

Home.

All this time, she'd been building a *house*, instead of looking for a *home*. How could she have missed the point entirely? "Grandma, I have to go."

"Go where?"

Alex smiled, then grabbed her keys off the kitchen table. "Home."

Chapter Thirty-Seven

Emma Douglas stood on the lawn outside the house her husband had built in 1978, tears streaming down her face, and wondered whether they all hated her.

They'd be justified if they did.

She clutched her handbag like a lifeline, the thin vinyl straps pressing deep into her palms, surely leaving a faux alligator imprint. "This was a mistake," she whispered. She turned around, to go back to her car. Then she saw him, standing by the picture window in the living room.

Roy.

Her heart trilled, and she wondered why she had ever left him. But then the memories filtered their way back in, insidious snakes, reminding her that the beginning didn't become the middle, didn't frame the end, and that things had changed between her and Roy. Changed a lot. Maybe changed in unforgivable ways.

She stood on the lawn, twenty feet away from the man whose heart she had broken. The same man who had broken hers a long time ago, and wondered whether the foundation of that house was as strong now as it had been back in 1978. Because if it was, maybe there was hope.

And where there was hope, there just might be for-giveness.

Or maybe . . . there might just be the same old fights as there had been before.

Roy had thought about what he would say to his wife for over a year. He'd had three different speeches prepared in his head. The outraged indignation. The angry recriminations. The sobbing gratitude for her return.

All three flew out of his head the minute he looked out his front window and saw Emma standing there. He held his breath, sure she was a figment of his imagina-tion, then she'd started moving, back toward her car.

He opened his front door, and she turned back, moved toward the door, then stopped a few feet short of the front step. Twelve months had passed—

But to his heart, his wife looked like she had twelve minutes ago.

He swallowed, and had to hold tight to the door-knob. "Emma."

"I . . ." She took three steps closer, bit her lip, then looked away. "I don't know what to say, Roy. I thought I did, but now that I'm here . . . I don't."

He could have yelled at her then, could have told her off for leaving him. Could have done a hundred other things than what he did. He pushed a smile to his face. "Why don't you just say . . . hello?"

She glanced up and met his eyes, her wide blue ones filled with so many tears, they looked like pools. "Hello, Roy."

"Hello, Emma." His voice scraped by his throat. "I planted your flowers."

A smile began in the middle of her face, then spread across her lips like honey. "I noticed." She wrung her hands together, knuckles white with tension. "There's so much to say. Where do we start?"

Roy released the doorknob and let the oak door swing wide-open. He nodded toward the kitchen. "There's coffee brewing. Do you want to start with that?"

She nodded. Tears slipped out of the corners of her eyes, puddling on her cheeks. Roy hurried down the steps and over to his wife.

"Don't cry," he whispered, brushing the tears away with his thumbs, doing what he should have done years ago, trying to heal her heart, trying to tell her he loved her. "Don't cry, Emma." Then he took her in his arms and began with that instead.

Chapter Thirty-Eight

Mack waved the truck into the driveway, and said a silent prayer. It was the only way he knew how to prove to Alex that he meant what he'd said.

He loved her.

Of course, the last time he'd tried to prove that to her this way, he'd given her a ceiling fan that had gone over about as well as a bottle rocket without any gunpowder. But what was inside this truck wasn't a ceiling fan.

And it packed a hell of a lot more bang for his buck.

The men climbed down from the truck, rolled up the back door, and started unloading the contents as Mack barked orders and stood watch, as anal-retentive as a Hollywood diva preparing for the red carpet. The stakes were higher here, though, and the appearances mattered even more.

"You do amazing work, Mack."

He pivoted and found his mother standing in the living room, admiring the house with a proud smile that seemed to take over her entire face. His heart filled, and the anger he had felt in the True Value dissipated like puddles on a hot day. "Mom. How did you know I was here?"

"Your father told me."

"You saw Dad?"

She nodded and crossed to him, her hand out-stretched for part of the journey, then, when she reached him, her touch dropped away, as if she was still unsure whether he would welcome her. "We talked for hours. Believe it or not, but that man had a lot to say." Another smile stole across Emma's face, this one the same smile Mack had seen on Samantha's face earlier.

And he knew—he knew his mother loved his father, despite everything. That love, it seemed, could weather any storm. "Dad talked? In multisyllable words?"

Emma laughed. "I know. He surprised me, too."

"A man will do about anything," Mack said, "for the woman he loves. Even change his ways. And he does love you, Mom. He told me he does."

Her face softened, and now she did reach out, her delicate palm meeting his arm. "Are you okay with this, Mack? Because if you're not . . ."

"I want you to be happy. You and Dad both."

"Your happiness is more important, Mack. It always was." She let out a sigh, and released him, then crossed to one of the new chairs and sank into the leather seat. "I thought you were old enough, that if I left, it wouldn't bother you . . ." She lifted her head, caught his gaze. "But it hurt, didn't it?"

A swell of emotion clogged Mack's throat. "You did what you had to. I see that now." He let out a ragged breath. "It's torture to love someone who doesn't love you back in the same way."

"You mean Alex?" She glanced around the room, taking in the new furniture, the freshly painted sur-faces. "This is her house?"

He nodded. "I'm finishing it for her. Getting it ready for her baby."

"Because you love her." The words sat there simply, the truth laid bare. He loved Alex, and she probably didn't love him back the same.

He tried to work up a grin, but the smile hurt his face. "What can I say, I'm a hopeless romantic. Just like Dad."

His mother laughed, and Mack joined her, their voices ringing in the house like happy bells. Mack opened his arms and welcomed his mother into a hug.

And for the first time since Emma had returned to Boston, she fully knew the sweet pleasure of being home.

Alex couldn't park in her own driveway. "What the hell?"

She parallel parked along the sidewalk, then strode up the driveway, past the delivery van, and through the open front door. Two burly men passed her on their way out. "Enjoy it, ma'am," they said, then headed off to the truck.

Enjoy what?

As soon as she entered the foyer, Alex halted and stared. The house was filled with furniture. Comfy, cushioned pieces that welcomed a person with a fabric hug. Thick area rugs in warm, rich colors. In the living room there was a low-slung coffee table holding a crystal bowl of fresh oranges and two matching end tables with delicate bronze lamps.

On the built-in shelves, there were books, lots of books. Paperbacks, hardcovers, the bright letters on the titles drawing Alex to the spines. Her favorite authors filled the shelves, their names greeting her like

old friends. Propped up on a gold stand was a copy of
The Season of Light by Willow Clark, flanked by the
porcelain pig she'd bought at Theodora's Tearoom.
In between the books, there were flowers, little vases
of fresh-cut flowers, providing a bright burst of color.

Mack. Who else would do this? But why?

Alex wandered the downstairs rooms, but didn't
find him anywhere. Finally, she grabbed the banister
and headed upstairs. At the end of the hall, the
master bedroom held a vast king-sized bed, topped
with a thick white down comforter, seeming to beckon
her to come in, take a nap.

But she didn't go into that room. Instead, she
turned right and entered the nursery. The walls had
been painted a soft, neutral mint. The wall-to-wall
beige carpet had been topped with a pastel area rug
made of concentric building blocks.

Tears welled in Alex's eyes, blurring her view of the
new white crib that sat in front of the window, filled
with thick blue and pink blankets, and more stuffed
animals than one child could play with in a lifetime.
Alex stepped inside, her throat thick, her heart
swelling.

Chester lifted his head from where he was napping
in the corner, beside a rocking chair draped with a
knitted yellow blanket. A matching changing table
hugged the wall, already fully stocked with diapers
and wipes.

How had Mack done this? How could he pull it off?
And again . . . why?

Alex drifted over to the window. Long sheer white
curtains reached to the floor and drifted gently in the
breeze. She fingered the delicate fabric, pulling them
back, and peered outside.

She pressed a hand to her mouth and gasped. "Oh. Oh, my."

There were flowers. Roses. Geraniums. Impatiens. Azaleas. A rainbow of Nature's colors, exploding through the landscaping. They seemed to be everywhere, a graceful painting of floral colors curving around the small backyard, creating an oasis out of what had once been nothing but a pile of weeds.

"I couldn't plant any tulips. It was too late in the season."

Alex wheeled around, surprise still lodged in her throat. "You remembered, about the books, the curtains, the flowers."

Mack grinned. The familiar smile she had known all her life and couldn't imagine not seeing, not for one second. "Of course I did. I've known you since first grade, Alex. I know everything about you."

"Everything?"

He crossed the room and took her in his arms, holding her so close her heart beat against his, their rhythms almost twins. "Absolutely everything."

"But why . . . why would you do all this?"

He tipped her chin, caught her gaze with his own. "Did you ever wonder why my best friend is a girl?"

She laughed, at the change in subject, at the way he'd asked the question. "Now that you mention it, it is a little odd. Why?"

"Because no one listens to me like you do." He cupped her jaw, his thumb tracing the outline of her bottom lip, his gaze soft on hers. "No one tells me when I screw up like you do. You're the only one who can call me on all my faults, not that I have many, of course—"

"Of course." She smiled.

". . . yet at the same time make me feel like the greatest person on earth."

"And drives you crazy?"

A grin spread across his face. "And drives me crazy."

"But that doesn't answer my question." She looked around the room, still not believing all that she saw, the sheer completeness of what he had accomplished in a matter of a day. He'd thought of every detail, not in a way that Steve might have, but in a way that came from the heart, that spoke volumes of how much he cared, how much he'd wanted to create the perfect space for her to come home to. "Why did you fill this house with furniture? Create a nursery for my baby?"

"Isn't it obvious? I'm in love with you, Alex. I've been in love with you for months. Maybe even years. It just took me a while to realize that. And not because you're my best friend, but because you are the most amazing woman I have ever met." His hands tangled in her hair, the touch tender, but firm. She inhaled the spicy notes of his cologne, holding the scent in her lungs, her heart. "You're smart and beautiful and, yes, you drive me crazy, but you make me happier than anyone I have ever known. I did this, so that you would have a home. For you, for the baby. No matter what happens with us."

"Oh, Mack—"

"Don't," he said, pulling back to press a finger to her lips, "don't interrupt me until I've told you what I need to say." He drew in a breath. "I know I'm doing exactly what you've always accused me of doing—taking care of you."

She nodded.

"But I can't help it. It's the only way I know to show you that I love you, Alex. And I'm on a new campaign to do that as much and as often as I possibly can. A wise man once told me that the biggest mistake he ever made was letting the woman he loved most in the world walk away. Well, damn it, I'm not going to do that."

Then he leaned down and kissed her, long and hard, so that when he pulled back, they were both breathless, panting, his heart thundering in his ears. Alex's face was flushed, her eyes wide. He knew he read desire in her gaze, her touch, and he'd be damned if he'd let her pass it off as something else. "If that's friendship," Mack said, his voice low and dark, and filled with the rumble of want, "then I think we need to rewrite the definition in *Webster's*."

"No, that definitely wasn't friendship." Alex let out a shaky breath. "And neither was that night in the pool."

"That night in the pool deserves a definition all its own." He grinned. "So, we're agreed that we're no longer friends. But are we something . . . more?"

Alex looked deep into Mack's eyes and knew, without one iota of reservation, that she couldn't walk away from this man. She'd made a lot of mistakes in her life, a lot of bad choices, but she wouldn't do that here. She'd be a fool to let him go, to let one more minute pass because she was afraid of what might happen down the road . . . when she already had an amazing present right in front of her.

"You want to know why my best friend is a guy?" she asked, her arms stealing around his neck. She didn't wait for him to answer, just barreled forward. "In the beginning, it was because you were stronger than me, and when I was little, I needed that. And, yes, at first, it was because you protected me, and made me feel safe."

"I'll always do that, Alex."

She touched his lips, stopping him from speaking, too. "But I'm all grown-up and I need something different now. You were right, Mack, about me." She leaned her head against his chest, a chest she had known all her life, and seen as a source of strength, of support. But now, after those nights in his arms, she knew his chest could hold her in other ways, warm her heart and body through to the bone. "Oh, Mack, I've been so afraid to love you."

"Afraid? Of what?"

"Of getting hurt. Of being left alone." She held on to him, knowing that if she let go, she wouldn't say what needed to be said. "But most of all, I was afraid that if I changed anything between us, I'd lose you as my friend."

"Alex, you could never lose me." His grip tightened around her, as steady as a cement pillar. Birds chirped outside, and a sweet summer breeze whisked in through the windows, kissing at their skin. "I won't let you go."

"I know that now. I saw the truth in that picture."

Confusion knitted his brows. "What picture?"

"The one you snuck into the box." Tears welled in her eyes, threatened to spill onto her cheeks. Her voice clogged, but she kept going. "You knew me better than I knew myself. You knew I'd want to keep it."

"I know. I did that a couple days ago, when I thought I was losing you. I wanted you to know you could always come home to me. He brushed a tendril of hair off her face. "It's the first thing you learn in rebuilding houses, and even constructing new ones. No matter how you go about it, the past becomes part of the present, the foundation for the future. It's like renovating this house. You have to use the footers you already have, and build the walls up from there."

"Sort of like starting with the big, hulking man you already know, and creating a marriage around that foundation?" She smiled, teasing him. "Warts and all?"

Delight lit his eyes, and his grin widened. "You want to marry me?"

"Does your offer still stand?"

"It was never off the table, Alex. I'll marry you today. Right now, right here."

She laughed. "I think we should wait a little bit. Grandma will kill me if I don't let her wear her new dress."

"Then by all means, we'll wait and make Grandma happy. But we won't wait too long, because I want to make you my wife. I love you, Alex Kenner."

"I love you, too, Mack Douglas." His words sang in Alex's heart. This was what she had been seeking. Who would have thought that the perfect man had been right under her nose all this time?

"I always thought all I wanted was a place to put a sofa. A house. And here, I have exactly that, a house. But I realized today that it would have never been enough because you . . ." She looked up at him, and smiled into his blue eyes, into eyes she had known for so long, she could have drawn them in her sleep. "You made it into a *home*. That's what I needed, Mack. That's what I wanted most of all."

He shrugged off the words, as if what he had done today was nothing. "I bought you some furniture, planted some plants—"

"That isn't what makes it a home, Mack." She raised on her toes, placing a kiss on his lips. "Having you with me does. You and Chester, and . . . the baby. Us, as a family. Whether it's here or anywhere."

A smile spread across his face, breaking like dawn on the horizon, reaching deep into his eyes. "A family. You think we're ready for that?"

"Who is? We'll just do the best we can—"

"With the tools we have," he finished.

"Exactly," Alex said, and joy rose in her chest, seeming

so appropriate in this house that had once held such sadness. Her happiness became a balloon, lifting the entire place with a helium of high hopes for the days ahead. By filling these rooms with love and joy, the last part of the renovation would be complete. Her mother, she knew, would be proud.

"There is one more thing," Mack said, with a grin.

"What?"

"Pancakes. If I remember correctly, they were part of the deal with the kitchen cabinets." He tiptoed a finger across her jaw. "You *can* make pancakes, can't you?"

"For you?" She thought about that for a second. "I'm willing to try anything."

"That's good enough for me." Mack swooped her up into his arms and carried her out of the nursery and down the hall to the master bedroom. He paused, just at the edge of the bed. Anticipation pooled in Alex's gut. "Wait. I remembered something else."

"Mmm?" Alex managed, her mouth now on his neck, tasting the hot skin she had missed so much in the past few days.

"I believe there's still an issue of payment for services rendered?" He nuzzled her lips, igniting a fire with nothing more than a preview of the kisses to come.

"Take me to bed, Mack Douglas," Alex said, her laughter deep and throaty, but her patience wearing quite thin, "and we'll see if we can settle on a figure."

"With pleasure," Mack murmured. "With pleasure." And he laid his wife-to-be in the bed of their home.

But just before he made love to her, he took a moment and pressed his ear to her stomach, and listened to the rhythmic beat of the greatest miracle life had to offer, the one gift he'd never known he wanted until he'd received it.

A family.

Did you miss REALLY SOMETHING?
Turn the page for a preview.

She picked up two rocks, bigger than the ones before, one in each hand, ready to fire them off, bam-bam—

"Hey! What'd that sign ever do to you?"

One rock had already flown forward, dinging the corner, leaving a permanent mark in the painted ivy border that danced around the edge. She jerked around, ready with her last piece of stone ammunition, half thinking of throwing it at the person who had interrupted her.

Until she saw who it was.

Oh, hell. Duncan Henry.

Of all the people she'd thought would leave Tempest on the first bus, Duncan Henry would have been at the top of the list. He was bound for bigger things, he'd always said, than this little spittoon of a town.

"So, are you mad at the sign or just looking for some target practice?" he asked.

"Darts," Allie said, thinking fast, swiping at her face, erasing the tears as he approached. All six-foot-two of him, lean and rugged. Dark hair with piercing blue eyes set off by the blue in his shirt. He had a way of walking, of commanding each step, that flipped a switch in Allie. A switch she'd thought she'd turned off the minute she'd left Tempest.

Obviously, it had just been waiting for Duncan to walk back into her life.

"Darts?" he said.

"Yeah. I couldn't resist the urge to hit a few bull's-eyes." She hid the second stone behind her back, her face hot.

Yeah, that was believable, considering the Swiss cheese she'd made of the welcome sign. If she hoped to make her time in Tempest work, she'd better beef up her lie-telling skills.

"New in town?"

She smiled. Friendly, out-of-town kind of smile. "Just arrived today."

He considered her for a moment. Did he recognize her? She waited, heart beating, but no recognition dawned in his blue eyes.

"If you're done beating up the sign," he said, jerking his chin toward the stones littering the grass in the shadow of the sign, "would you, ah, be interested in getting a cup of coffee? I could show you around, give you the scoop"—he gestured toward the sign's footnote—"no pun intended."

Allie had to look twice to be sure she saw interest in Duncan Henry's eyes, not the same twisted joke he'd played on her at the senior prom. The whole "pretend I'm interested and then dump the fat chick before the prom" thing.

But no, it was real, impossible-to-miss attraction. The kind that stirred an answering heat in her veins, the tribal music of desire.

In the last five years, she had met men—many of them—who had wanted to date her. Take her to bed. Some even wanted to marry her. She'd dated several. Married one. And over the years, her confidence had built until she could handle herself pretty damned well in the male-female sexual dance.

But none of those men had lived in Tempest, Indiana.

And none of them had been Duncan Henry.

The only guy who had ever been nice to her at Tempest High. The only one who had made her believe that maybe—maybe he'd cared no matter what she looked like.

"Uh . . . coffee?" she said.

"Yeah. Hot beverage, lots of caffeine, little nutritional value." He grinned, the same familiar sexy grin that had flipped her stomach in high school every time he'd sat beside her in Algebra II or Trig and marveled over her ability to whip through an equation. Told her she was smart. Good with numbers. His saving grace.

That had been his nickname for her.

Grace.

The memory hit her, fast, quick, darting in, overriding the pain of his senior-year betrayal. "Hey, Grace, how are you?" A smile, then him sliding in beside her, his book next to hers, two peas, same pod. Pencils twinning, her heart slamming in her chest, wondering if he would ever want more from her than help figuring out what X was.

She looked at him now and realized the power of his smile hadn't dimmed over time. Something tingled in Allie's gut and the first few words she meant to say got lost somewhere between her throat and her mouth. "Coffee sounds . . . good."

No, it doesn't. She wouldn't fall for Duncan Henry again like she had when she'd been twelve and trying on hormones with her training bra. She wanted closure. To show she was way beyond all that crap that had happened years ago.

Back in L.A., she'd told herself she was going to Tempest to find extras, to scout out a spooky house for the opening scene, a cornfield for the climactic moment. But she'd lied.

She'd come here for revenge. For a comeuppance.

And to prove to every resident of Tempest that losing one hundred and seventy pounds had made her into someone totally different. Someone who didn't need the approval of a single damned soul in Tempest, Indiana.

Especially not Duncan Henry.

"There's a diner right down the street," Duncan said, "about five blocks—"

"Margie's," Allie finished, forgetting to play it dumb.

"You've been here before? Do you live in Tempest?" He bent forward, studying her, and for a second, Allie held her breath, sure that he would see past the size six dress and see the size twenty-six she used to be. That he wouldn't see big green eyes deepened by colored contacts, but plain hazel ones hidden behind dark-rimmed glasses. That he'd miss the sleek blond hair, and instead glimpse the mousy, curly brown.

That he would see three times the woman before him, and that he would turn away—

And laugh.

But he didn't. No spark of recognition showed in Duncan Henry's blue eyes.

"No. I, ah, saw the sign advertising it on the road back there." That much was true. The faded, peeling wooden billboard still read MARGIE'S EATS—COME IN AND DINE ON A DIME. A friendly, perpetually young woman, presumably Margie, was smiling and holding a pie beside the words. Margie's husband Dick had painted that sign back in nineteen seventy-four and it had stayed there, on the outskirts of town, ever since. Never getting a touch-up or a change, although Margie herself had always gone into the Curl Up 'N' Dye for regular tune-ups. Allie doubted anything on Margie's menu went for a dime—if it ever had. There was no truth in advertising, at least not in Tempest.

People who met the real Margie, who had all the warmth of a porcupine getting a rectal exam, found that out pretty quick.

"I'll take my car and follow you." Allie sent him a smile, a little helpless-girl wave of her hand. She needed the time to clear her head. Get out of the "Duncan Henry is the cutest thing on the entire planet" thinking and back into "I am a capable woman who is here for a purpose" mode.

"Sure." Duncan tossed her another grin, then headed back behind her rented Taurus, climbing into a black Miata. He zipped away from the shoulder, spitting pebbles in his wake.

Allie turned back toward the welcome sign. She raised her arm, closed one eye. She let loose the last rock in her fist, watching with satisfaction as it landed squarely in the middle of the word *Tempest*, compressing the circle of the *p* like a well.

"Take that, Duncan Henry." Then she climbed in her car and did the exact same thing he'd done to her seven years ago.

Blew him off.